The
Morrigan Timelines

By Brigid Burke

D1715993

Chthonia Books

©2020 by Chthonia Books and Brigid Burke

ISBN: 9780578799711

Distributed by Ingram Spark.

Artwork by Brigid Burke

Chthonia Books

https://www.chthonia.net

PART I: OUTWARD SPIRAL

1

Mila Fell looked out at the evening sky; a dusky purple floated in over the fading light of day. She could hear a few cars go by in the distance, but these were overshadowed by the rustling of the trees in the gentle, late summer breeze. She looked at the green tree line, already starting to show a few signs of autumn colouring, and had an epiphanal moment. She could feel the strength of nature, its acceptance of death and certainty of renewal, its triumph over the cities.

Indeed, nature was triumphing over the cities. It was unfathomable that just a few years ago, urban sprawl was rampant. Technological advances raced on, there were more buildings, more cars, the pace of life was frenetic everywhere. Everyone floated about in their own self-contained bubbles with their smartphones, oblivious to things like the sight that greeted her now. But how fragile that civilsation was! It didn't seem like it took very long for it to reach near destruction—and to realise that our advanced technologies would not save us. No; as it turned out, it required something old, very old—older than humanity…

Mila turned back to her office, her conference table piled with notebooks, newspapers, and printouts. Just beyond in the adjoining room was a studio, with a video camera and audio recording equipment. This plethora of archival stuff was a marvel in itself; she found herself lost in these documents, and had to get up, look out the window, or go outside just to re-align herself with the present.

Mila had been born in the late twentieth century, so she was well aware of the people and circumstances that were involved in the short battle, which was more like a war. That battle was like no other; its participants were something other than humans—at least for the most part—and after it was over, no one really had any good answers about just what the hell happened. All they knew was that it seemed the world was just saved from certain annihilation.

She had attended film school, but also had an interest in history and folklore, and this combination led her to a career as a documentarian. She was fascinated by ancient history in particular, and had made films on the archaeology of Egypt, Greece, and Israel. However, her special interest was Pre-Celtic Europe, especially the British Isles and Ireland. The connection of the battle to the latter grouping made it an ideal project for a documentary.

So, here she was, sorting through as much primary source material as she could pull together—diaries, news articles, and interviews—both written and recorded. Many of those connected with the battle were still alive, as it had not happened that long ago, and she was fortunate enough to talk to many of them about their experiences with the key players. The story that was emerging was incredible—frankly impossible, she would have said, if they all hadn't witnessed it.

You see, the Western world had been largely monotheistic or atheistic (two sides of the same coin, really). The idea that the old gods existed—or ever did exist—was largely dismissed, except by those with more esoteric interests. In fact, religion in general was largely discarded as an artifact of a more ignorant time, when people did not understand science. The mechanistic view of the world had taken over; human psychology was reduced to a series of brain functions and chemical reactions, part of a purely biological system that had no more meaning than its survival function. Of course, the mystery of consciousness still hung about like a spectre, and deep down no one was convinced that biological survival and evolutionary function was "all there was to it." Yet that worldview prevailed as conventional wisdom.

Then the fateful day came, when the world was overrun by strange, creepy humanoid beings. They suddenly seemed to come out of everywhere—from the waters, from subway tunnels, sewers, out of forests and woodlands. In retrospect, it seems impossible that they just "appeared"; they had to have been around for some time, hidden, or just somehow unseen. Armies were mobilised to fight these invaders, but all of their weapons failed; the creatures seemed invincible. They were mindless destructive, charging at anyone and everything with horrific, gutteral cries, and people could do nothing but flee—or hide, if they could. These creatures were defeated by an army that also seemed to appear out of nowhere, one that was just as baffling as the creatures that appeared. This army was also largely made up of non-human creatures, but there were two humans—and each of them was recognised by someone near the scene. These particular humans had either mysteriously disappeared or had dramatic changes in personality in the preceding months, or had notable personality changes years earlier. They were musicians, and one of them in particular was a singer—one who seemed to open the gates of another world for the ethereal army, to close it again—and, somehow, to start the process of rebuilding through song. The other human was clearly a general or some kind of leader for this otherworldly crew. And technically, there was a third supposed human, a woman, who turned out not to be human at all. It all defied any kind of logic or reasoning, it seemed like the kind of thing from an old epic or fairy tale. And yet—it happened. Mass hallucinations don't leave that level of destruction and permanent change in their wake.

Or do they?

Naturally the world governments wanted to know about this mysterious army. An effort was made to find the recognised individuals who had participated, but all of them had disappeared. The task of reconstruction was left to their bewildered family and friends. With the immediacy of the event long behind them, Mila had picked up the trail. She knew that it would make a successful documentary, but she was finding that there was much more than the event itself. She was not only documenting a strange battle; she was documenting a major shift in humanity and life on the Earth.

She sat down and began to sort through the papers and piles of film cartridges on her desk, trying to put everything in order. It was not an easy task to say the least. To begin with, the centre of everything seemed to be a woman named Layla Black. But there also seemed to be two identical Laylas with different lives. Surely they were two different people? But they didn't seem to be. It was as though Layla, her family, her friends, were living in two different universes, and somehow came together in this one event. She could not even pretend to know how that would happen.

The evidence came from a variety of places. The main piece of evidence for at least one part of the story was Steve Abbott's diary. Steve was a very famous blues and rock singer, and was in fact identified as the man singing before and after the battle. She had managed to collect oral histories and interviews with family, friends, bandmates; some she conducted herself, some she got from other sources. And some of it—admittedly—came from her own imagination. As Mila worked on the project, she sometimes felt possessed by Layla in some fashion, as though she were channeling her. She would have very clear visions of events as they supposedly transpired. As you might expect for an academic, she was torn about this kind of "evidence." On the one hand, she should have dismissed them as wishful thinking or hallucination. On the other … the impressions were so strong that they felt impossible to doubt, and she had found at least some secondary supporting evidence for her ethereal interpretations. So, she decided to incorporate those notes where they were needed to fill in gaps in the full story.

The dueling timelines and events bothered her. She knew that just about everything she had from the accounts came from credible sources. How could there be such different accounts of the life of the same person? She started to research the whole concept of timelines, time shifts, and quantum mechanics. She felt like she was dealing with something in this realm, but it was unclear how it could happen. Quantum events took place at the particle level, and even those who theorised time shifts, wormholes, matrices, and other such space-time slips generally talked about momentary events that were often subtle and easily unnoticed. There was nothing subtle about these events. And as she learned more about Layla, she realised that she was not in any way dealing with an ordinary person. This was entirely new territory.

After months of work, Mila managed to snake her way through the evidence, and come up with some kind of multi-level narrative, one in which parallel universes seemed to collide, humanity pushed itself to the brink of extinction...

And a goddess called Morrigan--sometimes under the name Macha, and other times as Babd–appeared in the world to fight for a largely ungrateful and unworthy humanity.

2

Timelines

The idea of multiverses and parallel universes is not new. Aside from anything in fiction, quantum physics itself suggests the idea that there are multiple, alternate realities. The idea of a parallel universe stems from the theory of a flat space-time continuum, in which there are a large (but still finite) number of possible universe configurations. Since there are a finite number of combinations, such parallel structures are likely to be repetitive at some points. It is believed that in these various universes, our lives could be going on in an alternate reality—perhaps with a different ending. While some testing of this theory has happened on a minute scale, it is still very much theoretical in terms of how it might affect human lives.

However, if you accept the possibility that there are parallel universes and lives, then you have to ask: do these ever collide? It seems unlikely that everything runs on a straight line through infinity; the "arrow of time," from past to present to future, is an illusion.

There are many who believe they do collide. The explanations are various, and some are more credible than others. There is the idea that one can "jump" between timelines, and experience themselves in more than one part of space-time. But this doesn't seem to be the normal experience, so what are the circumstances that would cause these shifts?

For those who believe in the theory, a large-scale event is required to cause timelines to cross. It could be a change in world leadership, a seismic event, or some kind of mass change in collective consciousness. But the changes are permanent, if not always immediately apparent. Sometimes the changes are invisible to those who do not have eyes to see. But in some cases...

You know. And you can't help but to know.

THE EVENTS

3

It began with the nightmares.

The place was clearly an ancient part of Britain—no, perhaps it was Ireland—yes, Ireland. A young warrior stood in a rock ring, and placed his hand on a stone, and was repeating what appeared to be some kind of oath or vow—I didn't know the language. In front of the stone a beautiful dark haired woman appeared—her eyes were violet, and her skin like ivory, and a radiance shone around her like the sun. Her limbs were willowy, and she had long fingers. She took the hand of the warrior, and led him off; I didn't see what they did, but felt pretty certain something sexual went on, among other secret things. I then saw the young warrior being given a hazel staff—it felt like the dedication of a king.

Then the scene changed. I saw the young king again, but this time he was in a room with several other men, most wearing long robes like monks. Once again, I could not understand their words, but they made gestures that were familiar to me as a Catholic—it seemed that the young king was becoming a Christian. In the next scene he appeared before his tribe, indicating through his gestures and the new symbols that he wore that he had given his allegiance to Christianity. The people in the crowd did not look happy; some were angry, and some looked extremely fearful.

Next, the young king was going to battle under his new banner. His fellow soldiers stood with him, but I could not help but to feel their unease; they kept looking at the sky. It was deathly quiet, except for the sound of their marching feet. Then the crows started to settle in on the branches of nearby trees—a couple at first, then suddenly what looked like hundreds of them. The sky began to turn an ominous red colour. A feeling like panic seemed to go through the crowd, though I didn't know the exact reason. When the armies met, the crows suddenly took off, came together in a cloud, and formed into the image of a woman—the same dark-haired woman from the first scene, only now she came down from the sky like a violent storm and screamed. I woke up at this moment, as the scream was so horrible, I thought my ears would bleed.

My heart raced and I shook all over; I got up and ran to the bathroom. When I looked at myself in the mirror, my face was as white as a sheet. It took a lot of pacing around and a couple of whiskey shots to calm down enough to go back to bed.

But the dream didn't end there—when I returned to bed, the action picked up where it left off. I saw that the young king's army was decimated—their enemies were raging against them, and there were mangled and dismembered bodies everywhere. Among the heaps of corpses, I saw the woman again—she was only partially covered in a black garment that was half like crow's feathers, and she carried a massive battle axe. She ambled like a monstrous being across the mounds of bodies, her eyes almost demonic. Her limbs were spindly, and she was like a giant skeleton with an explosion of black hair racing toward him. The young king turned and saw her—she went right at him, throwing the battle axe at him and nearly chopping him in half. She grabbed him, pulled out his intestines, and then wrapped them around his neck, hanging him from a tree. She then shouted at the remaining survivors, her voice an angry howl—she was saying something, and again, the language was unknown, but it felt like a curse. After this she turned and shambled away, leaving the steaming, bloodied pile of bodies. I woke up a second time, and was unable to get back to sleep.

At first I thought I'd smoked some bad weed, or maybe ate something that was affecting me. But the dream went on for years after that. Night after night, it was always the same, though sometimes I saw certain parts of it with more clarity. It was as though I was being asked to pay attention to certain scenes in particular at different times. I couldn't make any sense of it, and I didn't know why it was happening. People say I was very irritable and short-tempered in those days; this is the reason why. I hardly slept for three years. Then, all at once, the dreams stopped, just like that. At first I thought it was a fluke, I was so used to them. But no—a whole week went by, then two, and I didn't have the dream. I felt like a new man.

Then in 1975 in Los Angeles I met Layla Black.

4

The "Incident"

From the Police Report:

At the Lowery Hotel, Los Angeles

August 10, 1975

1:30 AM

Officers responded to a call at the hotel reporting a sexual assault on three-year-old Layla Macha Black. The call was made by hotel management at the request of her father, Malcolm Black. Black was a guest at the hotel, and the girl was left with a nanny, twenty-three-year-old Andrea Lawson. He reported that he came back from an evening out to check on his daughter, and found her alone in the room, with a bloody discharge on the bedsheets. The girl was taken to the LAC Medical Center, where it was confirmed that she had been penetrated. Swabs were taken from the victim as evidence, but testing proved inconclusive. All that was gained from an interview with the girl was that a tall, long-haired man had entered her room and gotten into bed with her, but it was too dark to see his features. When asked if she knew the man or if he was familiar, the girl said no. The child did not appear to be traumatized, and the doctors reported that she was in stable condition with no apparent long-term injuries. The case remains open.

***

Mila's Interview with Steffan Brown

Well, let's see—Layla. I've known her since she was born. I played bass in the band Armadel with her father for a number of years. We never knew anything about her mother, which was strange, but it was not out of the question for Malcolm Black to be involved in some weird and wild things, so no one really questioned it as too out of the ordinary. I think everyone was very protective of her—she was cute with her long, black ringlets, and those rather unusual eyes. She tended to be very placid and calm—never threw tantrums, and never cried to my knowledge. Malcolm insisted on taking her along on tour, which many of us were against—it really wasn't a great place to have kids. I would never have dreamed of bringing my kids along, even if they came to see a gig with their mother now and again.

I have to say that her presence was never a problem, until one particular visit to Los Angeles in 1975. Malcolm had a nanny stay with her—I think her name was Andrea—and they always had their own room not far away from Malcolm's room. The usual routine was for Malcolm to go out to the bars, and when he finally returned to his room—usually accompanied by some girl— he would stop in and check on Layla, make sure she was safe in bed and say goodnight.

Well, on that particular night, everything occurred as usual, and Andrea took Layla to her room around 7PM. When everyone came back, at almost 2AM, we were surprised to hear Malcolm crying out—he was terribly upset. Naturally, we all came out to see what was going on. He held Layla in his arms and was sobbing. Andrea was nowhere to be seen—apparently she had taken off somewhere when Layla fell asleep. Malcolm had found Layla awake and sitting up in her bed—and there was a stain of what appeared to be blood on her bedsheets. After much alarmed questioning, Layla finally told him that Andrea had gone out—and always did so—and that a man had come into the room and gotten into bed with her. She was extremely vague about the identity of the man—she claimed it was dark and couldn't see him. But in her usual manner she was very calm about it; Malcolm was in a panic, and she told him he was making a big deal of nothing. He couldn't make her understand the gravity of what had happened to her, though she continually said that she "understood perfectly well."

Malcolm and our manager spent the rest of the night at the hospital with her, and waited through a host of police and counselor interviews. In the end, the counselor told Malcolm that it seemed clear Layla didn't understand what was going on, and that this might be to her benefit in terms of recovery. While we were all glad things weren't worse for Layla, everything else was thrown into chaos. It's not uncommon for mad things to happen on tour, but this just outraged everyone. Needless to say Andrea was fired, and investigated for child neglect. The tour didn't go on much longer, which was probably a good thing, as Malcolm now insisted on keeping Layla with him in his own room. She never toured with us again after the incident.

5

From Malcolm Black's Letters

It was the worst night of my life.

Layla was—and is—everything to me. I love all of my children, but she has always been my favorite. She's … different, to put it mildly. Not anything like the others. Sometimes I'm overwhelmed by her. Why? Because of what she knows, and what she can do. I can't explain it all—you just have to know her. She seems to know everything, or most things. She's powerfully strong—even as a child she had unnatural physical strength. People always comment on how placid and even-tempered she is; she's always been like that. Nothing seems to phase her.

I guess this was why I was so thrown by the incident. We knew most of the people staying in the hotel, as they were involved with the tour; I couldn't believe any of them, even in their drunkest or most strung-out moments, would ever touch a little girl in that way. I also couldn't believe that Layla allowed it; she could have thrown that chap right out of the room.

I remember entering the room, and seeing her there alone.

"Sweetheart, are you awake? Where's Andrea?"

"She's out."

"Out where??"

She shrugged. "I don't know. I think she goes out every night when she thinks I'm asleep."

I was really alarmed at this. "Layla, she is not supposed to leave this room."

"Well, she does."

"Why are you sitting like that?"

"Like what?"

"With your legs up?"

"No reason."

I walked over to her, wanting to pick her up. It was then that I saw the stain on the bedsheets. I could feel the color leave my cheeks; I shook all over.

"Baby," I said, my voice cracking, "what happened? Was someone here?"

She looked at me nonchalantly. "Oh. Yes. Someone came in."

"Who??"

"I don't know who they are."

"What did they look like?"

"I don't know. It was dark."

I knew she was lying to me.

"Sweetheart please—you must tell Daddy who came in here and did this to you!"

"Oh, don't worry about it."

"Layla! I don't think you realise how serious this is!"

"It's not that serious."

"Yes it is!"

She rolled her eyes, and shrugged again, saying nothing. I picked her up and carried her out to the hallway; my face was hot with tears at this point. I was shaking with rage, and held Layla really tight to my chest. Just about everyone in the nearby rooms came out asking what happened. I had lost it by now; Layla just put her head on my shoulder as I gripped her tightly. I did not want to let her go, even for an instant. The police were called, and we took her to the hospital. It was hours of questioning—questioning me, questioning witnesses back at the hotel, questioning Layla in a room away from me. All these questions, and no answers. I was beyond exhausted when we returned at daybreak, but could not sleep. I was scarcely fit to play the next day; I was totally drained, and extremely distrustful of leaving Layla with anyone.

Somehow I muddled through the gig. I returned to my room afterward and showered, Layla in tow. She sat down with her paper and pens, and a stuffed rabbit that she carried around. I had ordered food for us, and Layla sat drinking juice and doodling on her notepad. After dressing, I sat on the sofa beside her. I had so many questions, and was still trying to figure out how to get the answers. She looked so sweet and innocent, with her stuffed toy and in a little flowered dress, with socks on her feet. She seemed completely unmoved by the situation. I was torn up, because I hated to see her innocence victimised; at the same time, I felt like there was a lot more to this story. I had to try to find out.

I drew up close to her. "Layla, sweetheart…"

She looked up at me.

"…look—I know you think I'm making a big deal about last night. But honey, I don't think you understand what happened to you."

"I understand perfectly well."

"Honey, no one should be touching you that way. You are a little girl, not a consenting woman."

"What do you mean by consenting?"

"Consenting means that you've given permission—that you allowed someone to do it."

"Oh. Well, I consented."

"No, honey—a three-year-old can't consent."

"Why not?"

"You're too young! You don't understand what sex is, and your body isn't built for it yet."

"I understand perfectly well. I told you that."

I was getting frustrated. "Honey, it's a crime—it's illegal to have sex with a girl below consenting age."

"What's consenting age?"

"Well, a girl has to be at least sixteen to give her consent."

Layla stared at me. "Oh. How old was the girl you brought round last night?"

I winced. "Look, that's a different situation."

22

"Why?"

"Honey–just–you're too young!"

Layla just gave me a look. Then she said, "Well whatever. I had my non-consenting relationship, I guess you should have yours."

I was stunned by this retort. I really shouldn't have been.

"OK–if you won't tell me who did it–can you at least tell me why you consented?"

"I guess so."

"OK–so why?"

She shrugged. "He's an ancestor of the O'Connors. I'm interested in them. And I need him in particular for my work."

"What work?"

"The work I'm here for." She said this in a tone that implied it was obvious.

I did not know how to respond to this. Finally I said, "Honey, I don't have any idea what that means."

"Yes you do. You know where I came from." I felt a chill down my spine; I made great efforts to not think about where she came from.

"I may know that, but I don't know anything about you."

"You know enough. Anyway, he needed to do what he did. I tricked him into it."

"You *tricked* him??"

"Oh yes. He thought he was sleeping with someone much older—or, well, at least someone of 'consenting age'." She bracketed the last two words with her fingers.

The disconnect between the little girl in front of me and who she really was started to give me a creepy feeling.

I took a deep breath. "Why did you trick him?"

"Well, I need to have control over him. That's the way to get it." She was so matter-of-fact.

"And…why do you need control over him?"

"Well, no one believes in the old gods these days, do they? Maybe some do, but they think they're all in the mind. He's not going to understand anything about what he needs to do unless I have some control over his actions."

"What does he need to do?"

She looked at me steadily. "That is for him to find out."

With that, Layla returned to drawing her picture in earnest, and answered no more questions.

6

It was in the summer of 1975, and we were playing in Los Angeles. Armadel was also playing with us, and I was standing off to the side during their soundcheck. I was sort of aimlessly looking around, when I spotted her—a little girl sitting atop one of the unused amplifiers, with long black curly hair. I did not see her face; she had a flowery print dress on, and was sitting cross legged, drawing on a pad with a pencil. She seemed very intent on her work. I asked one of the roadies who came by about who she was, and why she was there.

"Oh, that's Malcolm Black's little girl—Layla. She goes everywhere with him. She does have a nanny, she's around somewhere, but he likes to have her around before the shows. I think the nanny keeps her in another room away from all the aftershow shenanigans."

"How old is she?"

"She's three years old."

"Three?? And he takes her on the road? Shouldn't she be at home with her mother?"

The roadie shrugged. "Something about her not having her mother—he has a girlfriend and another daughter, but he doesn't want to leave her with a woman who isn't her mother. I

25

don't know where her actual mother is, and maybe he doesn't either. In any case, she's very low maintenance—does just what she's doing now, never really fusses. No one minds having her around."

That was the end of the discussion, and I still found myself looking at her. All at once she lifted her head and looked straight at me, and it was like I was hit by lightning. Her face was remarkably beautiful, but there was something really familiar about it, as though I had seen her before. And it wasn't as though I'd just randomly passed her somewhere; it seemed like she was important. But I couldn't place her, and it bothered me. I also started to have some startling thoughts, and that bothered me too. I turned away to get back to my business before the show that evening.

After the show was over, I was undecided about staying in or going out. I ultimately decided to go out for just a little while. As I walked down the hall to my hotel room to get showered, I saw the little girl Layla again, this time with her nanny. I saw them enter the room diagonally across the hall from mine—room 256. The girl glanced at me before entering the room with her nanny. *Where the hell had I seen her before?* It was really bugging me. I also found myself thinking about fucking her, a thought I immediately tried to shut down. What was wrong with me? Why the fuck would I even think of such a thing? She was just a little girl, and I was no pedophile. I jumped into the shower, got dressed, had a smoke and went out.

I came back fairly early, around midnight, as I wasn't really in a social mood after all. Before I made the turn into my corridor, I saw the girl's nanny and another woman walk by. I heard the woman ask her, "Is it OK to leave her alone?" The

26

nanny replied, "Oh, it's fine, I do it all the time. She's asleep, no one will be back for awhile. We'll be back well before her father comes to check on her." I then saw them get into the lift, and watched the doors close.

So here I was, in the hallway, facing room 256, knowing that Layla was in there alone, and no one else was around. The disturbing thoughts I tried to fight earlier now took over; I felt like something had taken over my body, and was impelling me toward the door. "It will be locked," I thought, "and that will be that."

But the door opened when I turned the handle.

I stepped carefully into the room, looking around. I expected it to be dark, but the lamp near the second bed was on. There were two beds, and Layla was in the second one. She was not asleep; she was propped up on one side, hand on her chin, looking at me almost expectantly.

"Come in, Steve Abbott. What is it you want?"

I was startled to hear my name, but it occurred to me that she might have pointed me out to her father, and he might have told her my name. The words rolled out of my mouth: "I want to make love to you."

She gave me a look that was hard to decipher; I felt like I was being scrutinised, and maybe there was a shadow of a smirk as well. She replied, "Well, then don't stand there—come over here!"

I obediently walked over to the bed, and moved towards her. What happened next—well, it really upsets me, and when I talk about it as I'm going to, it sounds like I'm trying to evade responsibility for my actions. Really, I am not—I should not have been there, period, and in spite of the bigger picture I had later, I still have not been able to shake a terrible sense of guilt. But I really felt like my actions were not my own, and she did not in any way behave or look like a three-year-old child. In fact, when I loved her, I felt like I was in the arms of an experienced woman—she knew exactly what to do. Everything about her seemed much older. I think if that hadn't been the case, I might have snapped out of this psychosis and run as far away as I could. But I didn't. At one point I must have hit something sharp, because I cut my thumb. I swore, and went to suck the blood, but Layla beat me to it, putting the finger in her mouth. She then ran her own finger across it, and the bleeding stopped. This was when I noticed she had only three fingers on her hand—on both hands? No, just the right one.

When we finished making love, she sat up in the bed, and grinned at me. "You'd best not stick around; my father will be up soon, and he always comes in." This was the first inkling I had that maybe I'd done something I shouldn't, but I was still disoriented. She put her nightdress back on, and sat by the window. As she sat there, a number of crows lined up along the sill; she opened the window, and one jumped onto her shoulder. I thought this was strange; I was still deeply fascinated by her, and still trying to recall how I knew her. I was also a bit reluctant to leave; she had been a spectacular lover. She seemed to read my mind, and said, "Don't be foolish—you don't want to stick around now, you'll have trouble. Don't worry, you will certainly see me again—it will be a few years. I'm not going to tell on you, and you shouldn't tell either—especially not your gran, who will be displeased that you slept with the Morrigan."

I literally jumped at the last thing she said; I stammered something unintelligible and turned to leave. She directed me to a side door, which would take me to the other part of the hallway –it would be too risky to go out the way I came in. I found myself running out of the hotel, looking to go somewhere–anywhere– where I could be alone to think. Her last statement got to me. Gran always said it–"Stay away from the Morrigan!"–and never explained. I had no idea who the Morrigan was, and I still didn't know. No one took it seriously. But suddenly something started to come together in my head–the crows, her statement and– then I realised it–the nightmares.

Layla was the same goddess I saw in my nightmares–that was where I had seen that face. And she had shapeshifted from a flock of crows, and then back into them again. Was that a dream of the Morrigan? And why was my Gran warning me against her? I also remembered the roadie saying she "didn't have her mother"–she was Malcolm's child, but where the hell did she come from? I heard rumors that he fooled around with the occult, but I didn't know if that had any bearing or not, or if that was even believable. Anyone who had the slightest interest in anything fringe or esoteric was labeled a Satanist or occultist, and it was mostly bollocks. I finally slipped back into my room about 2AM, but couldn't sleep. I was torn up with self-loathing, guilt, and fear–the nightmares had stopped, but now the goddess of the nightmare had enticed me to make love to her– or something did–and she was only a child. I really didn't want to believe it, but it was there, I could tell no one, and no one would believe it; the feeling sat in my gut like I'd swallowed a rock. The whole thing was seriously fucked up, and I couldn't make sense of any of it. But I wasn't likely to get any answers at 2AM in Los

Angeles; everything had to wait until we packed up and flew home the next day.

7

I came home from the States after that incident in a rather foul mood. I wanted nothing more than to talk about this incident, to admit guilt and accept the consequences, or just to have someone make sense of it for me. I couldn't do it. Any time I went to open my mouth to say anything at all, it was like my jaw had frozen up. If I did speak, it would always be about something unrelated. I felt like I didn't have control over my speech or actions in this matter, and it was really frightening.

A few days after I got home, my wife was trying to get in some appointments for herself, but had promised to take my daughter to the library. I volunteered to take her, as I wanted to look up a few things myself. I got my daughter settled with a book in the children's room, and grabbed an encyclopedia to look up "Morrigan"—it was a place to start, anyway. I learned that she was a war goddess, and treated as a kind of demon by the monks of the church. She was associated with crows, and seemed to have multiple aspects with different names. The stories about her were confusing and a bit contradictory. Ulster had its own stories about the Morrigan, in which she appeared as a beautiful young woman, and in Connacht she was associated with a cave that was an alleged "gate to Hell." But the stories didn't feel quite right. I couldn't find anything specifically about her appearance in a battle like the one I saw in my dream. I looked up a few books on Irish folklore, and I read over some of the stories, but they didn't help very much. Nonetheless, I was getting some level of confirmation that the scary dream-woman—and perhaps Malcolm's daughter—were connected to this "Morrigan."

About a month later we had a family birthday party near Doncaster, and my Gran was going to be there. I'm not a fan of extended family gatherings; much of my family is very Catholic, and their conversations are often xenophobic and superstitious. That said, I needed to know more about my Gran's "warning" about the Morrigan, though I really didn't want to bring it up. Fortunately, I didn't have to.

They began to talk about family members who were ill or had died. There were a large number of tragic deaths in the family, especially of young children. Gran suggested that the family was cursed, and swung around at me, wagging her finger.

"Steve, be sure to stay away from the Morrigan. I went to see Maeve the other day, and she said the Morrigan is back—she can feel her energy." Maeve was one of those "spiritual advisors" that good Catholics were supposed to avoid, but Gran trusted her because her house was loaded with images of angels and saints.

"Gran, you always say that. I don't even know what you mean. Who is the Morrigan? What am I looking out for?"

She leaned in, looking serious. "The Morrigan is a false god. You probably don't know that you're the descendant of an old king of Connacht in Ireland, of the O'Connor family. When Duagh, bless him, made his vows as king to the Morrigan—they all did in those days, she was considered the land goddess—he then converted to Christianity and renounced that old, evil

32

religion. The official history says that Duagh was blessed by St. Patrick himself, but the Morrigan story isn't told. Well, the Morrigan destroyed him and cursed the family—one male child in every generation dies. We've prayed and prayed to remove the curse, but it always seems to happen. They say that if the Morrigan mates with a descendant of Duagh, and if she tastes his blood, he will become enslaved to her will. God only knows what will happen then."

I had been standing at the sink with my back to my Gran, and I was glad she could not see my face at this moment. The dream was now starting to make sense, as well as Layla's actions, but none of this seemed like it could be real.

"Steve? What is the matter? You're not answering me."

"Oh, sorry Gran. I was thinking."

"About what?"

I couldn't say what was really on my mind, though something else occurred to me. "I wonder about this story. I mean—if Duagh took an oath, and broke it…I don't see why he and the family wouldn't be punished."

"He broke his oath for the true religion," said Gran, raising her voice. "He was blessed by St. Patrick."

I shook my head. "OK—so, if she is a false god, then why should I worry about her at all? False gods don't exist."

"Well, she's false as a god—but she's really a demon."

"A demon…"

"Yes!"

"OK—so—if Christianity is the true religion, and Duagh did a good thing by converting and was blessed by St. Patrick, then why would the Morrigan be able to destroy him and curse us? Wouldn't Jesus save him? Save us?"

"Steve, you need to stop."

"Stop what? Look, you're asking me to take this seriously. I'm trying to take you seriously. What has the family done to try to break the curse?"

"We go to church and pray about it, and have masses said."

"How long have you been doing that?"

"I don't know—it's been going on so long, at least a thousand years, 1500 years."

"More than a thousand years? And nothing has changed?"

"Enough of this Steve! I will not listen to you defending a demon."

"I'm not defending a demon. Maybe you need to look at this differently. You're defending an ancestor who committed treason. Maybe that's why you can't solve this problem."

Everyone gasped when I said this, and I realised that I needed to stop talking. I thought my Gran would actually get up and hit me at this point—Gran would not tolerate arguing, and it was just the sort of rubbish I hated dealing with when it came to my family. But it was clear to me, if I took this story at face value, that the Morrigan was the one who was betrayed. Why they would assume there were no deserved consequences for that was beyond me. Surely their prayers would have some effect if she was false or evil by this point—or perhaps there was no real curse at all, it was a superstition, though my dream and my encounter with Layla made me take it seriously. And why didn't the monks mention it? Probably because it made their super saint look less powerful.

"Whatever, Gran. Where is Fiona?" I got up to go look for my daughter, and to definitively change the subject. I was getting a better picture of the situation, and the bottom line was that if I was to avoid the Morrigan, it was too late for that. What I still didn't know was what it would mean to me and to my family in the future. This was the first time I'd heard of a curse, and it might be worth researching. After all, if children in our family died at a young age, it might be evidence of a genetic defect rather than a curse. Some of the puzzle pieces fit together, and others didn't—I would research what I could, and I just had to wait on everything else.

8

Interview with Jack Evans

I think it was sometime in 1977; our band was finishing up its ninth studio album, and we happened to be renting studio space in the same building as Malcolm Black, who was working on the production of a record for Armadel. While our interactions were always polite, we can't say that we were terribly close to Malcolm or his bandmates. We'd never toured together; even though we both played rock and roll we took it in very different directions. They were a bit more edgy and blues based; we used to be like that early on, but ended up moving in a more "electronic" direction, if you will. We liked playing with synthesisers and other new electronic gadgets. So, we probably had a lot of the same fans, but weren't necessarily crossing paths very often.

I should note that our group was not getting on so well; there had always been personality conflicts. I tend to be a bit more laid back; I'm a stickler for getting things right, but I like to give everyone breathing space to sort things out in their own way. I also realise that things don't always have to be exactly "right"; that's what makes it rock and roll. Not everyone in the band felt that way; Aaron in particular was an extreme perfectionist. I didn't always mind, it was good to have someone who was being extra attentive to quality. However, over time, he was becoming more of an obnoxious and arrogant nuisance.

While never explicitly stated, the rest of the band was treated like we were perfect morons when it came to playing music and production; he was the "only one doing any work," at least according to him, and he was resentful. The rest of us were also working our asses off, so naturally we were also resentful. This eventually destroyed the band, needless to say. At that time, however, we soldiered on, regardless of the tension in the studio.

On this particular day, we happened to pass Malcolm coming into the studio, and nodded our polite hellos. This was the first time I'd seen his little girl; she was with him, with a flowered tote over her shoulder, her stuffed rabbit under another arm, in a flowery print dress, white socks, black patent leather shoes with buckle straps, and a wide-brimmed hat. She had long, rippling black hair, and was a stunning little girl, absolutely adorable. I can still see her in my mind to this day, she was so striking. Gavin, our keyboard player and I both loved kids and couldn't help stopping to say hello to her. She was very soft spoken and polite, and looked at us shyly, with the softest eyes. Her eyes were a strange violet colour.

Aaron had been milling about, impatient to get started with work, though he did come over and politely nod and smile to both father and daughter. All at once the girl looked up at him, and her face changed. She pointed at him, and in a very bold voice said, "Who is that man?"

I was a bit taken aback, but I smiled. "That's Mr. Aaron Langley."

She looked at me, and then at him. She repeated his name, almost as a question. "Aaron Langley?"

He turned around suddenly at the sound of his name and looked at her, with a surprised and slightly puzzled look on his face. "Yes," he said. "I'm Mr. Langley."

"My name is Layla. Layla Black," she said, staring at him.

Aaron was starting to look uncomfortable, but he managed to smile and say, "Hello, Layla."

She cocked her head, and looked at him through harder eyes, as though she were thinking.

"Do you like war, Mr. Aaron Langley?"

The question took all of us by surprise. We looked at her, and at Malcolm, who was also staring at her with an aghast and clearly confused look on his face. Aaron, who was very anti-war, was trying to be polite, but we could tell he was offended by the question.

"No," he said somewhat sharply. "War is terrible. Why would you ask me that?"

She just shook her head. "That is too bad." Then she turned to her bewildered father and said, "Let's go. I want to draw a picture."

"Yes, yes, we should get on," said Malcolm hastily. He said a few words to us that were a bit apologetic in tone, and they walked away. As they were nearing the end of the hall, we could hear him ask the little girl, "Why in the world would you ask him that question?" They turned into their studio room before any of us could hear the answer.

Naturally this bizarre encounter was the subject of talk in the studio for the first few minutes while we were setting up to record. Aaron was trying to pretend that he wasn't affected by the conversation, but you could tell it rattled him. "Malcolm Black, figures he'd raise a daughter without any manners," we heard him mutter to himself.

"Come off it, Aaron. She's only a child."

"Yes, and what child likes war? Especially a little girl?"

I couldn't help but grinning. "Maybe she understands your personality. Kids are perceptive, you know."

"Oh, fuck you."

Aaron went about in his snit, but the rest of us chuckled among ourselves in amusement. It was a strange question, and we were sure there was no malice in it—Malcolm had no reason to try to prod at Aaron in that way, nor did Layla—and it was clear that Malcolm was as stunned as everyone else by the question, and he did not laugh when she said it. As we got to work, the subject receded into the background, and we almost forgot about it.

Later that afternoon, we were taking a break. Malcolm was taking her out; I don't remember if they were leaving for the day, or if they were just heading outside for a break themselves. However, Layla marched right up to Aaron, with a piece of paper that she had clearly drawn on in her hand. She tugged at the bottom of his shirt.

Aaron turned and looked at her, his eyes wide. "Yes?" he said, with something of an edge in his voice. He couldn't figure out what her interest was in him.

"Here, Mr. Langley. This is for you." She handed him the picture, and then marched off without another word, taking her father's hand. I looked at Malcolm, and again I could tell that he was perplexed by her behaviour. He said a hasty goodbye to us, and they walked out.

Aaron looked at us, and it was clear that he was baffled. He looked at the drawing in his hand. "Did she actually draw this??"

We passed the drawing around. You would expect children to draw trees, and houses, and maybe even people, suns, stars in stick-figure fashion, the kind of childish refrigerator drawing that we've all gotten at one time or another from our own children. This, however was different. It was not drawn in crayon, it was done in coloured markers. And it was an elaborate kind of mandala, very Celtic or old Pictish in its look. The scrollwork on it was extremely detailed, and there were intertwined snakes in the middle, with some other weird kind of geometric figure. I don't remember the details exactly, but it had circles and curves, and what looked like a stylised "M" at the bottom. The colours she chose for the background were somewhat ominous; the sigil itself was green, yellow, and blue; the background was a deep, bloody red, oranges, and black.

"What the hell is this?" Aaron asked, and I could see his hand was trembling.

"Well, if she drew that, she has remarkable talent," I said.

"Yes," said Aaron, still staring at the picture.

"Does it look familiar to you?"

"No. Does it to you?"

"No. I've never seen anything like it."

Aaron shook himself, folded it up, and put it inside his coat. "Right, well. I don't know what that was about, but we should be getting on." You could tell he didn't want to talk about it. He went back to being his usual blustery self. But there was a look in his eyes that suggested he was troubled.

There is a postscript to this story. When we were done recording, we did a small gig up North, just over the Scottish border. It wasn't our usual, just a small acoustic set to try out some songs in a local pub. After we finished, we sat at the bar with the locals having a drink.

There was an old man there, who looked like he could have come out of a folktale. He had braces to hold up his trousers, a balding head with white hair around the fringes, and a somewhat lengthy beard. He smoked a pipe, and spoke with a thick Scottish accent. But he was friendly, and chatted with us. Somehow the topic drifted to actual folktales and legends, and he mentioned that it was believed there was a lot of crossover between Irish and Scottish folktales in the time before Christianity. There were some sources that referenced it, and some things could be worked out by looking at old artwork, particularly the kind of spiral art done by those ancient people.

We had been listening with interest, but I noticed that Aaron's face was very intent on the old man. When he mentioned the artwork, I saw him reach into his coat pocket, and pull out the same folded-up drawing that he received from Layla. He handed it over to the old man.

"Speaking of artwork," he said. "What do you make of that? It looks a bit like it could be Celtic or Pre-Celtic." I wondered if Aaron had been trying to research the drawing. He hadn't mentioned it again, but it must have bothered him.

41

Our companion's face changed when he saw the drawing. His eyes widened. "Where did you get this?" he asked.

"From a little girl. Layla Black. Her father is the guitarist Malcolm Black."

"Oh. THAT girl," he said, stroking his chin thoughtfully.

"Why do you say it like that?"

He looked up with serious eyes, and then looked down thoughtfully, as if he was trying to decide what to say. "She is… something other."

"Other?"

"Yes. Well, I've always suspected it from what I've heard about her from others. If she drew this, then it just makes me more sure that I'm right."

"But—what is it?"

"It's a military insignia—an extremely ancient one. So ancient, in fact, that you will have an extremely difficult time finding references to that army anywhere. It's the insignia of the Dagdachoris, which was the elite fighting force of the Tuatha de Danann."

We all stared at him. Aaron was turning pale. "Why…why would she draw that? How would she know what that was?"

He looked at Aaron pointedly. "From the anecdotes I've heard, I've suspected that little Layla Black is actually Macha de Danann, otherwise known to us as the Morrigan."

"Um…and what does that mean?"

"It means she's an ancient goddess of war. In fact—another obscure legend suggests that she united the De Dananns with their enemies, the Fomorians, in the Otherworld, and that she rules over it. I've also heard that at least one Fomorian faction never stopped being enemies of De Danann, and of her in particular. But…" he shook his head and paused. We were all silent, waiting for him to continue.

"…if that's really her, and she's doing things like this… then she anticipates a war."

"With whom?"

He looked uneasy, and looked around him, as though paranoid. "Probably best not to talk about it. It's something beyond me."

"Okay, but why would she give that to Aaron?"

He looked at Aaron again, as though he were sizing him up. "I don't know. She has some message for you there. But I couldn't say what it is." Somehow we felt that he could, but felt he shouldn't say anymore. But I was still curious. So, I told him what Layla said to Aaron before giving him the picture. Aaron looked grim, but didn't give me any dirty looks; I think he wanted to know himself.

"She said that to him? She asked if he liked war?"

"Yes. It was an odd question for a child."

He shook his head firmly, and he reached over and grabbed Aaron's hand.

"I'd put this away and not show it to anyone else. You don't know who might be looking. And take care not to put yourself in any danger."

Aaron was clearly perturbed by this. "Why would I be in danger? What is a child going to do?"

"It's not what she's going to do. It's what her enemies might do. Keep this to yourself." He then excused himself, said goodnight, and left abruptly.

We all left the pub in silence. The next morning, I made some allusion to the previous night, but now Aaron was full of bluster again, writing the old man off as a drunken sot. The subject never came up again among us, and after awhile I stopped thinking about it–

Until that day, years later, when Aaron disappeared.

LAYLA'S TEEN YEARS

∞

9

Interview with Rosa Price, Layla's best friend at school

Layla and I were friends for a long time. I met her when we were in the first form together at our school in Esher, and we just clicked. I knew her father was a rock guitarist, but like me, she was into punk music. She didn't dislike his music, but she wasn't all that into it, either. As we got into our teenage years, we were a troublesome lot, along with our friend Angie. Angie preferred the girls, and I think she had a huge crush on Layla—and I think Layla also obliged by sleeping with her, even though she wasn't a lesbian.

Anyway, that's a side note—you'll have to ask Angie about her experiences, if she'll allow herself to be interviewed. Truthfully, I don't think we were all THAT bad in retrospect—we were just always out at clubs that we shouldn't have been at, because we were too young. That's where Layla met Iain James, the bass player for Witchfell—I think he was gobsmacked when she told him she was only thirteen. She came across as older and more experienced, I think, though she didn't look "old."

She was definitely a magnet for the blokes—I always loved watching her make them nervous. Many of them were too shy to approach her, but she was not shy at all if she was in a flirtatious mood. She was kind of a "fantasy girl"—they all talked about her, but none of them could imagine that they would ever be with her, and many of them were not—she preferred experienced men for the most part. I remember that she was not interested in having a steady boyfriend—she would sleep with lots of different blokes, but would not commit to any of them. Iain really wanted her to commit, but she put him off. She said she was too young, which was the truth, really. Her father was in a band with Steve Abbott at that time, and while she never openly said she was having sex with Steve, I kind of felt like she was—they had a weirdly close relationship, and she sometimes dragged him into our shenanigans. He always went along with it, though I think it annoyed him at times. In any case, I knew her way, and some of the offhand comments she made about him, along with the way he behaved around her, suggested that they'd probably been involved. She was cautious about saying too much about her relationships, as most blokes were considered too old for her by law, even if they were only in their early twenties. She didn't want to get anyone in trouble, and she didn't want to be labeled as anyone's "bird."

There was one relationship, if you want to call it one, that I did know about, and that was with Father Peter. He was our Christian Ethics teacher. He was really good looking—green eyes, dark wavy hair cut short, a rather boyish face, if I recall correctly. Layla and I walked into his classroom, and I saw the look on his face when he looked at her—it was hilarious. He was struggling to be serious and pious in his teaching, and she really did not make it easy for him. I know that Layla was not raised as a Christian, so I was continually amazed at her knowledge of the Bible—and he was too. She really didn't "get" Christianity, and truthfully, neither do I, though she was much better at arguing the points then I was. I think he was hoping to convert her, but that was absurd. Why? I don't know—there was something very pagan about her, I don't know how to explain it. I think about her differently after all the things that have happened over the years, and about some of the things that I noticed about her, but thought perhaps I was mad. At the time I felt there was something extra special about her, but she could behave so normally, I just thought I was blowing things out of proportion. I remember that she was physically strong, and fast. Our P.E. teacher was desperate for her to run track—said she could compete in the Olympics she was so fast. But she had no interest —she said something odd about "having raced significantly once, and not willing to do it again." She never explained what she meant.

One day she and I were out in town, and we saw Father Peter with this horrible woman; from the overheard conversation, we guessed it was his mother. She liked to belittle and berate him, and he just seemed depressed and resigned to her criticism.

Layla elbowed me and said, "I'll bet you twenty quid that I take his virginity and defrock him."

I slapped her arm. "You are terrible! But you're on."

"Why, do you think I can't do it?"

"No, I think you can, and you like a challenge."

She just grinned at me. We were in a coffee shop, and we saw them go out to catch the bus. She beckoned to me, and we jumped on the same bus, paying our fare to another street in town. The bus was crowded, but there was one seat open next to Peter and his Mum, and she plopped down next to him. "Oh, hello Father Peter," she said, rather seductively. "Fancy seeing you here." He turned several shades of red and said, "Yes, hello Layla," while his Mum gave her the evil eye. The bus lurched along, and she conveniently slid into him. I could tell that he was extremely tense; with his mother there he could do absolutely nothing. Our stop came up, and she jumped up to get off. But before she did, she slid her hands along his thigh and said, "Ta! See you Monday," before running off. I saw the look of shock and anger on his mother's face, and the look on Father Peter's face could only be expressed as bewilderment.

"You are so evil—you did that on purpose," I said to her.

She giggled. "I did. Mainly because his Mum was there. She's a proper twat."

I remember that he asked to speak to her on Monday after class, and I think he wanted to scold her for what she did on the bus. I wasn't there for the conversation, but she looked pleased when she left. He did talk to her about it, but she had no apologies. She was vague about how they left off, but she said, "we still have a bet!"

I know her own father was not pleased about Father Peter. He'd gone to Parents' Night and had met him, and told Layla to watch out for him. He didn't like the way Father Peter reacted when he mentioned that he was her father—he felt that Peter could scarcely hide his desire for her, even though he made a great effort. It was strange to me that Mr. Black had such a distaste for Father Peter in particular—it's not as though Layla lacked for admirers, and I know he knew that. In any event, Layla was not in the habit of listening to her father, and dismissed him if he scolded her. I did notice that he ultimately yielded to her in any argument, and I heard him say once that he had no control over her. She responded by saying, "No you don't, and you know better than to think you should."

49

Well, one day something did happen. I don't know all the details—Layla kept them from me—but I remember a weekend when her father called frantically, asking if she was at my house. She wasn't, and I didn't know where she was. This was on Sunday. Monday came, and I saw her in school, and asked her about it.

"Yeah, my father came home early and wanted to know where I was. He wasn't supposed to get home until 7:00."

"Well, where were you?"

She grinned at me. "Let's just say I'm halfway to the twenty quid you owe me."

"Layla—you were NOT out with Father Peter…"

She laughed. "I may have been…"

"May have" was code for "yes, of course I was." I wanted details, but she gave me very few. All I knew was that Peter's family had a house in the Cotswolds, and that they somehow met up and she went there with him, and had sex with him for almost two days. He got her home just in time, before her father called the police. She said an argument ensued, but she put her father in his place.

I might not have believed her, but Father Peter's rather tense and repressed manner changed after that. He seemed more relaxed, and it actually seemed that he no longer was so serious about what he was teaching. Later, I heard that he changed his name and disappeared, and left the seminary. Needless to say, I gave Layla twenty quid.

10

Interview with "Father Peter" (real name withheld).

I was in an Anglican seminary near Esher, and was in my first year as a novitiate. My name was Peter Walsh, and I later changed it—I will get to the reason why as part of my story. It would be a couple more years before I was expected to take final vows as a priest. I entered seminary at my mother's urging, and I thought I had a zeal for the calling; I wanted to make people into better Christians, at least according to my understanding. I was assigned to teach at a public school in the area, and was teaching Christian Ethics to students in the fourth through sixth forms. I remember my first Autumn term, going over the student roster with Father George, who had worked in the school previously but was now reassigned. He scanned the list, and read the name "Black, Layla" out loud.

"God help you, son," was all he said, handing the list back to me.

I asked him what he meant. "Oh, you'll soon find out, believe me."

"Is she troublesome, or a troubled student?" I continued to venture.

"No, she's a very good student. But she will test you."

I continued with questions, but he would only say, "trust me, you'll see." The only other thing he mentioned was that her father was that famous guitarist, Malcolm Black. He didn't exactly have a reputation for ethical living. Maybe this had some effect on her.

I was puzzled, but put the discussion out of my mind.

The first day of Autumn term arrived. This was my first time teaching, and I think I was a bit naive; I was certainly nervous. I had three earlier classes, and these were fine. I got to the last class of the day; as the students entered, I suddenly felt an overwhelming sensation in the room, like it was filled with something numinous. I looked up, and saw a young woman with long dark wavy hair and violet eyes. Her skin was like ivory, and her figure was willowy. I noticed that she had long fingers. She entered the classroom chatting with another friend, who I later identified as Rosa Price. As soon as she looked at me, I felt my courage wilting; I looked down at my hands and they were shaking. She hadn't done anything at all, not even spoken to me, but I felt very disoriented by her. What was wrong with me? And what was it about her? There seemed to be something uncanny about her.

As the term went on, I began to understand Father George's warning. She was indeed a good student, and attentive in class, but she asked a lot of questions. I learned that her sister was baptised, but she was not, which baffled me. When I asked her why, she simply said that they had different mothers with different wishes. She was always questioning points of dogma, and her very detailed questions suggested that she had read the Bible, and was trying to make sense of contradictions as an outsider. I would give her the canonical answer, but she always just shook her head. When I asked if she understood, she would always reply, "No. But I believe you when you say that's the rule."

Initially I used to ask why she didn't understand, but this generally led us into dangerous theological territory, so I stopped. I told her we could talk more about these things before or after class if she preferred. Sometimes she came to the office and asked questions, sometimes she didn't. I couldn't tell if she had a genuine interest in converting, but I'd foolishly hoped so. I convinced myself that this was why I allowed extended conversations with her—I was anxious to show people who were not Christians how this was the "right way".

But that really didn't carry any weight when I would return to the seminary for the evening. During prayers, meals, any activity—I found myself thinking of her. At night when I slept, I had the most outrageous fantasies about her, even to the point of having nocturnal emissions. I was sick at heart, and prayed to be delivered. But things only got worse, not better.

Before the beginning of class, students would come in and continue their hallway and lunchtime conversations in the classroom before the bell. One day another student mentioned something about the upcoming Witchfell concert, and directly asked Layla if she was going. Layla shrugged, and said, "possibly, if I'm given a ticket." Then the other student said, "Someone said you were dating Iain James; is that true?" Iain was the bass player for the band, as I later discovered. Layla shrugged again. "We've met..." was all she would say. Instantly I found my jealousy stoked. I managed to stifle it during class, but after school I found an excuse to get away from the seminary, and drove by the concert venue. As luck would have it (or not), I saw Layla being given a backstage pass, and greeting one of the long-haired fellows in the band, who kissed her passionately. Eventually when I saw a photo of the band, I realised that the rumour was true.

Well, it bothered me and tore at my heart, even knowing that it was none of my business, and I had no business thinking of this at all, especially not about one of my teenage students. It occurred to me that she was too young to be involved with this bloke as well—he had to be in his twenties, and it wasn't legal to have sex with a minor. Maybe that was why she demurred about their relationship. In any case, my fantasies about her were off the charts in their sadism; I felt grossly ashamed of myself, and even briefly engaged in self-punishment to stop the sinful thoughts. It didn't work.

Around this time I noticed that Miss Black looked at me rather curiously during class, as though she was reading me—I don't know why I thought that, but it was how it felt. I was determined to be as authoritative and cool as possible, but I was more nervous around her than ever. However, nothing was said, and I wasn't sure whether I wanted her to say anything to me or not—really, I desperately wanted to have her, and to have her go away at the same time.

The other thing significant thing that happened around this time had to do with my mother. I had always felt intimidated by her, and she made me feel guilty if I indulged in the slightest thing for myself. In retrospect, I'm pretty sure that I didn't have a true religious vocation—she told me I had one, or was going to have one. Everything was forced on me, and I felt like a bad and ungrateful child who had to make it up to her. God! I can't believe I lived with that for so long.

Well, one day she came to visit me at the seminary, and I took her out shopping in town. I remember that she was critical of everything I did, how I took care of myself, how I carried myself—it was really draining, but I felt I had no choice but to put up with it. She was Mother, after all. I thought God was testing me, and that I had to show patience.

My car was in the shop, so we took a bus around town, which clearly annoyed her. I remember sitting, feeling dazed, when suddenly I realised that Rosa and Layla had gotten onto the bus. My adrenaline immediately kicked in, and I could feel my heart racing. Layla pinpointed me with her eyes. *Oh God*, I thought. *Don't sit next to me…*

Well, of course she sat next to me. I instantly had an erection, and I felt that I had flushed as red as a lobster. She was looking at my mother with some amusement, and I realised she was looking to start trouble. I felt paralysed; I needed to do something, but I felt I could do nothing. She spoke to me, and I responded to her politely–but then she touched me rather suggestively, and I thought I would go through the roof. My heart was pounding; I didn't know what to do. She was leaving the bus, fortunately, so there was no time to react.

My mother, however, read me the riot act once we got off the bus. She said that the girl was a whore, and that I was weak and ineffective at putting her in her place. Now, I had always allowed my mother to dominate me–I was quite weak, truth be told–but I remember snapping back at her, which surprised both of us. I don't exactly know why I defended Layla, as I suspected she was something of a "loose" young woman, but I felt like she was disrespecting something sacred. It really didn't make sense to me at the time.

My mother turned on me, purple with rage. She told me I was a horrible son, and that it was obvious that the devil had taken a hold of me, and I ought to have been beaten within an inch of my life. I no longer remember how I responded to this harangue, but when I finally got back to my room and she had left, I just blacked out. Something inside of me was ready to explode.

I didn't want to do real self-examination, because it didn't take much to reveal what I didn't want to acknowledge—that I absolutely lusted after her, and was insanely but impotently jealous of any competition. I wanted to control her, and yet I had never been in control of any of the women in my life. The argument with my mother didn't help matters. Was that part of the problem? I didn't know; all I knew was that something would break soon.

Layla came to class the next week, and somehow I muddled through, though I was restless and irritable. I was becoming totally unhinged over the situation. And all at once, on Friday afternoon, after class, she marched into my office and sat down. I looked at her crossly.

"Yes, Miss Black, what can I do for you?"

She gave me a strange smile. "You have some interesting fantasies, Father Peter."

I froze. How did she know? She'd caught me off guard, so I stammered, "I...what are you talking about, young lady?"

"Oh, you know perfectly well what you want to do. I just want to tell you I'm intrigued, and if you want to have a go, meet me Saturday morning behind the house at 10:00 in the morning. My father is out all weekend, and if you want the weekend away with me, no one will ever know."

I stared at her in speechless astonishment. I am sure I sounded like an idiot in my response. "I…I don't know what you're talking about."

She shrugged. "Of course you do. You just don't think you can admit it. So, tomorrow morning at 10." She then glided off before I could say another word.

I could not focus at all during evening prayers, and ate and slept very little that night. I knew that there was no way I was not going to take Layla up on her offer, no matter what it cost me. I felt I would go mad otherwise.

As it so happened it was my free weekend at the seminary, and I told them I was going to visit my mother. Instead, Layla and I went to a family cottage in the Cotswolds. I kept her there for the entire weekend, bringing her home on Sunday night. The sex was insane—she allowed me to carry out some of my weirdest fantasies. After the first night, I felt a crushing sense of guilt; what I was doing was clearly wrong by any legal or ethical standards. When we sat down to a late supper together, I expressed my guilt. She just waved a dismissive hand.

"Rubbish," she said. "As I told you, you have had nothing but negative experiences with women—in fact, no experiences except your mother, who wouldn't allow any other women around you, and kept you a virgin. It's a kind of reverse Oedipus Complex. In any case, you feel completely alienated from women, and from your own body. You need to do something drastic to break out of it. I intimidate you, so you've projected all that angst onto me. I don't really mind, because I hate boring sex, and the stranger, the better, as far as I'm concerned."

I stared at her, feeling a little more relaxed after she said this, but everything still felt unreal. "Layla, can I ask you something?"

"Yes, of course."

"Who is your boyfriend? Is he that bass player bloke..."

"I don't have one. I'm not interested in serious relationships. I'm only fourteen, for heaven's sake. Iain desperately wants a serious relationship, but I can't give that to him. I am also involved with someone else, someone who is married—but that is also a special situation."

"Well, that does qualify as infidelity..."

She wagged her finger at me. "I am his goddess, not his girlfriend. The gods may have even the avowed virgins."

"What do you mean, you're his goddess?"

She smiled. "Exactly what I said. Why do you think my father didn't baptise me? I don't worship anyone; they worship me."

I was taken aback by this display of apparent narcissism. "Well, I mean you're a beautiful girl, but..."

"But not a goddess? That's where you're mistaken. You don't believe in the old gods, but that doesn't mean we don't exist."

"Layla—while I admit there's something rather uncanny about you, I don't know that I can accept that. I am a priest, you know."

She stretched her arms over her head. "Accept whatever you want. It doesn't change the fact. You may not believe it now, but you will later on. The world in general had better start accepting its goddesses; you're all headed for extinction if you don't. You have lost touch with the earth."

I didn't know whether she was delusional, if this was a joke, or if this was serious. I decided to treat her declaration as serious.

"What does your father think of all this?"

She laughed. "He doesn't know a bloody thing about my relationships. I deliberately keep him in the dark, because he worries too much about things out of his control."

"But—does he know what you say about being a goddess?"

"Of course he does. He knows how I was born. He was there, you know." She chuckled.

"And…how were you born?"

"Ah, that is a secret. But never mind—you can meditate on that in the future. In the meantime, we need to talk about you."

"About me?"

"Yes—about you and your so-called 'vocation'."

"I don't understand."

"Peter, you are not meant to be a priest. You haven't taken final vows yet, so you're free to leave. And you are allowing your life force to be sucked away by that harpy who calls herself your mother. You deserve much better than this."

"But…there's really nowhere else I can go." I think this was the first time I admitted that I felt trapped.

"Nonsense. You have options. Here is what I recommend. First, you have paintings, yes? You may have put them away, but you should take them with you. I can introduce you to a friend of my father's who runs an art colony in Portugal. I feel like you will do well there, and that you will meet a nice young woman that you can love and respect. You should change your name entirely, and change your papers at the same time—that should take a few weeks. Once you have that—book yourself a ferry to France and a train to Portugal, where I will have you meet up with Daddy's friend. The night before you leave, send a letter resigning from your job and from the seminary. And whatever you do, tell NO ONE. Your mother will find out and throw a fit, but she will not be able to find you—I will make sure of that. And very quickly you will see how happy you are to be free and doing what you love."

I have no idea how she knew that I'd painted, but I suppose that was the least strange thing about the conversation. In retrospect, I had to have been in quite a state to have simply accepted what she said as I did. When I talk about it out loud … her idea isn't a mad one, not exactly, but I still marvel that I was so willing to listen to her, one of my teenage students, telling me some very strange things. Perhaps when you are desperate, you are open to anything.

Ultimately I did what she suggested, and she was right—I was very happy away from the seminary, away from my family, and with a woman I loved. I felt a tinge of remorse, as I wanted to be with Layla initially, but she told me that she was too dangerous to be relationship material. We did, however, meet up several more times outside of school before all that went off.

Layla gave me a new name, and it's like it made me a new person. I can hardly believe that I had such a miserable existence before this, and that I'd actually put up with it. I've been cut off from my family of course, but I can't say I miss them; they were a kind of curse, truth be told.

I think I would have always seen her as a remarkable young woman rather than a goddess, if the battle hadn't taken place. I now realise that God was looking out for me—but it wasn't the god I expected.

11

Jesus…Layla…

I met Layla in London. The band was having its after show party at a club in Chelsea; I can't remember the name of it now; I think it's become something else anyway. On the weekends she and her girlfriends would take the train into the city and go there. I'm not sure how they got in, as they were all too young, but I'm sure that the fact she was Malcolm Black's daughter helped.

When I saw her for the first time, I didn't know anything about her. All I knew was that I was looking at the most beautiful woman I'd ever seen. I could not stop staring at her. She actually made me weak in the knees. Most of the men there were staring at her, and I'm sure I wasn't the only one who wanted her attention.

Her friend must have noticed me staring at her, because she nudged Layla and pointed at me. Layla looked over, and we made eye contact. She smiled, and at that moment I knew she had me; I would literally do anything for her, or to be with her. She did not come over right away; I desperately wanted to talk to her. She finally walked my way, and I approached her before she could walk past me.

"Wait! Please—can I talk to you?"

"But of course! What do you want to know?"

"What's your name?"

"Layla Black. And you are Iain James?"

"Yes, yes I am."

"After show party, is it?"

"Yes, it is."

"Where did you play?"

"At the Roundhouse."

"Oh, this is a bit out of the way from there, isn't it?"

"Where are you from?"

"I live in Esher."

"Do you live alone?"

"Oh my, no. I live with my father and sister. I'm only thirteen."

"You're thirteen??"

She nodded sadly. "Yes, I'm afraid so."

"But you look older than thirteen!"

"Yes, I do look a bit older, I think. But I don't know that you want to take a chance on me; I don't want you to get into trouble."

My heart sank. She was probably right, but I couldn't bear to let it go. "I don't want that to be an issue—please don't go away."

She laughed. "Well, if you wish, but we'll have to keep it a secret."

I was prepared to do that. I didn't like it, and I should have walked away right then and there, but I would take whatever I could get. I brought her over to a corner where we could sit alone, and we talked for some time. I took her to a private room in the back, and must have kissed her for about twenty minutes. I really wanted to make love to her, but that seemed too quick and too presumptuous. I didn't want her to be a one-night stand; I hoped we could see each other for awhile, and that we could be in a real relationship when she turned eighteen. She gave me her private phone number before she left, and kissed me goodnight. She told me I could call her late at night, even after midnight. If she was home and in her room, she would answer.

When she left I was on a real mental roller coaster. I was so happy to have been able to touch her, to kiss her, and have her close, but I hated her being away, and I was extremely paranoid about the whole setup. I was less worried about being caught with a thirteen-year-old and more worried about other blokes; there was no way I wasn't going to have competition for her. But there wasn't much I could do about it.

I would call her almost every day; sometimes she answered, sometimes she didn't, and it drove me crazy when I couldn't speak to her. Trying to arrange to see her was difficult; I loved it when she could sneak away for a whole weekend and come to my house in Derby. Sometimes she also came to gigs; I would make sure she was hooked up with tickets and backstage passes, and I could have time alone with her before and after the gig. The time we spent together—to this day, I would say that there was nothing in my life that made me more happy or blissful then having her close to me.

But the flip side of this was that she was so detached. When I wanted to talk about the longer term, she seemed lukewarm about it. She told me she wasn't in favour of marriage, and did not want to make any long-term love commitments; she had too many years ahead of her to think about that, if she would ever do it. While she was probably being sensible, I couldn't take it. I hated not having any control over her, or the relationship; I was not used to a woman who wasn't jealous, possessive, or needy. While that should be great–I don't know. I wanted her to be a little possessive, honestly.

I also had the feeling that she was involved with other blokes. She told me she was not in a relationship with anyone else, but technically in her mind she and I were not in a "relationship" and we were having sex. I desperately wanted to know if there was anyone else, but I was also too terrified to ask. I wanted to believe that she would change, that things would change once there were fewer limits on being together.

She never mentioned that Malcolm Black was her father; I found that out quite by accident when he was on tour with Steve Abbott, and I saw a photo of her there with them. I admit it gave me a start; I thought she was sleeping with one of them, and I was relieved, but also shocked that she never mentioned it. The next time I spoke to her I asked her about it. "Oh yeah, that's Daddy," she said, and laughed softly, as she often did. Malcolm Black was an idol to most of us, so it just made me that much more in awe of her.

Things were more or less alright for a while, but then one of our roadies, who had worked on the Black/Abbott tour as

65

well, told our singer Zach that he thought Layla was sleeping with Steve Abbott. He saw Abbott slip her his spare room key at hotel check-in, and he knew that Malcolm wondered where she went in the evenings, as she was not in her own room.

I remember that I went home and cried after this revelation. I tried to reason it away; maybe our roadie didn't see what he thought he saw. But it really ate at me, until I couldn't think of anything else. I finally had to ask her about it; my stomach burned and my head ached as I made the phone call.

"Hello, Iain! How are you, love?"

"Well, not so good actually…"

"Oh? What's the matter?"

I let out a shaky breath. "Layla—I heard something about you today, and I have to know if it's true."

"Did you? What did you hear?"

I explained what the roadie told me. She laughed. "Of course I spend time with Steve Abbott. His wife doesn't come on tour, you know. My father's girlfriend comes along, and I know she wants him to herself. So, I keep Steve company."

I calmed down a little, but still felt some panic. "You're… you're not having sex with him, are you?"

"Does that make a difference?"

Now I was upset again. "Of course it makes a fucking difference! I don't want you sleeping with anyone else!"

She was silent for a moment. "Hmm, well, Iain—as I've told you, I don't mind dating you, but I can't be committed. You tour and have lots of beautiful women at your disposal—I would never stop you from getting involved. While I enjoy being with you, I'm not your possession. And you're not mine."

"Layla, I have NEVER cheated on you with any woman who has come backstage."

"Well, you could if you wanted to. I never said you couldn't. I don't see that as cheating."

"Look—we obviously don't view this relationship the same way."

"Yes, I guess we don't. What do you want to do about it?"

"Layla—I love you. It already breaks my heart that I can't be with you every day. I don't even think you care about me; I can't even bear that thought."

"Oh now really, Iain, enough of the dramatics. Of course I care about you. But I have already told you over and over again that I am not looking for serious attachments—and in spite of any feelings, it makes no sense whatsoever for us to get so attached. You will get into deep trouble."

I really did not know what to do at this point. I should have just broken up with her, but I couldn't do it—I felt like I would stop breathing if she wasn't in my life. So I finally said, "OK, I'm just going to have to deal with it, I guess. When will I see you again?"

"Hmm...well, it may be a month or so."

"A month??"

"Yes. I'm thinking about the next four weekends, and there's something happening every weekend."

"What exactly is going on?"

"Different things—mostly related to family and school."

"But doesn't school get out for you soon?"

"Yes, it does—and my father wants to go away when school gets out."

I sighed. "Just tell me when I can see you again, if I make it that long."

I could almost hear her eyes rolling on the other end of the phone. "I can see you during the second week of July, if you're around. I'll let you know if I'm free sooner than that."

"I'll make myself be around."

"Alright then. We'll be in touch before then. I have to dash now—ta!"

I held a dead phone in my hand. I felt sick inside. I was supposed to go out with my mates that evening, but I ended up canceling. The band had more work to do—we had an album to finish. But my heart was not in it; I was depressed.

Finally Zach and our guitarist Andy took me aside one day. "Look Iain, something's up with you. You're not yourself. What's going on?"

I told them what was going on with Layla, and had a hard time containing tears. They both looked at each other, and then at me. Zach spoke up:

"Look mate—she's an unbelievably beautiful girl, she's Black's daughter—I get why you're really into her. And I can tell it's really bugging you—I'm sorry. But you can correct me if I'm wrong—I don't think she's promised to be committed to you in any way. I've overheard more than one of these discussions—she's pretty clear that she finds you attractive and likes it when she sees you, but she's not making a commitment. Frankly, I'm surprised that a thirteen-year-old girl has that much sense. She's really doing what's best for you—she doesn't want you to get in trouble, she wants you to be free to do what you want on tour. Maybe it's because she's Black's daughter; you know she grew up around all that."

"It doesn't change how I feel about it. I'm sick about it."

"I know you are—and maybe you just need to get out of this situation."

"I am NOT breaking up with her."

"Iain—your choice is to either do that or miserably wait around for her, when I don't think she's ultimately going to do what you want."

"You don't know that."

"No, I guess I don't. But it's making you crazy, and I really do not think she is the marrying type."

"She may change her mind. She's only thirteen."

They both gave me an exasperated look. "Mate, you are OBSESSED. This is not healthy—even if she did change her mind."

"Look, I don't want to talk about it anymore." I got up and walked out of the room. I knew deep down they were both right, but I still couldn't bear the idea of leaving her. Anything was better than nothing, as far as I was concerned.

I should have listened to them. Things didn't get better; they got worse. The rumours got worse—I heard she was having a go with a priest at her school, with one of her female friends—and there was speculation that she was a little too intimate with her own father. That last one could have just been slander, or maybe someone just trying to push me to the last straw. But I felt there had to be a grain of truth to some of the rumours, at least.

I think I officially blew it when I confronted Abbott about his relationship with her. He denied they were in a relationship, and was not very forthcoming about the time he spent with her. We almost came to blows over it, but fortunately he was able to calm me down. I did have an emotional breakdown after that; I realised that I was deluding myself, and I just couldn't deal with it. Breaking up was the only right thing to do, but it felt like self-castration.

As it turns out, I didn't have to initiate that talk; Layla had already made up her mind. The next time I managed to see her, she rather gently told me that she wanted to end the relationship. I was too stressed and strung out by the circumstances, and she was not going to string me along. I was absolutely devastated; I didn't think I'd ever get over it. I did not want to let her leave, but when I confronted her, she grabbed my arm, and said, "Don't." I was absolutely shocked by the power in her grip; I felt like she could snap my arm in two, and she wasn't holding me that tightly.

I couldn't accept the breakup. I would go to places that we frequented, but she did not turn up. I tried to call her, but she did not answer her phone. She was deliberately avoiding me, and it hurt like hell. I felt like I'd been stabbed and left to bleed to death.

It took me a long time to recover emotionally from my involvement with her. I realised when I had time to clear my head that something was really strange about her. I can tell you that I've fallen in love with other women, but never like that; there was something about her that really brought you to your knees, and it wasn't just that she was beautiful. In retrospect, I understand that I could never have lived with her, and I really am better off—but I still have an emotional wound that just will not heal.

12

Steve Abbott's Diary

It's been almost ten years since I originally wrote about Layla. Not much happened in the interim, which is why I put this aside for so long. The only thing I can add looking over my previous entry is that I did research the Morrigan's curse, and found that a male child, usually aged two or three, dies every nine years on June twenty-first. No two children died of the same thing; some had sudden illnesses, some were in accidents, some ate or drank things that caused a severe and fatal allergic reaction. The theory about a genetic weakness didn't add up. 1976 would have been the last death, and that was when my cousin's child died. The next death is due this year, if this curse is a real thing. I think my daughter may be old enough to be safe—at least I hope so. The fact that they all occur on the same date and in the same cycle of years is hard to discount; I wish I could write it off as something logical.

So, Malcolm Black is no longer with Armadel, another great band destroyed by internal politics and egos. He's very pale, looks sickly, and takes a lot of drugs, cocaine mainly. I have heard from others that Layla is not happy about this, and has threatened to disembowel his drug dealers; she's been scary enough that they have been staying away as of late. Knowing what I think I do about her, I'm not surprised. In any case, I hope it helps Malcolm; we're not spring chickens anymore, but he's still too young to die.

Malcolm and I met up recently at a concert, and he asked me if I'd like to write some songs together. I think he has one particular song in mind that he'd written, but of course you don't record just one song, you make an album. I actually like Malcolm a lot, so I'd agreed, though I tried to stay away from his house. As I am about to explain, I have been unsuccessful at this. I go there often, and it's been very much against my will.

We worked together a bit at my London house, but Malcolm has a studio in Esher that he's recently fixed up; we can do a lot more there in terms of creating tracks without incurring the expense of studio time. I was hesitant; I thought, "No, I'll just commute from London to Esher, it's not that far away." But as I was about to say that to him, the words that came out were, "That sounds great, I appreciate your hospitality." I hadn't discussed this with my wife, who had already complained that I was on the road too much. Surprisingly she did not give me a problem; I was kind of hoping she would, so I would have an excuse. There is nothing wrong with Malcolm's house, but I dreaded what might happen next with Layla.

I arrived on a Thursday morning, and Malcolm welcomed me into the house. We sat and talked for quite awhile, both business and pleasure. The time went by, and Malcolm said, "Oh shit, look at the time—my girls will be home from school soon. I just have to talk to them when they get in, and we can get back to business." A few minutes later, Layla and Anika Black entered the house in their school uniforms, deep in conversation about something. Malcolm introduced Anika to me, and then Layla. Layla smiled and said "Yes, we've met before."

Malcolm looked puzzled. "You have? When? I don't remember that."

Layla waved her arm noncommittally. "It was a long time ago, you probably forgot. Where is Mr. Abbott staying?"

"I haven't even offered to bring up his bags yet—I was thinking the second floor guestroom."

"Oh no," said Layla, "not there. Anika has her school project spread out in that room. Why don't you put him in the new guestroom on the third floor? He'll have his own toilet and privacy that way."

"Oh yeah, good idea, I tend to forget that we redid that room. Is it OK for you to be on the third floor, Steve?"

"Yes, fine—whatever works for you works for me." I was congenial, but felt very nervous around Layla. I was overwhelmed by how beautiful she was, and the powerful charisma, or aura, or something, that she had. I was both captivated and terrified at the same time.

"Brilliant. Come, Steve, I'll show you your room," said Layla. She looked at her father, "We'll be right back down."

She led me up the stairs with my baggage, and took me into a turret room with a skylight, and as she had noted, its own bathroom. "What do you think?" she said, turning to me.

"It's lovely—this is more than fine, thank you very much." I put my things down. I felt her eyes on me. When I turned around, she was smirking at me. I felt uneasy. She broke the silence, saying "Come now, you should go downstairs. I will see you later on." As she said this, she ran her hand along my back, and brushed it across the front of my trousers. I felt immediately aroused, and I'm sure I blushed; my face felt hot. She pulled me to face her, and she kissed me on the lips, pushing her tongue into my mouth. Then she released me, and led me to the staircase.

My encounter with Layla left me feeling disordered, and seeing her come downstairs, changed out of her school clothes and now wearing a short skirt, just made me feel more off balance. I forced myself to be present, and think about why Malcolm had invited me, trying to put her out of my mind. She told her father she was going out and would be back later.

"Will you be back in time for tea?"

"What are we having for tea?"

"Um...er...I was kind of hoping you could cook..."

Layla rolled her eyes, and shook her head. "Men, you are so useless for anything. Fine, I'll be home by 6:30, and I'll cook something."

Malcolm smiled, "Thank you sweetheart, I appreciate it." She kissed him fully on the lips, which was startling, and not just a bit uncomfortable. She then said goodbye to both of us and flounced out the door.

We went into Malcolm's studio, and started playing around with some song ideas. We were absorbed in doing this when we suddenly heard the front door open, and realised that Layla was home. "Oh, that means tea will be ready soon," said Malcolm. "We can finish up with this and then take a break."

We all chatted over the meal, and I felt odd trying to make small talk. I mainly let Layla talk to Malcolm, who asked about her day, her classes, and about one of her teachers in particular, an Anglican priest who taught her Christian Ethics course. Malcolm said he was suspicious of the man, because he

75

felt that for all the piety of his office, his reaction to Layla suggested that he wanted something else from her.

"You think so?" said Layla.

"I know so. I know how blokes are; I am one, you know."

"I hadn't noticed."

Malcolm shot her a look as she smirked at him. "I'm serious, Layla."

"Aren't you always?" She was buttering a piece of bread and popped it into her mouth.

Malcolm put his fork down. "Look—I am your father, and I have a right to be concerned, and also to know what you've been up to. You share very little with me, which only makes me more concerned, and frankly, hurts my feelings."

"Oh cut it out. I tell you what you need to know. It's not good for you to know some things."

Malcolm sighed. "Promise me that nothing is going on with this chap?"

She shrugged. "What if something is?"

"Layla!"

"There isn't anything going on, but I'm not necessarily unwilling. He's rather attractive, you know."

Malcolm grabbed her hand. "Layla—I don't want you involved with him. Period."

"Why not? It's peculiar that you have it in for this chap, and not others I've been around."

"I just don't. That should be enough."

"Well, whatever. Are you finished?" She stood up and began to clear the table.

We finished eating, and Anika volunteered to take care of the dishes, as her sister did the cooking. Layla helped her anyway, and then announced she was going upstairs to do her homework.

Malcolm and I sat up late into the evening, enjoying a nightcap, and then eventually said goodnight. I went up to my room, remembering the extra steps, and got ready for bed.

I'm not sure how long I dozed; it might have only been an hour—when I awoke and realised I was not alone in the room. The moonlight shined brightly through the skylight, and there was a silhouette in front of me, illuminated by the moon.

Layla.

When she saw that I was awake, she immediately slid onto the bed, and pushed my arms down into the mattress. She smiled at me, and pulled my trousers down. I realised that she had no knickers on underneath the dress she was wearing. She climbed on top of me and rode me in a manner that no woman ever had before—it didn't seem natural. But I was deeply aroused, and came violently. She put her hand over my mouth as I cried out in orgasm. She gave me a wicked grin, and then leaned over and kissed me passionately. It was probably only a few minutes, but it felt like she was there for hours, as I was somehow anxious and blissful at the same time. Then she waved her hand over my eyes, and I remembered nothing until morning.

13

It wasn't often that Layla toured with us, due to her school schedule. However, if we toured over her Easter break, or during the summer, she usually joined us. Mal's girlfriend Lisa would also come along; I'm not sure how well she and Layla got on. I think Lisa was jealous of her, and the place she had in Mal's life. Whenever she raised any kind of fuss about Layla, Mal basically told her to mind her own business; Layla was his worry, and if she didn't like it she could leave. This didn't go over well with Lisa, but she would usually shut her mouth, more fearful that she would lose what she had with Mal. When she got pregnant a couple years later, I think she thought she would have more say in the household. Mal did marry her, but nothing else changed; Layla still dominated the household. I have a feeling their later divorce happened at least in part because Layla was clearly first in Mal's life, and he was hostile to any competition. As long as his partners respected her place, it was fine.

At any rate, when we were touring, there was the potential for a lot of tension, as Mal wanted Layla to spend time with himself and Lisa. But Layla wasn't interested; she said his girlfriend didn't come all this way to hang out with his daughter, they should have some time to themselves. You could read the relief on Lisa's face, but Malcolm was ambivalent. On the one hand, she seemed to be respecting his relationship, but on the other—he knew what kind of mischief Layla could get into, and didn't fancy leaving her on her own. He didn't really think her refusal to spend time with them was in any deference to his girlfriend.

What Mal didn't know was that Layla spent her time after gigs in my hotel room, and often stayed all night. My wife never came along on tour; occasionally she would come to a gig with our daughter, but it was rare. She certainly never came to the American gigs. When the lot of us were checking into the hotel, we usually got two room keys; I always slipped the extra one to Layla.

When she came by we usually dined together in the room, and usually polished off a bottle of wine or two. We would talk for long periods of time, and we always ended up having sex. Truthfully, it made touring bearable; I was getting to an age where I didn't want to go out partying so much after gigs, and this kept it from being boring. When she wasn't there, I always missed her; I would be invited out to do other things, but it wasn't the same. I was becoming extremely attached to her, and I wasn't sure how I felt about it. On the one hand I was happy to be with this extraordinarily gorgeous young woman; however, she was still underage, I was married, and this was my good friend's daughter. Neither he nor my wife had any idea what was going on.

On one such night I brought this up to her. She gave me a sour look. "You need to be constantly reminded that I am your goddess, not your wife, and not your girlfriend. There may have been ethical questions if I was an ordinary mortal. You forget that I am not."

"But why is this different? Why don't those ethics apply to this situation?"

She tapped her fingers on the wine glass in her hand. "Have you ever read any mythology from any culture?"

"Well, yes…"

"Mmm-hmm. And what do relationships between gods, and between gods and mortals, look like?"

"I'm not sure I understand the question."

"Well—let's take the Greeks for example. Zeus is king of the gods; Hera is his wife. Hera is also his sister. Do you think Zeus is bothered about incest? No. He's a god, he's a force in the universe. In spite of any mortal appearance, human rules don't apply to him. I'm always amused by philosophers and your priests who use the same measuring stick for gods and mortals. We're not like you; your rules don't apply."

"Well, you look like us. What makes you different? I mean, I can see that you have an extraordinary mind, and a lot of physical strength. But it has to be more than that."

"Yes, much more than that. Let me show you." There was a sharp knife that had been brought to the room with dinner and was unused. She took it and slashed her arm; I almost jumped ten feet when she did that. But what came out of her arm was not blood; it was a purplish kind of substance. Within an instant of seeing this, the skin suddenly closed up over the wound as if nothing happened.

"That's the first thing; I can't be wounded or killed. I don't bruise, break, or bleed. I'm immortal in body." She put the knife down and picked up a heavy paperweight that was in the room, probably made from iron. She handed it to me.

"Try to break that."

"What, with my hands?"

"Yes."

"I can't possibly break that with my hands. It would have to be melted down."

"Just try."

I gave the thing a squeeze as hard as I could, and as I expected, nothing happened. "Now give it to me," she said. I obeyed her, and she squeezed it in her own hand. I could hear it crack and crumble. What she dumped in the rubbish bin was nothing but iron dust and shards.

"That's the second thing; I am physically stronger than you, not just in being more physically fit. I could snap you like a twig if I wanted to. Now then, tell me this. Can you teleport your body around the room? Could you be sitting here in this chair and suddenly disappear and reappear on the other side of the bed?"

"No, I couldn't."

She then proceeded to do just that; I watched her vanish and reappear on the other side of the room. "That is the third thing; my body is not like yours, and thus I can rearrange my molecules at will. On the same subject—can you change shape into something else?"

"No."

I suddenly watched her body contract like flowing water, and she turned into a crow. It sat on the bed looking at me. The whole thing was starting to freak me out.

She changed back into herself. "I can change into whatever I want; that is the fourth thing. In addition I can speak all languages, I know all texts, and can accurately tell you the future most of the time. I have control over the fate of the dead. The only thing I can't do is to change what is fated; sometimes I can mitigate a disaster, but I can't always prevent death, or other such things. But I have control about ninety percent of the time. Now, do you need any further examples of how I'm different from you?"

"No, I think you've amply proven your point."

She returned to her chair, sitting cross-legged, and picked up her wine glass. I was thoughtful. "You know—I do want to ask—my grandmother always says you're a demon. I don't really believe that. What's the difference between demons and gods?"

Layla shrugged. "Demons are largely an invention of your religion. I mean, there are all kinds of spirits, and many more races than the human one. To call something 'demonic' means that you consider it inferior. The original word has nothing to do with evil spirits; a daimon is a helpful spirit, a mediator between gods and humans. Socrates claimed his knowledge was from a daimon. There are certainly other beings with evil intent, but there are humans with evil intent as well; it's a character trait. Humans in general have more evil traits than most of what you call pagan gods. In Christian-speak, "demon" basically means anything that's "not Jesus." That is why your grandmother thinks of me as a demon, or a false god. But she has no understanding of pagan gods whatsoever—or of her own." She emptied her wine glass, and held it out to me to pour her another.

"What doesn't she understand about her own god?"

"Well, for starters, her god is one of many; she may believe in one god and reject the others, but they still exist. And," she said, taking another drink, "her Jesus doesn't like treasonous behavior any more than I do."

I was silent for a moment. "So—she goes to church, as have other family members before, and prays for deliverance from the family curse, but Jesus is just as annoyed about the transgression as you are?"

"That is correct."

"But I thought Jesus was a forgiving god?"

"It's not his forgiveness that you need. It's mine. Think about it—and I know you have—what if someone came in and slaughtered your family, but did it in 'the name of Jesus' to save you? You'd be furious, and you'd want justice. And the perpetrators don't apologise—they call you evil for not accepting that, they've done it "for your own good." Things are not OK just 'because Jesus'."

"I definitely agree with that. But surely he was not the only king to convert to Christianity at that time?"

"No, he was not. But none of those kings broke their vows. Some mixed the two traditions, following Christian teachings but also giving me my due. Others simply said they could not take vows to me, because they were Christian. Others tolerated Christianity in the kingdoms, but still kept me as their main goddess, leaving the next king to decide what he would do. In all those cases, no solemn vows were broken. Duagh is the only one. And he was not exactly respectful about it either. Do you remember your dream, where he was addressing the people after his conversion?"

"So that dream WAS about this whole thing…"

She waved her hand impatiently. "Yes, you already know that. Do you remember that? But you don't know the language; you don't know what he said."

"I do remember the scene. But you're right, I had no idea what he said; all I know is that it seemed to make people upset."

"Indeed it did. He said he had converted to the true religion, and he was not going to bow to a woman, one he basically called a filthy devilish whore."

I whistled. "OK, I definitely did not catch that. That is really bad."

"Yes it is. Especially for a warrior. Warriors who reject the war goddess never end well."

"But isn't war a very male thing?"

"No, it isn't. Yes, there are war gods, obviously. But the root force is feminine. Back to Greece—there is Ares, the god of war. But there is also Athena. And who is the one who gives warriors their victories? Athena. When the two go head-to-head in combat, who wins? Athena. In Ireland I am a goddess of war; I provide the battle fury. Warriors who dismiss me, especially because I am a woman, do not succeed and usually die horribly."

"Well, if the dream is to be believed, he certainly did die horribly."

"Yes, that's exactly how he died, and how your family came to be cursed."

I sat back thoughtfully. "I only had this discussion with my Gran once; she was very angry with me for suggesting that Duagh committed treason; said he was blessed by St. Patrick."

Layla snorted. "St. Patrick! The bollocks that he spread around, and that is written about him...if anyone thinks he could best the pagan gods, they've taken the mick."

"Really? That's what I always understood."

"Of course. That's the only formal written account you have. Druids didn't write things down, you know; everything had to be kept in here," she pointed to her heart.

"Surely you mean here?" I pointed to my head.

"No. That is another mistake. Here." She pointed again to her heart. "In any case, there was a lot of propaganda, and the previous Roman rule really set the stage for that. I've never seen such a rigid lot. It doesn't have to be a problem, but when you only allow for one god...I suppose that's the one thing Caesar didn't do, though he still lied about the Druids. In any case, Christianity won out in the end because we withdrew; humans were going through a bad cycle, were becoming more aggressive toward us, and it was better that we regroup before returning. When the consciousness of the people changes, sometimes it is better not to fight the tide. Christianity happened to fit that change, Patrick or no Patrick. He just became a poster boy for the monks, a kind of comic-book superhero. But it was bollocks."

I was fascinated to hear all of this. "So—what is the truth anyway?"

She smiled. "You will find out one day, if you ask the right questions."

"What questions are those?"

"The ones that will remove your family curse."

Now I was sitting up. "And what are they?"

"Well, I can't tell you."

"Why not?"

"Because that violates the terms of breaking the curse. You have to come to it yourself and act on it; if I tell you, it's no good. You're actually quite close, you just need to make another mental leap."

Now I found myself wondering what the question was; did I already know it? She read my mind. "Don't stress yourself about it now; let it come naturally. There's actually a lot that you need to let go of before you figure it out, and are committed to action. But it will come."

"I suppose. But now it will bother me."

"Don't worry—you have more trials ahead before you get to that point."

"Trials?"

"Yes. Remember this too—I am your goddess, and everything I do with you and for you is meaningful. When I have sex with you, it's to empower you, and to strengthen the bond between us, which is critical to so much more than just your

86

family situation. While you haven't taken the final step you need to take, you essentially gave yourself over to me when you came into my room in 1975. Which, in spite of what your Gran says, or society, or anyone else, is not a terrible thing. I have much to teach you, and you actually can do a lot for your fellow humans. But I have to break you of certain beliefs and mindsets."

With that, she exhorted me to finish my wine, and come to bed. I had many strange dreams that night, but I couldn't remember them.

14

Steve Abbott's Diary

It was a week after we returned from our American tour that the story broke in the newspaper. A gruesome set of murders had occurred in London, and the perpetrator was still at large. The victims were all young girls in their late teens to early twenties. All of them had been raped, and had vicious looking lacerations all over their bodies, and fearsome bite marks. The dead girls' faces were all frozen in a look of terror. Most of them had been out partying until midnight, in the southern part of London near Brixton, but in one case, a girl disappeared while walking home from school in the West End. It was on the edge of one of the rougher neighborhoods in the city, but not one with a particularly bad reputation. The whole thing raised considerable alarm in the city center, and also in the surrounding communities.

Though Esher seemed reasonably safe from all the action, the schools were still taking precautions. Parents were still told to drive the children to school, and to pick them up again, at least until some progress had been made on the case, and Malcolm insisted on doing this for Layla and Anika. Anika didn't mind, but Layla, as expected, found it ridiculous, at least for herself.

Later that week, a description of the killer appeared in the newspaper, with a police sketch. It was at this point that Layla took a particular interest in the case. One of his intended victims managed to escape, and the description she gave police was horrifying; she was severely traumatised and had to be under psychiatric care for awhile in order to recover. He sounded rather scruffy, with long scraggly blondish hair with lots of curls. His eyes were brown and rather menacing. But what was really frightening were his teeth and his hands—he was described as having long needle-like teeth, and long claw-like fingers. It was as though he was half-human, and half-monster.

Malcolm read the description at the breakfast table to Layla, Anika, and me. "Good Lord," he said. "Are they sure the girl wasn't on hard drugs or something when she saw him?"

"Well, those features are consistent with the bite and claw marks they found on the other victims," I replied.

"But that's just impossible, unless the guy is wearing a disguise."

Layla gave him a sharp look. "Is it?"

"What do you mean?"

She stared at the drawing thoughtfully. She had a curious look in her eyes. "He's from a different race..."

"I don't know of any races that look like that," I said.

She gave me one of her looks. "You're thinking of humans."

"What other races are there?"

"You know perfectly well. We've discussed it."

I was puzzled, but soon realised she was talking about our tour conversations. Malcolm didn't know about these and asked, "He has? When?"

But Layla did not answer. She tapped her fingers on the table, and seemed to be thinking.

Malcolm looked at her disapprovingly. "I know that look. You mean to do something."

"Of course I mean to do something. He can't keep murdering people. I'm sure he's doing it because people don't understand what he is, and treat him like a monster."

"Well, you haven't told us WHAT he is."

"It's hard to explain. But he's a kind of elemental being. They're not necessarily evil, but they look scary. If he's been treated like a monster, he's likely to act like one."

"If he's out killing and raping women, that sounds pretty evil."

"Yes—but what's not known is whether or not he is that way because he is just purely evil, or if he has become evil through monstrous treatment by others."

"So, what exactly do you intend to do?"

"Nothing you should worry about."

"Layla!"

She looked directly at Malcolm, with some irritation. "What?"

"You're planning to confront that bloke, aren't you?" he said.

"Yes, I am."

"No. I don't want you getting involved."

I was surprised at how fast she turned on him. "It's not your business to tell me what to get involved in. I may have reasons you don't know need to know about." Her eyes were fierce.

Malcolm cowered a bit. "Well, you know how I feel. I'm responsible for you, you know."

"And it doesn't involve you at all. You have no need to be concerned."

Malcolm opened his mouth to say something else, but thought better of it. He still drove the girls to school, and had them picked up. In retrospect, I wonder why he never questioned Layla's mention of these things in my presence. After all, he didn't know that I knew about her...

That night, the girls went to bed as usual, but Layla never came to my room.

***

Mila's Vision

Layla stood on a South London street corner, and sniffed the air. All of her feelers went out, trying to home in on where the killer was at this moment. She felt that he was not far, maybe a couple of blocks over. Layla had an image of an abandoned warehouse, and walked in that direction.

Sure enough, she rounded the corner, and there was the place in her vision. She entered the building, which was pitch black. The floors creaked, and felt rotten in parts. In the slivers of moonlight that passed through the boarded-up windows, graffiti could be seen on the walls, and rubbish everywhere. She stood inside for a moment, and then headed down to the basement.

Layla cast an eerie shadow as she headed down the stairs. She could see a faint light. Moving toward it, she saw him—he had a small fire going in an old stove that had undoubtedly been out of use for years. He had heard her coming, and turned and stared at her with wide eyes. He rose to his feet.

"I wasn't expecting company." He eyed Layla, looking her over with a mixture of interest and suspicion. "Not very smart coming down here."

She continued to walk toward him, clearly unafraid. This puzzled him, and made him more suspicious. "Who are you?"

She responded to him in a strange tongue: "Can you take a guess?"

Now he was taken aback. "Who taught you to speak that way?"

She shrugged. "It's natural. I'm the queen of the De Dananns and the Fomorians."

He groaned in disappointment. He had hoped that his visitor was somehow lost, and that he could have his prey without even having to leave his lair.

Layla read his thoughts. "Sorry to disappoint you. You won't be able to kill me."

He grumbled.

Layla reached into her bag, and pulled out a bottle of whisky. "There now, don't look so pouty. I didn't come to make your life difficult. You may even get part of what you hope for."

He took the bottle from her, and now looked curious. "Why are you here?"

"I'll get to that. But come, let us sit—I have things to ask you."

He laughed. "Surely you notice this isn't much of a sitting room."

She shrugged. "It is no matter. I will make do." They sat down on some broken down furniture. "Tell me—what is your name?" she asked.

"Well, I was named Judas, though my mother had other names for me, even less complimentary, as you might imagine." He chuckled. She put me out of the house as soon as I was born, and became a born-again Christian from what I hear. I was bounced from orphanage to orphanage, but I was always kept in the cellar. The nuns hated me; thought I was a demon. Really, I've grown up quite feral."

"Now, that means your mother is human. So your father is a Fomorian. How did that encounter manage to happen? Fomorians are rare in these parts these days."

"Ah, yes indeed. She never told me how she encountered him; I think she was off on a holiday somewhere, in an isolated part of the woods. Somewhere in the West Country. She encountered him when she was out very late one night, and we can just say that it wasn't a mutual love encounter." He took another swig from the bottle.

Layla shuddered. She couldn't imagine what that would be like for a mortal woman.

"Well, anyway, she had me. I think she wanted to abort me but couldn't. So here I am. I can't die, no one wants me, and I basically exist by hanging out in abandoned buildings and sewers. It might not be so bad if I was alone, but I'm not."

Layla scowled. "Who else is with you?"

"From what I've gathered, they're called White Watchers. Tall scrawny white pasty things. Nasty bastards. I've killed a few of them. Apparently they do die, they just feed on mortals—both body and mind."

Layla did not like to hear this. "How many have you seen? A couple? A large group? A massive army?"

He scratched his head. "It depends. Sometimes there are just three or four lurking about; sometimes it's a bigger group."

She looked thoughtful. "Are they just in this area?"

"Nah, I've seen them other places as well. Always underground. Sometimes they do come to the surface, and in a couple of cases I think I've been blamed for their kills. Not that it matters much."

"Hmm, this is moving faster than I thought," she said.

"What is?"

She looked at him. "Listen, Judas—do you really want to stay here and live like this? I can offer you a better life, back home where there are others like you. And if you go back, I have a special position for you."

Judas looked at her with surprise. "Why would you do that for me?"

"Because you don't belong here. You are one of the tribes I am bound to defend. I need someone among the Fomorians who has human blood in their veins. The one drawback to no human contact is that the bloodlines are becoming weak. And I would need you to head up the Fomorian branch of the army."

"Why me? I doubt I'd make a decent warrior."

"Yes, you would. You have survived by living in tunnels and on the edge. You've encountered and killed White Watchers. It's better than making it bad for yourself by killing innocent human women."

"Well, maybe I enjoy that part."

"Maybe you do, but you'll have a much better pick of willing women where we go."

He tapped the side of the bottle with his long fingers. "It's all quite tempting. But what do I get from you if I agree to go?"

She had the shadow of a smile. "What is it that you want?"

"I think you know what I want."

"Very well. But," she said, tossing him an axe, "you'll need this first, I think."

"What, am I going to fight you?"

"No," said Layla, pointing at the hallway. "We need to fight them."

They both turned, and a huge crowd of what Judas called "White Watchers" were gathering in the hall, no doubt drawn to the light of the fire and the sound of their voices. She looked at Judas and nodded. "Get ready!"

With that she made a backwards flip and landed with her feet on the ceiling. She was decked out for battle, with a bow and arrows, and a massive axe. She spun herself around like a fiery tornado and began slashing her way through the crowd of monstrous beings, disintegrating them with her touch. Judas followed suit, and they chased down the stragglers, with Layla shooting at them with her bow and arrows. Soon the tunnel was quiet again.

"How did you know they were coming?" Judas asked her. He was impressed, and not just a bit intimidated by her.

She tapped her ear. "Astute listening. You need to develop that. I think you have it, really, but you need to be alert."

With the threat now over, Layla gave Judas what he requested.

At 4:00 in the morning, Layla finally got up to leave, and convinced Judas to go with her, after the rather sketchy copulation that occurred on a dirty mattress on the warehouse floor. She opened a portal with her axe, and walked him through to the Otherworld.

15

Steve Abbott's Diary

    I woke up the next morning, with the realisation that Layla had never visited my room that night. This was unusual, as I'd seen her every night that I'd stayed in the house up to that point. I looked at the clock—it was 6AM, and it was a Saturday. It was way too early to be up, but I was awake. As I got up to use the toilet, I heard a faint singing from downstairs.

    I carefully opened the door and tried to walk as quietly as possible down the hall, so I would not wake anyone. I saw that Layla's door was open. I peered in, and saw it—the battle axe I had seen in my dream from years ago. It looked like the same one she'd used to disembowel my not-so-illustrious ancestor. It made me a little nauseated, but curiosity got the better of me. I walked into her room to look at it.

    It appeared to be made of iron, or some kind of iron alloy that looked more like silver. Or was it silver? I touched it; it was ice cold, and if I tried to move it, it wouldn't budge. It was extremely heavy; it was like trying to move a concrete building support. I had no idea how she managed to pick this thing up, never mind to use it.

    I left the room quickly and headed toward the stairs again. The singing was getting louder, and as I rounded each corner, I discovered that the kitchen was the source of the sound. I peered around the corner, and found the singer—Layla. Her voice was positively angelic; I had no idea she could sing like that. She was singing in a language I couldn't decipher, and she was kneading dough on the counter as she sang. I had woken up some weekend mornings to freshly-made bread, so this seemed to be her routine. She did not look up from her work, but she stopped singing, and said, "Come in Steve. You're up early. I'll make you a coffee."

"I didn't know you had such a beautiful singing voice."

She smiled, and said nothing about it. "Come in and sit."

Within about ten minutes I had a cup of coffee in front of me, and she put her kneaded dough into a warming oven to let it rise.

"I didn't see you last night."

"No, you didn't. I had business to attend to."

"Did it have to do with...that fellow mentioned in the newspaper?"

"Yes."

"What did you do?"

"I brought him to a place where he will be happier."

"You didn't kill him, did you?"

She gave me a funny look. "No, that wasn't a euphemism. He's immortal, like me. You can't kill him."

"I saw your battle axe in your room..." I hedged.

"Yes."

98

"It's quite heavy."

"Ah, you tried to move it, did you?"

"Sorry—I was curious. I recognised it...from the dream."

She nodded. "It's the same one."

"There was blood on it. That's why I wondered if you killed him."

"No. That is White Watcher blood."

"White-what?"

"White Watchers. They are these weird clammy skinned all-white creatures that populate remote and underground areas. They like to devour things. I think they're a bit like what Americans call wendigos, now that I've seen them."

"Okay—I've never heard of those. And that sounds rather scary. "

She gave me a serious look. "One day you will know about them firsthand. You will know what they are, the rest of the world won't."

"What do you mean?"

She sat back. "There's a war coming."

"A war? With whom?"

"With them. And other beings created by human fear and stupidity. And … perhaps some of my old enemies. I wonder sometimes if they are also involved in their manifestation."

"Humans created them?"

"Yes."

"I don't follow—did they mate with something monstrous to create them?"

"No, they are products of human fear. They're a bit like poltergeists—energetic beings built up out of energy that is nothing short of vampiric. It's a mindless, devouring energy."

"But how can beings be created by the mind?"

"There is a lot more to the mind than you realise."

"What about your enemies? Who are they?"

"I'd rather not talk about them at the moment—but you will learn about them as well, I assure you."

"When will this happen?"

"I don't know yet. I'm watching for signs of their growth, and other things. But I will need the help of two individuals; this murderous fellow I met last night, is one of them. The other one I have encountered, but he will need some convincing to do what I need, though that will happen soon. And I will also need you."

"Me? What am I going to do?"

She smiled. "That is what you will find out. We are reconnecting, and you have to take the final steps. Once you do, you can do a lot to save your own race."

I stared at her. This was getting incredibly surreal, and I still hadn't had enough coffee to really absorb what she was saying. "I can't imagine I'd be any use to anyone."

"You will be. But don't worry about it now—you will get to where you need to be. I should warn you, though, it won't be without troubles."

"More than I have already?"

"My dear, you don't yet know what trouble is."

She stood up and took the bread out of the oven, kneading it a final time before putting it back.

16

I was always a bit nervous about the time I spent with Layla. We went out of our way to be discreet, but someone was bound to pick up on it sooner or later. And someone must have, because I found myself face-to-face with an angry Iain James not long after the tour ended.

It was entirely unexpected; I was at a charity event, and the guys from Witchfell were among the other musicians there. I chatted briefly with Zach Graves, who I knew quite well, and noticed that Iain was frowning at me intently; he looked angry. I was puzzled by this, but said nothing at the time. After it was over, a few of us stopped at a local pub to have a drink, and this was where he cornered me.

"Listen mate, can I talk to you?" he asked.

"Of course. Is anything the matter?"

"Yeah—I think so." His face was tense.

"What's the problem?"

He closed his eyes, and seemed to be thinking about what to say. Finally he blurted out "Are you having a relationship with Layla Black?"

"How do you know Layla?" I wasn't about to commit to an answer, and at the time I didn't know anything about his involvement with her.

"I consider her my girlfriend."

I was taken aback by this. "You know I tour with her father. I see her all the time. She's never mentioned being involved with you. She's only thirteen, you know."

He looked irritated. "Yeah, she's a bit too casual about it. Which is why I ask you—are you involved with her or not?"

"No, I am not involved with her. I have a wife and children."

"That's not what I've heard."

"Well, what HAVE you heard? And from whom?"

"I prefer not to name my sources—I'm not getting them in trouble. But they say they've seen you give her your room key when you've been on tour with her father."

"Oh for fuck's sake. People need to learn to mind their own business."

"Look—for God's sake—can you please just tell me if you've been involved with her or not? It's tearing me apart." He looked like he would actually cry.

I sighed deeply. I didn't know how to answer him.

"You have been, haven't you?"

I shook my head. "It's not what you think."

"She suggested to me herself that you were sleeping together."

"What? What did she say?"

"I asked her about the rumour, and she said yes, she did go to your room, because her father wanted to spend time with his girlfriend, and she kept you company."

"Yes, that's entirely true."

"I said to her, 'You're not having sex with him, are you?' and she said 'Would it matter if I was?'"

"Well, that's a funny thing for her to say if you're her boyfriend."

He looked angry and frustrated. "Like I said, she's a bit too casual about all this. All I can say is if you've been sleeping with her, I want you to stop."

Now it was my turn to get annoyed. "You don't know anything about my relationship to her. She's the one who solicits it from me, not the other way around."

"So you HAVE been sleeping with her." He was starting to raise his voice, and people were starting to look our way. "Enough!" I said. "Do you want to get yourself in trouble? She's too young for either of us."

"I don't give a fuck! I don't want anyone else touching her!"

I turned away at this point and went outside. He followed me. I had a feeling this wasn't going anywhere good. I was bigger than him and could have beat the stuffing out of him.

When I turned and sized him up, he backed away for a moment, as I think it occurred to him that he might be going too far.

"Listen, mate," I said sharply. "You're getting a bit out of control about this. As far as I know, Layla doesn't get seriously involved with anyone. If you're sleeping with her, count yourself lucky, because that's as close as anyone gets. She isn't my girlfriend." *She's my goddess*, I thought, mentally repeating her words. But I didn't say them out loud. "And I doubt she's as serious with you as you think—she dislikes being tied to anyone. I suspect you and I are far from being the only ones she's been interested in or involved with in some way. I think you'd be happier if you didn't think about it."

He started to cry, and I could see how hurt and frustrated he was. I did feel bad for him; it was tempting to want to possess her, to have her all to yourself. I finally put my hand on his shoulder.

"Listen," I said more gently. "I know how you feel. I don't even have the option of really competing for her attention—as I said, I already have a wife and family."

He looked up at me. "Then why are you sleeping with her?"

"I don't know how to answer that," I said truthfully. "I spend a lot of time working on tracks at Malcolm's house, and she's just appeared in my room at night. But she seems to be interested in me for reasons that have nothing to do with love or attraction."

He looked puzzled. "I don't understand what you mean."

We both sat down on the back step, and he continued to look at me with the question in his eyes. "Layla...is...let's just say she's very different from other women. Do you understand at all what I mean?"

He looked up. "Sort of. I think. There's something a bit—unnatural about her."

"Yes," I said. "Though she's entirely natural—it's the rest of us who are unnatural."

Iain looked at me, baffled. "We're unnatural?"

"Yes. She's like a force of nature. That's why she doesn't care much about who she fucks, what their level of commitment is, or anything else. She's not able to have children, and in many ways she's uncontrollable. And—if I can believe things she's said to me—she never fucks anyone without a good reason. The reason is rarely that she's in love—I wonder if she really does fall in love."

"What other reasons are there?"

"I don't pretend to know. In my case—I have an old family connection to her that makes her keen on getting close to me. In your case—well, I'm not sure. How did you meet her?"

"She was at a club down in Chelsea with her friends. We were there for an aftershow. I just fell in love at first sight." You could hear the misery, and some resignation, in his voice.

"Alright—I'd wondered. In that case—I don't know, I would guess she does fancy you and is willing to have a go. But she's not going to treat it the way other girls do. She sees it more as an amusement."

"Great. That makes me feel better," he said bitterly.

"I'm sorry. I'm not saying that to hurt your feelings. You should be complimented, because I've seen her turn down a lot of lads. Many are too scared to even approach her."

Iain shook his head. "I don't know if I can take this. But I also don't want to leave her."

I just nodded. "Well, I'm not going to tell you what to do. You have to decide what you want to put up with. But if you're asking me if I'm her boyfriend, or a boyfriend—no. She doesn't see it that way, and I guess I don't either."

"How do you see her, then?"

I had to think for a moment. "She's a test, really."

"A test? Of what?"

"I'm not entirely sure yet."

17

After the tour was over, I had something of a break at home. Our first album together was reasonably successful, so we were going to work on another one after taking some time off. I should have welcomed this, but I tended to be a workaholic; I got restless if I was at home for too long. I always promised my wife that I'd make more time for her and the kids; I really did mean it, but never seemed to be able to do it. Now I was home and had a real opportunity to do that.

But so much had changed in the last nine months. I felt like Layla was a more intimate partner than my wife, and in spite of the ways she made me crazy, it was hard not to be around her. But there was no way I could talk about this with anyone.

In any case, it wasn't long before I found myself having trouble in the bedroom; I just couldn't get aroused. I was starting to worry—did I have some kind of disease? I just couldn't face the idea of impotence; it was psychologically and physically devastating. My wife tried to be understanding, but I could tell it was putting an even greater strain on our marriage. I went through the motions of family life for a while, and was glad when Mal asked about getting around to recording the next album. I felt tremendous guilt, because I loved my family; I didn't want to separate myself from them all the time.

I'd felt ambivalent about Layla for some time, but now some resentments were really starting to rise to the surface. I loved and missed her, and I was angry at myself for it. I knew she had a lot of control over my life, and that I had given it to her– unwittingly, but I gave it to her nonetheless. I wanted to be in control of my feelings and my sex life; I felt like I had no control at all.

And there was something else too, that I couldn't quite put my finger on. It was like a voice I my head, telling me to stay away from her, that she was a liar, evil, demonic. Sometimes I could see my Gran's face saying these things, and at first I thought perhaps it was just a memory of her nattering on about "avoiding the Morrigan." But there seemed to be more to it than that–was this really Gran talking to me? I kept hearing another word, and I felt it was a name: Duncluan. Was this another one of my ancestors, or someone connected to them? Somehow I didn't think so. But I didn't know what the name meant.

So, even though I was anxious to get back to work, I felt some irritation about returning to the Black household. I suppose I could have asked Malcolm to come to my house, but he really did have a better working setup, and it was cheaper and more efficient than renting studio time. I did not discuss my problem with either Malcolm or Layla; I was feeling victimised, and was sure I must have some terrible disease. I had a doctor's appointment scheduled for the following week, and felt nervous about it.

However, if I thought I was going to get away from Layla, I was wrong. I hadn't spoken to her much, and she had more or less left me alone. But I had taken a break from working while

Malcolm took a phone call one day, and she accosted me. She looked disdainful.

"Impotent! Nonsense."

I cringed. I hadn't told her anything, but she always knew. "I really don't want to talk about it."

"Yes you do. And there's nothing physically wrong with you."

"Well, the doctor will determine that, won't he?" I was tired of her telling me things, and I started to push back.

"Go if you must; there's nothing physically wrong with you. I know what the problem is."

"Really?"

"Yes."

"Did you cause the problem?"

"No. You are causing it yourself."

"Well, that's great. I'm suffering and I get blamed for it."

She rolled her eyes. "Stop with the childish whinging. You're experiencing impotence because you are resisting connecting with your power. You won't let go."

"Won't let go of what?"

"You want to be the man in control. You want to be the powerful one, in control of your destiny. You have never been in control—that's a lie, and it will only drive you mad. You need to learn to yield."

"To you?"

"Yes."

"Why?"

"Because I am the source of your power. In fact, I'm the source of everyone's power. But you unconsciously make the same mistake as your ancestor—what can the little woman possibly do for you? You should be in control. But the female power controls everything. If you yielded, you would be astounded at how much control you have over everything."

I grunted. I'd had enough of this kind of talk. "Well, I don't know what exactly you expect me to do."

She looked me over thoughtfully. Then she said, "I know what to do."

"What?" I could hear the irritation in my voice. She ignored it.

She smiled. "I need to break you."

"Excuse me?"

"You heard what I said."

"And what does that mean, exactly?"

"I guess you'll find out!" She then stood up and flounced off, humming to herself.

I was feeling flustered and angry; I was as angry at myself as I was at her. I felt like everything I was doing with her was wrong, I felt like the impotence was somehow her fault, and I hated being manipulated like a puppet all the time. I was determined not to yield; I needed to be a man and stand up for myself.

She left me to go back to working with Malcolm. Over the next week she was busy with schoolwork, and I was commuting between home and Esher. I did stay over one night, but she wasn't there.

18

Steve Abbott's Diary

I went to the doctor, and as Layla said, nothing was wrong. He suggested I see a therapist. I thought about it, but decided to wait on it. My wife took the kids to visit with her family for a few days, as there was a short school holiday. I was glad to have the house to myself, and thought about how I might use the time. I had a guitar that needed re-stringing, and it was one that I preferred to use. That was the first thing I wanted to do. But when I went to look for the guitar, I couldn't find it. What the hell did I do with it? I combed the house looking for it, and my car—nothing. I realised with a groan that I probably left it at Malcolm's house.

So, I called the house, and Layla answered. I asked her if I'd left my guitar in her father's studio.

"Half a minute. I'll go check."

I heard her footsteps move away. A couple of minutes later, I heard them come back.

"Yes, it's here. Do you need it?"

"Yes, I do. Is your father home?"

"No, he's gone away for a few days. At the moment it's just my sister and I."

"I see. Well, can I stop by tomorrow morning and get it?"

"Yes, of course. What time do you think you'll pop round?"

"About 10:30ish?"

"OK, that should be fine. One of us should be here. If I'm not here, I'll leave the guitar out with a note for my sister to give it to you."

"Great, thanks Layla. Ta."

"Ta."

So, the next morning I headed to Esher to pick up my guitar, and pondered what else I would do for the day. It was first things first, so I pulled into the driveway of the house.

I got out of the car and noticed that the front door was open, though the screen door was shut. I knocked, and heard Layla's voice. "Is that you, Steve?"

"Yes."

"Come on in. Sorry, I'll be right out."

"Thanks." I walked into the house. I didn't see my guitar anywhere; it must have still been in the studio. I could hear Layla's voice somewhere; she was softly singing to herself again. I walked through the rooms looking for her.

Suddenly, without warning, I was grabbed from behind, and then I didn't remember anything.

When I woke up again, I was laying in a darkened room. I couldn't tell where I was exactly; it was as though I was covered in a blanket of darkness. Was it an actual blanket? I couldn't move enough to tell; it was as though every one of my limbs tightened and would not move. If I tried to move it was like try to swim through dense water. Or maybe earth?

That was the feeling—like I'd been buried alive. But I was certain that I was not in the earth. Then where the fuck was I?

I could feel my breathing get harder; I was trying not to panic, as I was using up the little air I felt I had. I started to sweat, and my face was flushing; now I was getting angry. How dare she do something like this? What the hell was she doing anyway? I tried to call out for her, but I felt like my voice was going nowhere; it was like I was in a void.

I struggled to move, to see, to breathe, to do anything, to have control over anything, but it was all fruitless. I just felt more drained and more constricted the more I fought. My mind filled with a thousand curse words, and what I would do once I was free from this situation…

But what if she wouldn't set me free? I obviously had no power to escape. When the thought came to me, I had a new sensation. It was a creeping feeling in all my organs, like they were dropping one by one. I could feel the vibration in my arms, torso, and legs; my head started to pound. I could not deny it anymore; not only was I afraid, I was absolutely terrified.

I don't know how long I was in this state, but something finally broke. I began to weep. The tears felt like hot acid on my face; I was burning up. I was starting to choke a bit. I felt all the rage draining out of me, and I felt totally lost. I remembered my first encounter with her, what I'd done…and I realised with a really stark clarity that I had never been in control of my life from that moment forward. No matter how strong I thought I was, how independent—she controlled everything. And she was much stronger than me; I was not going to win this battle. Now I desperately wanted her to come back to the room; I had no idea when she intended to return, or what she would do when she did.

19

Suddenly the darkness lifted; the sudden light was like a stab in the face, and I cried out. It took me a few minutes to see where I was; I was in Layla's bedroom, and she sat on a chair opposite, looking at me with an impenetrable gaze. I could see my reflection in her mirror; I was disheveled, sweaty, and pale; my body was trembling all over. I wanted to speak to her, but all I could do was start crying. The sobs came up from my throat, and the shaking in my body became more violent. Finally she moved from her chair and walked over to me. A shadow of a smile crossed her face.

"Remind me what you said about being in control?"

I put my hands in my face, and started to weep again. All I could say was, "Please…"

"Alright," she said, though her tone was gentler. "Get up. You're in need of a shower."

She took me to the bathroom, and I asked her not to leave; I was dizzy and unsteady on my feet. She undressed me and made me sit down while she threw my clothes in the wash. Then she helped me stand up and get showered. The water hit me like a slap, and I felt myself slowly starting to become more lucid, and less shaky. She dried me off when I was done and handed me a bathrobe; she then motioned for me to come with her. We went downstairs together, and she began to prepare a meal for both of us. I looked up at the clock; it was already 5PM. I tried to ground myself, to get a grip on where I was, who I was…I found the latter part was not so easy.

I finally felt able to speak to her, though only a whisper came out. "What happened?"

She did not look at me, but shrugged and smiled. "I told you. I would break you."

"Why?"

She laughed. "Certainly you know why!"

"But what IS it that you want from me? I know what happened a long time ago, you've made it clear that you're in charge–but are you just tormenting me for what my ancestors did?"

She sighed and shook her head. "You just don't get it, do you? Doesn't your family already have a curse? Does it include tormenting direct descendants? I know that you've been able to think about this the right way; what do you say to your Gran when you argue about it?"

I paused. "Well…that Duagh probably deserved what he got, because he broke an oath."

"Yes. And breaking the oath caused the curse, and crying to Jesus isn't going to help. There's only one thing that will help."

"And that is…?"

She smiled. "I can't tell you exactly. The terms of the curse are that you have to work it out for yourself. And I'm trying to help you do that. The longer you resist and give me an attitude, the harder it will be for you to do the right thing."

"But why all these things? My Gran says you're a demon..."

"And do you believe that?"

I didn't answer right away, and she read my thought. "You don't really know, do you? You're too deeply programmed, even though you vowed to throw away all that orthodox religious bullshit that you were taught." Her tone was somewhat irritated.

"Look," I said, "nothing in my life has prepared me for this. I can't even believe most of what's happened. My rational mind can't accept that this is real. And when I start moving into that realm, I don't know what to believe about anything. I don't WANT to believe that you're a demon, but I have to honestly face the fact that I don't know that—I'm just trusting you."

Layla pulled herself up. "That's it, isn't it? You have to drop your rational mind and trust me. You don't really know anything about anything."

"But it's not easy to drop the rational mind. I don't know how else to function."

"Or your superstitious one, apparently."

I didn't know how to answer her on that.

She continued. "We've talked about all this before, so it's not new. But I suppose it's good that you're admitting you've had doubts. To answer your question—if you view the demonic as evil, then no, I am not a demon. I'm neither good nor evil. Neither are any of the other gods. And in spite of whatever your silly traditions tell you, we are still around, watching, and controlling. We were not "conquered" by some other religion. We have merely shifted into the background. And now you need us more than ever. But it's not just about the gods, and it's not just about your curse, you know."

I looked up. "What else is there?"

Her face was serious. "It's about keeping our universes from being destroyed."

"Universes? Plural?"

"Yes."

"How many are there?"

"Thousands."

I shook my head. "I can't even comprehend that. Are they all different?"

She paused, and her eyes moved back and forth, thinking how to answer. "They are the same in many ways but different too. Different things happen in them. But many of the players are the same. Everything happens at the same time."

"Even things that we think of as past and future?"

"Yes."

My head started to ache again. "It's all beyond me, really."

She smiled again. "It won't be soon enough."

"Come again?"

"I suppose I should tell you—you're not going home yet. I've softened you up, now I need to educate you."

"I hope it's not like what I just came out of—I beg you not to put me through that again!"

"What's terrible about that? You were in darkness, and frankly, you're in darkness most of the time, you just distract yourself from it."

"I don't understand."

"Exactly."

I shook my head, but then suddenly remembered something.

"Layla?"

"Hmm?"

"I have to ask you something–thinking about what we've just said–whenever I would get those ideas about you, the negative ones, I saw my Gran's face, but I kept hearing a word that I think might be a name."

"And what name is that?"

"Duncluan."

Suddenly her face changed into a scowl. "How long ago did you start hearing that name?"

"I don't know exactly…it hasn't been that long. Maybe a few months."

"And you became impotent then, and started to be resentful of me?"

I had to think for a moment. "Yes, I think that's about right. But are you saying they are connected?"

"I'd be willing to bet money they are." Her face did not have a pleasant aspect to it when she spoke. But it did not seem to be directed at me.

After a bit of uncomfortable silence, I finally got up the courage to speak again. "What does it mean?"

She looked at me, and I could tell that anger was building in her. "It's a name."

"Of who?"

"Of an enemy who needs to be finished off. Permanently." Her face then softened, as she looked at me. "Enough about him for now. I need to focus on you."

20

Steve Abbott's Diary

The previous day with Layla had left me absolutely exhausted; I had no trouble falling asleep that night. I slept in her room with her, but I barely remembered anything that happened that evening.

I was awakened the next morning by sunlight streaming through the curtains. As I sat up, I felt rather dazed; it took me a moment to remember where I was. I looked at the clock; it was 8:00 in the morning. I rubbed my face and stretched my legs.

That was when I realised that something was off.

I looked at my hands. They were smaller and thinner. I hadn't shaved in a couple of days, but my face felt very smooth. I shook myself; was I awake, or having a dream? I seemed to be awake. Layla was already up; I could hear her humming to herself in the next room. I pulled the covers back and swung my legs over the side. They looked different too. My heart was starting to pound; carefully I removed my clothes and turned to look at myself in the mirror. I wished I hadn't.

I have what you might consider a very "masculine" look; hairy chest and body, ample genitalia, and a muscular chest, with slightly thinning hair. What I saw in the mirror was a female body; no hair except around the genital area, full breasts, and a curvy body. I looked down at my genitalia; I definitely had a vagina. I found myself touching it numbly; the labia on the outside, the

123

knob of the clitoris on top, and the rather weird pinkish fruit of the opening. I felt a sharp pain in my lower abdomen, like a vice grip on my insides. I felt dizzy, and managed to sit down on the bed before I fainted.

When I came to consciousness, probably only a few seconds later, Layla was back in the room, shaking me awake. I looked down at myself quickly, hoping it had been some weird illusion, but all of the female biological indications were still there. I looked up at Layla, and the horror must have been evident in my face. She only grinned.

"I told you today would be different."

I found myself stammering. "Layla..what...what...please, oh God, please tell me this isn't real!"

She shrugged in her usual indifferent way. "Of course it's real."

Now my heart was really racing. I could feel panic rising in my throat. "Why...why...why is this happening?!"

She sat down and looked at me, just as she had the day before. "Because I want you to experience what it's like to be a woman."

I stared at her in disbelief. My voice was trembling, and was definitely higher. "Please tell me this isn't permanent."

"Of course it's not, silly."

I let out a long breath. "How long...?"

She shrugged again. "Probably just for a day or two. Longer if you annoy me."

"Probably??"

She rolled her eyes at me. "I swear, such drama from you. Worse things could happen to you, you know. And you know it's temporary. What's so terrible about being a woman anyway?"

"Uh…that I'm not one?"

"Well, as I said, now you get to experience being one! You've always said women have such charmed lives, so you should be happy!"

I realised at once that I was going to regret every statement or action I had ever made that tasted at all of misogyny.

"So, are you going to stand there naked all day, or get dressed?"

"Well, I don't think my clothes will fit…" I was feeling a bit lightheaded again.

"Here, I have clothes for you." She tossed some articles of clothing at me. I realised that I'd taken off a lot of women's bras, but had no clue how to put one on. She sighed, and came over and showed me. I felt another twinge in my lower abdomen, and cried out.

"What is that pain?"

"That? Oh, you're probably just getting ready to menstruate in a day or two. Fortunately for you, you'll have changed back by then."

"It can't just be that–the pain is awful."

125

She looked me over. "And why do you think menstrual pain isn't awful? Because your wife doesn't complain about it? No, women are taught to take some aspirin and get over it, because, you know, 'women are so hysterical about nothing.' And frankly, your pain is only mild compared to what usually happens."

I knew I was not going to get any sympathy, so I got dressed, but the twinges really bothered me. She got me downstairs for breakfast, and gave me some rather heavy-duty painkillers to take. "Here's the more potent stuff, since you're clearly unable to take it like a woman."

It was clear I was going to be in for a challenging day.

I started to feel better after the medicine, but I still felt unreal, like the real me was floating around somewhere else, but I knew I was in this body. I helped her clean up the breakfast dishes. After she dried her hands, she said, "Right. We have some errands to do, so we need to go out."

I stared at her. "Out? Like this?"

She looked at me like I was crazy. "Yes. Out like this. How else are you going to go out?"

"I'm not sure I want to go anywhere at all."

"Rubbish. Come on."

We walked to the nearby High Street to pick up some groceries, and to get laundry from the dry cleaners. As we walked, I could hear catcalling from men as we went by. One bloke even grabbed me by the ass as we walked by; I could feel the rage coming up in my throat. But Layla just grabbed my arm and pulled me along.

"Did you see what that bloke did?"

"Yes."

"I want to go back and punch him."

"Why? He thinks you're hot. Take it as a compliment." She gave me a sly smile.

"That is not a compliment. That's degrading."

"Really? Then why do you blokes do it? I mean, according to you, women should be appreciative! Right?"

I stopped talking. I knew I was in for a lesson, and I was getting it. In retrospect, nothing that serious had happened, but I was still horribly uncomfortable. I didn't want to admit that I'd done similar things in the past, and probably had reason to be ashamed. But Layla knew.

We finally made it back to the house, and I was emotionally rattled, and not just a little drained. But Layla was not done.

"Let's go upstairs," she said playfully. I could tell she wanted to make love.

"But…I can't make love to you like this…"

"Yes I know! I'm going to make love to you!"

I stared at her. "What do you mean?"

She grinned evilly. "Come on."

We went upstairs, and she came on to me rather aggressively. We undressed, and she ran her fingers over my body until I was aroused. She then got off the bed, but returned just a few minutes later with a strap on. My eyes widened. She was going to…

And the next thing I know, she was on top of me, entering me. As she pushed, pain just shot through me; I cried out, but she just pushed harder and harder. I found it hard to breathe, and I gasped in pain. When she pulled out, I saw that I was bleeding slightly, and the whole inside felt like it was peeled raw. All the organs in that area throbbed.

She looked at me, again with a grin. "So, how did you find that?"

"Awful."

"Really? Why? Women are supposed to like big cock. You know, the harder the better."

"That really hurt."

"And so it does!"

"Look, I don't believe that—women do like it if it's done right, I can tell by their reaction."

"Bollocks. Some women are experienced enough, have enough nerve endings inside, or have pelvises shaped in such a way that they're fine with it. I'm fortunate that way. But many women absolutely hate it. And blokes are never careful; they think huge size is the only requirement for pleasure, and only think about getting themselves off."

She undid the strap-on and sat next to me. "Give me your hand."

I did as she said, and she put it right in the middle of the top of the vagina. She pointed to the clitoris. "You see that? You see that it has a hood? That's what stimulates it. Give it a go. And don't be stupid and do it backwards—THAT will hurt."

So, I did as she said, and I suddenly felt a surge in my loins that exploded throughout my body. What's more, the sensation lasted for some time, probably about ten minutes.

"That," said Layla, "is where women get their pleasure."

"But surely they can get it the other way as well? I mean, they do?"

"Possibly—if you're careful. But not as often as you would think. And it's a good idea to do that BEFORE doing the other."

My whole lower body ached and burned. She suggested that we give it a rest, and relax for the rest of the night. I gratefully agreed, and I got dressed again, and sat with her watching telly. But I realised now why women were not always as anxious to have sex, unless they were young and horny. And I realised that for all of my macho behaviour and belief in my sexual abilities, that I really did not understand how women felt while having sex. I finally said as much to Layla before we went to bed.

She smiled at me. "That, my dear, is the point of what I'm teaching you."

"I have to know—are you done teaching me? Will I wake up tomorrow and be as I was?"

"Yes. But something else will be different."

I was curious. But I was also afraid to ask.

21

Steve Abbott's Diary

It was the third morning at Layla's house. I was starting to feel like I lived here all the time. I woke up earlier this time, around 6:00. Layla was still asleep on her side of the bed. I cautiously got up, and made my way to the bathroom. To my relief, I was back to my old self—my hairy body was back, my cock was back, and I looked as I expected to look. I relieved myself, and returned to the bedroom. Layla was just waking up at this time. She smiled at me.

"Up already? Are you pleased?"

"I'm relieved, that's for certain."

"Ah well, don't get too comfortable."

"Why?"

"Come. Let's have breakfast. You'll see afterward."

I went downstairs with some trepidation. I was starving when I woke up, but now my stomach was fluttering. I had no idea what was going to happen today.

"You really are keeping me in suspense here, aren't you?"

She sighed. "You don't know how to go with the flow, do you? Surely your life isn't that pre-planned?"

"Layla, I can handle some unexpected twists and turns. These last two days have been a bit beyond that, I think."

"Only because you still don't want to let go. You need to look at a reality bigger than your own. And you'll get another chance to do that today. No, don't ask me, you'll find out soon enough."

So, we finished breakfast and cleaned up as usual. She then brought me back to her room, and sat me down in a chair. "Close your eyes," she commanded me. I did as she said, and I felt her put her hands over them. She was massaging my eyes, my temples, and the back of my head, and I could hear her softly chanting something—I couldn't understand it. Then she stopped, and took her hands away. "Okay, Steve, you can open your eyes carefully."

Carefully? Why carefully?

It didn't take long to find out why. As my eyes opened, I saw a room in utter chaos. There were people coming out of the walls, the ceiling, and weird creatures everywhere. I saw pale human figures that I immediately knew were dead souls, and they were crying out at Layla, as if in supplication to her. There was barely a spot to move forward on the floor.

I looked at her, with that panicky feeling coming back. "What is all this?!"

"That," she said in a cheerful tone, "is what I see every day. You are experiencing the vision of a goddess."

"You see this every day?!" I was incredulous. I had no idea where I ended or began, whether the room was real...or what was real. None of this was here a few minutes ago.

She read my thoughts. "Of course it was here. You just didn't see it. You never see it. Come, let's go downstairs."

"But…there's nowhere to walk!"

"Rubbish. There's plenty of room. You're just seeing other dimensions. In our three dimensions, nothing is different." She took my hand, and as we walked through the room, I realised that we were walking through a lot of the figures. Leaving the room was not any better; there were figures literally coming out of everywhere; they almost looked like mandalas of beings, massive complicated artistic formations of just bodies, bodies, bodies…and not all of them were human.

What were they? I still don't know.

We went downstairs in a sea of bodies and cacophony of voices. Layla was unperturbed by any of it; I was ready to have a nervous breakdown.

"Please tell me we are not going outside."

She looked thoughtful. "We are—but not to the High Street. We're just going to the park. Fewer people there. But enough." I didn't ask her "Enough for what?" and she didn't answer that question, though I knew she heard it.

"Why do we have to encounter anyone at all? Aren't there enough—people—or whoever they are—here?"

"Yes, but none are in this dimension. You need to see someone from this dimension. You need to hear."

"How can I hear anything will all of this noise?" The voices were getting louder, and there was a persistent vibration, like a hum, that pulsated through my brain.

132

"You'll know when we get there."

So, I clung to her as we went out. I wondered if crazy people had these visions, if the schizoid person or old person suffering from dementia who saw and spoke to "invisible people" saw anything like this. If they did, it must be terrifying for them to do anything or go anywhere. And obviously, they weren't hallucinating; they were seeing SOMETHING that the rest of us, thankfully, cannot see.

In the park we passed several couples walking by, a couple of joggers, and they were walking and running in this sea of people and places that seemed to be everywhere. And as they passed us, I realised I could hear other voices–their voices, though they never spoke a word. I could clearly hear their thoughts. One woman jogger was thinking about the boyfriend who just left her; others were wondering if Layla and I were related, or if I was her father, or if we were a couple. ("He's too old for her, certainly!") The voices went through my head like the newsfeed at the bottom of the screen on the news channel. It was too much to process; I thought my head would explode.

Layla seemed to notice my intense discomfort. "Come on, let's get back to the house."

I was grateful to get out of there. I found myself wanting to push through the sea of entities that seemed to be everywhere; I got strange looks from passersby. Layla finally said, "No need to do that. They're not in this layer."

"But I can see them."

"Yes, you can. But you haven't learned to filter. Your human brain does that for you normally."

"So, what does your brain do?"

"Well, my vision is different, and my ability to process information is different. I don't need the filters."

When we returned to the house, she immediately took me back to her room and sat me down. She covered my eyes again with her hands, and repeated the process of the morning. When she finished and took her hands away, everything looked normal again. I breathed a sigh of relief.

"Is that…?" I didn't know if I dared to finish the sentence.

"Yes," she said, "That's all. But we still need to talk. Take a nap first."

I was exhausted, and all too happy to wrap myself up in the duvet, in my male body and with my normal brain filters. I need to calm down on too many levels.

When I awoke, Layla was not in the room. I got up and went downstairs, where I found her making supper. I sat down at the table, still feeling a little unsteady. So much had happened in the last three days, and I realised that I really didn't know who I was anymore; everything comfortable and familiar now looked different, and somewhat alien.

Layla spoke up. "So, how do you feel?" I told her my thoughts.

"Well, of course you feel that way. Your soul has gotten a workout. But you needed it; you're out of shape."

"I don't think I know anyone else who's had that kind of a 'workout'."

"No, and you probably never will. But you're going to find that it's critically important for what comes next."

"What is that?"

She sat down beside me, bringing me my plate. "If you can't think outside your own tunnel, you'll never know what you need to do, not only for your family curse, but…"

"But…?"

"But for everyone."

22

My sister had a son who was about three-years-old, and I loved him as much as I loved my own child. She lived in Oxfordshire, which was not far, but we didn't see much of each other with our different and busy lives.

One day the phone rang. My wife answered it, and I heard her say my sister's name. Suddenly my wife gasped, and said, "Oh God, Miriam, it can't be true. I am so sorry. Let me get Steve for you." I saw that my wife was weeping, and she handed me the phone. "It's your sister. She has bad news."

My heart pounding, I took the phone. "Miriam? What's happened?"

"It's Jacob…"she broke into sobs.

"What? What happened? Is he ill?"

"He's dead."

I almost dropped the phone on the floor. Shaking, I said, "How…how did he die?"

"It happened so fast. He had a fever, and was developing a rash. You know, kids get so many weird things…but he seemed to be in terrible pain, so we rushed him to the emergency room. He died within 10 minutes."

"Of what??"

"I don't know. It appears to be sepsis–he must have had some kind of hidden infection."

I sat down and began to weep. It was too much; everything I'd been through, and now this. I was too upset to even speak. Eventually my wife took the phone from me again, and managed to get the details about the funeral arrangements from my sister.

"Is there anything you need from us? Do you need us to come up?

"No–it's okay. I'll see you at the funeral. I've got so much to do right now..."

I was supposed to go work with Mal, but I was just too numb to do anything. I called and explained what happened; he told me to take my time, not to worry about work, and that they were all there if I needed them.

In spite of my sister's insistence that we didn't need to come over, we did anyway. My parents, my Gran, and my other siblings and their children revolved in and out of the house. There was a cloud of depression over everything. My Gran was angry. She looked at me with some venom.

"This is the work of the Morrigan's curse!"

That shook me with a jolt. I thought about the math I'd done years ago, and it made sense–Jacob was the right age, and in the right 9 year time period to be the victim of the curse. I remembered Layla saying that I was "close to breaking the curse, but not there yet." I now felt a mixture of guilt and rage. How could she let this happen? Couldn't she cut me a break with everything that went on? After all I'd done for her, and been through—how could it not be enough?

Frustrated as I was at Layla, it did occur to me that something bigger was going on. I could not believe for a moment that she would do this on purpose to hurt me. From what she had said, it sounded like the curse was something that had a life of its own; she had set it in motion, but certain conditions had to be met to stop it. *What was it I was supposed to do?*

Gran spoke up again. "I told you not to get involved with the Morrigan. This is your fault."

Now I was angry.

It took me a moment—I recall getting up very slowly, and turning to her. When I spoke to her, it scarcely sounded like my voice. "Don't you fucking dare, you hag. You're the one who won't make peace with the Morrigan. All the deaths are your fucking fault, and everyone in the family who wants to persist as traitors." I don't know how I looked, but everyone's mouth dropped open, and several of my family members backed away from me. Gran herself was clearly taken aback. But she was back at it again in no time.

"Don't you dare speak to your grandmother that way!"

"I'll speak to you however I choose." I was not backing down.

My sister intervened. "Steve! Stop it!"

"I beg your pardon? She is accusing me of killing your child. I am in fact the only one who was trying to save him. I am not going to stop it."

138

"Well you didn't succeed!" hissed my Gran. "The Morrigan didn't stop her curse!"

"Neither did your stupid masses."

"Steve—I think you'd better leave." It was my father.

I looked at him and everyone else incredulously. "Is that it? You're going to side with her on this? None of you have any understanding of what is going on, and you're just going to perpetuate this forever. Nothing I've done for you so far matters a fuck to you, does it? Well, I'm going to solve this fucking curse if it kills me, and it's nice to know how much appreciation I will get."

With that I beckoned to my wife and children, telling them we were leaving. My wife was apologising to everyone on the way out. "I'm very sorry—he's still very disturbed, we shouldn't have come..."

We drove home in silence. You could cut the tension in the car with a knife. I didn't care. I was angry that this wasn't solved, angry that this was happening…I DID blame myself, but not for the same reasons my Gran blamed me.

23

Steve Abbott's Diary

When the day of the funeral came, I knew we had to go, even though I had no desire to set foot in a church, or to see most of my family. I felt guilty, as I'd just created more anxiety for my sister, and she was still coping with the loss of her son. I had no idea how I'd be received when we arrived.

The reception when we pulled up was rather frosty; my Gran wouldn't speak to me at all, and I got uneasy looks from the rest of the family. I resolved to say nothing. We went into the church, and the Mass began.

It was impossible to describe how I felt; I was depressed and exhausted, and also enraged. But enraged at whom? I barely heard what the priest was saying, until he launched into his diatribe against the Morrigan. He prayed that God would deliver them from this evil monster who systematically tortured our family.

At this point I had enough. I was ready to stand up and tell him to go fuck himself; I was so disgusted with all of this rubbish, of defending someone who had committed treason "because Jesus." But all of the sudden I had a revelation. I now knew what I had to do.

I immediately stood up and walked out of the church, to the bewilderment of my family. As I walked through the doors, I saw my brother. He knew I wasn't feeling well, and had initially volunteered to drive my family home. I asked him if I could take him up on his offer; I had somewhere I had to go immediately.

"Well, sure Steve, I can do that. Are you alright?"

"Not at the moment. But I intend to make things right. Thanks, I owe you."

I then got into the car and drove off, my brother staring at me with a puzzled look. I knew my leaving was going to cause problems, but I didn't care. This was more important than anything.

24

I knew where Layla went to school, and judging from the time, I knew I could make it to Esher right at the time she would be dismissed for the day. I parked the car in town and walked to the school. The timing was perfect, as students were just being let out.

She came out as expected, and we made eye contact. She dismissed her friends, telling them she'd see them later. She told her sister to tell their father she'd be home late, and then she approached me. "I need to talk to you, privately," I told her.

Layla smiled. "Of course. Follow me." She led me to a nearby park, and to a spot behind the common area into a small patch of trees. There was a bench in the midst of this, and she motioned for me to sit down. "Now, what is it?" she asked.

"My nephew just died. He was only three. I loved him dearly."

Layla touched my hands. "I know. I'm very sorry Steve."

"How...how could you let this happen? After what I've been through?" I felt frustrated.

She shook her head. "Steve, the curse is out of my hands. You have to solve it. You now know what to do. I'm sorry you didn't know sooner."

I looked at her hard. Then the words came out: "Layla, what exactly do I have to do to atone for my ancestor's treasonous behaviour?"

She smiled at me. This was the right question, apparently.

"What you can do is renounce Christianity and become my priest–I suppose you would call that a Druid. You would be my link between the other world and this one. As part of it you would reaffirm and repair the vows that Duagh broke. I would then revoke the curse, provided you keep your vows."

I looked at her puzzled. "How would I become a Druid? Are there any left?"

"Ah well, see, that is the difficult part. Not impossible, mind you, just difficult. There are modern Druids, but they were never taught the old ways; they make their best guess, and that tradition is entirely new. There are old-school Druids on Tir na nOg."

"Where is that?"

"It used to be accessible from this world, from the cave near Rathcroghan. But after your ancestor's treachery, and the rising of Christian influence, we pulled it back into another dimension. Basically you have to cross dimensions to get there."

I stared at her, incredulous. "How would I do that?"

"Well, there are four possible ways to enter Tir na nOg. One is through death, but we're not interested in killing you. The second way would be if you had an immortal body, like mine–you could shift easily between dimensions. But you don't have that, either. So–it's either bringing you over bodily, or bringing over your subtle, astral body along with a layer of the physical. I only bring people over bodily if I plan to keep them there, or make them immortals. There are reasons I can't make you immortal—not yet, anyway—and you're not going there to stay. So, that leaves the last method, and it's highly unpleasant."

"And how does that work?"

She sighed. "Well, let me try to explain." She opened her notebook, rubbed her eyes, and began drawing an outline of the human body, detailing the different "layers" of substance and consciousness.

"Basically, we need to separate out about three layers, which is far less dense than the whole body, and bring them over. Part of your physicality does have to be there for the initiation. You can consider it a shamanic rite; the shaman learns to move between the worlds, but it's a painful process. Two things are required to separate the layers; one is a drug that I will give to you, that will start the astral process. The other is physical torture; I have to break the physical form to some degree to get that partial physical layer to jump out with the astral. The hardest part is that breaking away, and then the re-entry to the body. We have to take precautions to keep your body from becoming corrupted in any way while you're out of it, and to keep anything else from trying to get in. The good news about taking initiation in Tir na nOg is that time is contracted. So, you can learn what would normally take twenty years in about two days. The bad news is that you have to go back to your body, and even if the body hadn't been tortured, it's a suffocating process—like being encased in lead, moving back to human physicality from the clear lightness of the other world. So, you will be in a lot of pain when you come back. I'd give it three days for initiation, and at least three weeks to recover."

144

I put my head in my hands. I'd been through so much in the last year; could my body and mind take anything else? But if this was the last step; I couldn't stop now. "I'll do whatever it takes. And please know that I am scared to death. I'm not only doing this for my family, but because I implicitly love and trust you." I couldn't believe I'd just said it—but it was true. Layla gave me a smile that lit up the park around them; I was amazed to see flowers sprout under her feet. She seemed genuinely touched by this statement.

"Very well, then. Let us see when we will do this. It has to be a time when no one else is around. School is out in a couple of weeks, so that's one obstacle out of the way. Is your wife going away any time soon?"

"She's going away with the kids for about a month as soon as school gets out to visit her family."

"When does she leave?" Layla opened up a calendar that she had with her school books.

I looked over her shoulder. "She leaves on the fourth, that Saturday."

"OK—and I am done that weekend as well. Now, with regard to Daddy...he's going to meet Lisa in New Orleans on the tenth. He's invited me along but I already declined. Anika is leaving on the ninth to go to France with her mother. So—I think the eleventh is a safe day to start this. Does that work for you?"

"Yes, that should work. I have no other immediate plans."

"Good. Now, here is what you must do. As of the tenth, you may not eat anything at all; you can drink water, that's it. I don't recommend exerting yourself on that day, I'd rest up. The process of physical breaking may be more extensive if you don't. So, be sure to follow those instructions. You will not tell ANYONE about what we're doing—not even a hint. If that means avoiding your parents, grandparents and siblings until then, so be it. Are you clear? Do you have any questions?"

"No—I think that makes sense. I'm scared to death, though."

"Yes, it's scary. But you won't die or be permanently damaged. I will make sure of that."

I sighed. "Alright then—when do you want me on the eleventh?"

"Come by around noon. We will begin the preliminaries at 1:00."

She gently kissed me, and we parted ways.

25

Mila's Visions

Malcolm saw Anika come up the walkway to the front door, but Layla was not with her. "Hello, dear," he said, giving her a kiss. "Where is your sister?"

"She said to tell you she was going to be a little late getting home."

"Oh? Did she have to stay after school for something?"

"No—it was really strange. I saw Steve Abbott waiting outside the school, and she went to talk to him."

Malcolm sat up. "Steve? What is he doing here? He's supposed to be at his nephew's funeral!"

"Oh, that must be why he was wearing a suit. He did look rather distressed. But I don't know what he wants from Layla. She seemed to know, though."

Malcolm began to feel very anxious. "What is going on with her and Steve? I have the feeling something is up, and neither one of them is talking about it."

Anika shrugged, and gestured indicating her ignorance. "I don't know Daddy; she's not said anything at all."

Malcolm gave a frustrated grunt. "Well, I guess I'll have to wait until she gets home to find out. But I want to get to the bottom of it."

Anika nodded, and went upstairs. Malcolm found he could not sit still; he contemplated going out to look for them, but eventually decided just to wait. His patience was rewarded when Layla turned up about an hour and a half later.

"Where were you, young lady?" he asked.

"Didn't Anika tell you I'd be late?"

"Yes, but she also said she saw you talking to Steve Abbott."

"Yes, that's right."

Malcolm's eyes widened. "Layla, why is he talking to you? He's supposed to be at his nephew's funeral."

Layla poured herself a glass of juice and sat down. "Yes, he was there. But he got very aggravated at the funeral sermon and left. He came to talk to me."

"Well, I'm confused—why is he coming to you about that?"

"Oh. Well, you see, the Morrigan placed a curse on his family many years ago, and the death of a male infant generally is a result of that curse. They always say it's because I'm evil or demonic, but Steve realises this is not the case."

"Wait…wait…wait—Steve knows that you're…?"

"Well of course. He's known for years."

Malcolm now looked alarmed. "How did he find out initially?"

"Oh, that's a long story—it will have to wait until you're back from New Orleans. It will make more sense then, anyway."

"Why did the Morrigan curse his family?"

"Because one of his ancestors was an oathbreaker. Breaking an oath to the high goddess was treasonous—it was viewed as badly as murdering someone's family. I took care of the oathbreaker, and cursed his family. Steve is the only one smart enough to realise that it's the family and his ancestor that are the problem, not me."

"Well, I still don't understand why he had to seek you out, away from me."

"Oh, you will. For now, don't think about it. You will know everything soon."

26

Steve Abbott's Diary

I brought my wife and children to the airport, and said goodbye to them. My return home after visiting Layla was met with a tense and chilly reception, as I expected. My family did not know why I left suddenly, and I'm sure they were questioning my mental health. Some of them may have given me a pass, believing that I was under stress and overly affected by Jacob's death. At the moment, I didn't care. I drove back home, feeling very surreal, like I was watching a movie of myself driving. My upcoming appointment with Layla weighed on my mind; I just wanted to get on with it. But I would have to wait another week.

Somehow I distracted myself for those few days. Malcolm called me before he left, discussing plans for the next album, which we agreed we would work on over the summer, as Malcolm was leaving soon for New Orleans. I had no idea at that time that Malcolm was aware of the upcoming meeting; several times it seemed like he wanted to ask me something, and then stopped himself. I didn't give him any information. The day before everything was to happen I prepared as I was instructed. Even with Layla's description, I still didn't really know what to expect, and was not going to risk doing anything that could make the process worse, or more dangerous.

The eleventh finally came. Layla had suggested I pack loose-fitting clothes, so I put together what I needed, locked up the house, and went out to my car. Taking a deep breath, I began my journey to Esher, arriving a little before noon. As I pulled into the drive, my head was spinning; part of it was anxiety, part was the lack of food. I remember getting out and taking a deep breath to wake up. Then, grabbing my bag, I headed to the front door.

Layla answered the ring of the bell, smiling. "You're very punctual. Come in."

27

Steve Abbott's Diary

She led me upstairs, stopping first at her own bedroom. "Leave your things in here. When all is finished, I will clean you up and bring you back here to rest." I obeyed, and she then ordered me to undress. I removed everything, and she took my hand and led me into the same guest room I had slept in during the prior months. The bed was stripped of its duvet and pillows, and plain sheets were draped over it—I was pretty sure there was plastic underneath. He also saw that there were shackles placed on the headboard and linked to the footboard of the bed. The whole thing had been moved to the middle of the rounded floor. She had a number of bottles on a side table, some were liquid, some were solids—at least one was salt, I was sure. She had a censer, and some matches next to it, as well as some other odds and ends.

"Sit down." I sat on the edge of the bed. She was lighting a piece of charcoal inside the censer, and now added what smelled like frankincense to it. I remember the smell from being in church as a child. As the thurible smoked, she took the salt and drew a circle around the bed, and marked out certain sigils in the corner and behind the bed. She then took the censer and swung it in a circle around the whole perimeter, chanting something in a language I could not understand. There was an immediate change in the room; it felt normal before, but now it felt lighter, as though clutter was cleared from it. She then put down the censer and took a glass jar with liquid from the nightstand. She poured it into a glass, and ordered me to drink it. It was a light blue color, and had a taste I could not quite describe, but it wasn't unpleasant. After finishing it, I began to feel a bit lightheaded. She picked up a scarf she had brought and secured it over my mouth. Then she pushed me back onto the bed, pulling my hands over his head and securing them with shackles; she did the same thing with my feet. There was enough give with the chains that she could turn me on my side. She was now behind me, and suddenly began a guttural chant, and as she chanted she lashed me violently with what felt like a rattan cane. I was half delirious already from fasting and the drug she gave me, but the pain of the strokes went through me like fire. The chant was rhythmic, and the lashes were in time with her chanting. At times she would stop, and take a whip, beginning the same process. The pain was excruciating; I could feel tears in my eyes, and my breathing was laboured. My whole body ached and trembled; at first I flinched at the lashes, but eventually I started to become numb to them. Suddenly she hit me with something that felt electrical—it was like a cattle prod with a sponge on the end. I cried out, and suddenly lost consciousness.

28

When I became aware again, I was standing on the shore outside a gate. Layla stood there with me, looking more like the woman in my original dream; she had a radiance that was unearthly. She shook her head. "I thought I was going to have to kill you before you jumped from your body. The shocks finally did it. Now we're here, let's get on with things."

She sang out, and the gates suddenly began to open. She led me in, and I gasped. This had to be a kind of heaven; it was the most beautiful place ever, and the air was so light. I had never breathed easier in his life. I looked down at myself; my hands looked younger, and my body was slim and tight, like it was when I was younger. I felt longer hair around my face. Layla noticed my wonder at this, and said, "Yes, this is Tir na nOg–that means 'Land of Youth.' You have gotten younger." We walked along, and the sand on the shore was soft; it was like walking on silk. We moved through several groves of trees to a large castle. As we made our way up the walk, I started to see the denizens of this place; they looked strange. There were unusually and unnaturally beautiful men and women, as well as fairy-like creatures that didn't look human at all. They stopped to stare at me; apparently (as I learned) there hadn't been a living human on Tir na nOg for a very long time–thousands of years, to them. She led me inside the castle, where she was met by two servants who were part of this strange race. She spoke to them in a language I did not understand. They bowed and hurried off. She turned to me, leading me to a bench where she sat beside me. "Open your mouth." I obeyed, and she grabbed my tongue, muttering something and pinching the end. When she took her hand away, I suddenly realised that he could understand the chatter around me. When she spoke to me in the unfamiliar language, I could understand and speak back. "I had to give you the language," she said. "You will need it for your next tasks."

Presently the fey servants returned with a man in a white robe with a long beard. He looked at me with some surprise. "Gwydion, this is Steve Abbott. He is a descendant of Duagh O'Connor. He has come to renounce Christianity, become a Druid, and re-make the broken vows with me."

Gwydion nodded, and looked at me. "Have you come to do this of your own free will?"

"Yes" I said, and I meant it.

His stern and surprised countenance relaxed. "I congratulate you, young man, for your decision. I don't think you have any idea how important it is that you do this—especially as O'Connor's descendant. Come with me." Layla nodded at me to go, and I rose and went with Gwydion further into the castle.

Gwydion gave me a white robe trimmed with intricate designs to cover my nakedness, and took me into a room with others similarly dressed. He explained who I was to the others, and there were murmurs of surprise and relief. "We did not know if we would ever recover the heart of Connacht. Now we know that can happen, and then everything else can happen."

155

"I know about my ancestor, and what he did, and I know about the connection to Connacht. But I don't know anything else," I said.

Gwydion sat down, looking serious. "Your race is on the point of extinction. You're not quite there yet, but a series of events are coming that have the potential to destroy you. From our perspective, the problem is a race of parasites that has been created, that is eating away at that firmament. We may be in another dimension, but we are directly affected by what happens in your world. If that collapses, then we collapse with it. There's going to be a war with this race, which grows in intelligence every decade, and I think it will only speed up as the time draws nearer."

I was alarmed. "What can be done about it?"

"Well, that is why the Morrigan returned. After Ireland turned to Christianity, she withdrew what was left of the sacred precincts, as she didn't want this world destroyed as well. Men used to be able to come here when they performed the right rituals, but that time is long gone. She has done the unimaginable by uniting the tribes of De Danann, the Firbolgs, and the Fomorians. Now that she has done that, she is turning her attention to the human world. She has two missions. The first is to reconnect to the heart of the earth at Connacht by getting O'Connor's descendant to reconnect to her. That is happening now, so one thing will be accomplished. The second thing is to find two warriors and bring them back."

"Two warriors?"

"Yes. She has identified both, and brought one already. He was half-Fomorian, which was a boon; the Fomorians needed a new captain, and now they have one. Human blood is good for the races here, as it strengthens them. How a Fomorian and a human mated, I cannot imagine, but I will not question that at this time."

I wondered about this. "Can I see this person?"

We stood up and went to the window. I now saw the bustling town below. Gwydion pointed–"that is the man there."

I looked at him in amazement; he looked human for the most part, but had the jaw and teeth of a Fomorian, as well as clawed hands. Suddenly I remembered where I had seen him-in the newspaper article Malcolm had showed them at breakfast the one day. He was the murderer/rapist terrorising the area. I said this to Gwydion.

"I have no doubt," said Gwydion. "I don't imagine humans would treat a Fomorian hybrid as anything other than a monster. When you treat someone like a monster, they become one, though they don't always have the most pleasant nature to begin with." We returned to our seats.

"What about the other one?" I asked.

"Well, the other important position is the Captain of the Dagdachoris."

"What is that?"

"They are an elite fighting force, the most formidable in the universe. Apparently she has someone in mind for this, and has already given him a sign that he will be chosen. I don't think he has understood it, though. His time will come soon enough, and I predict you will be involved in getting him here. "

I raised my eyebrows, but said nothing, letting Gwydion finish. "So far everything is going as planned, but there is at least one obstacle, and I'm not sure how serious it is yet."

"What is that?"

Gwydion looked grim. "Duncluan."

I gave another gasp; this was the name that had crossed my mind when I'd become impotent and very angry at Layla. I told the whole story to Gwydion, who looked alarmed.

"Then he is active in your dimension as well. He was trying to derail you from your purpose; he succeeded long enough for the death of your nephew to occur. He was hoping you would rebel against the Morrigan. And he's using your grandmother as his mouthpiece."

My jaw dropped. "You mean...my Gran is possessed by him?"

He nodded, his face like stone. "She, like many in your family, have been set against the Morrigan because they've been told a false story. She's easy to manipulate, because he validates what she wants to believe—she thinks he's the voice of God. And because she's a kind of ancestor matriarch figure, your family will not oppose her. But I am grateful that you did not allow yourself to succumb to family allegiances in this case. Rarely do you see anyone, even of the dark elven race, that is so evil. But he is truly hateful of the Morrigan and sees the Fomorians and Firbolgs as traitors. He is actively encouraging what is happening in your world, and he's amassed a lot of power through human weakness. He is wreaking serious havoc on the Morrigan's incarnation in another dimensional timeline; I thought she was

158

reasonably free of his influence in this one. But he's striking out everywhere, if there is someone integral to the Morrigan's plans."

"But—surely he must know that he will also be destroyed if he persists?"

Gwydion shook his head. "You are right—he will be destroyed—but he doesn't seem to care. Revenge and power are everything to him. He is so blinded by his desire to overthrow her, he doesn't realise he will be destroyed in the process as well. But—we must move on and begin your training. There is not a lot of time."

I was taken to a room, where I was asked to memorise the songs and spells given to me by the Druid bards. Gwydion taught me how to go into myself and open my mind, to make it receptive. I listened to the songs, and absorbed them; I would be asked to sing them back, to make sure I really understood. After a couple of days of this, they finally brought me before the large group and tested me, to make sure I really knew everything. I was surprised at how well I did know what was taught to me; there were songs for the seasons, songs to affect nature, songs to affect people, and other secret things like the song that opened the gates of Tir na nOg, which Layla sang upon their arrival. I passed the test, and was brought to finish my initiation.

My hands were tattooed with the Druidic insignia. I received a ring, a hazel wand, a cup, and a dagger, and was re-dressed in white robes trimmed with purple, as I would be an ArchDruid in the outer world. There were no others, so anyone who was worthy of learning would have to learn from me.

Once this was over, I was brought into a magnificent hall, where a large stone sat atop a golden seal on the floor. I was told this was the original Stone of Destiny, upon which the Irish kings swore their allegiance to Morrigan. It was taken away along with other sacred relics.

Layla now entered the room—she was definitely the Morrigan in her role, and I saw her as I had in my dream. She approached the stone. I was told by Gwydion to put my left hand on the stone, and the right hand on my heart. The Morrigan approached and placed her clawed right hand on mine. I was then asked to take an oath, renouncing my Christian baptism, and giving myself entirely to the Morrigan. I made the vow, repeating the words after Gwydion. I looked into the Morrigan's eyes as he made the vow, and I could feel the force of my words. When I finished, she spoke. "I accept your vows, Steve Abbott, descendant of Duagh O'Connor. As long as you keep your vows, the curse on your family is revoked, and I will give you back the child you recently lost. I also give you the sacred name (omitting here for, well, secrecy) which you will keep secret."

The Druids banged their long staves against the floor as the vows were sealed, and I felt a rush through his body as though electrified. The Morrigan took my hand and pulled me up, telling me to come with her. In her private chambers, I made love to her. I have no words for how I felt; the bliss was too much beyond anything I'd ever experienced, or might ever experience again. When we finished, she brought me out again, and we celebrated, pouring the wine and raising a cup at this victory.

After this little ceremony, the Morrigan turned almost apologetically to me. "I'm afraid you'll have to return to your body now. This might be harder than your getting here, be warned."

I gave a deep sigh; I'd almost forgotten about the body I'd left, and she had been right when she said I wouldn't want to go back. But I knew he must, so I took leave of my new brethren. At the gates, she took my robe and my other tools, and led me back through the gates. I saw my battered and bound body, and had a revulsion at the thought of re-entry. She gave me a bit of a shove, and I dove back into my body.

29

When I re-entered I felt like I was drowning in a pit of sludge. The pain I felt was excruciating, and I almost couldn't breathe. Layla unshackled me, and pulled the scarf from my mouth, encouraging me to take deep breaths, with her hand on my chest. My erratic and panicked breathing began to fall into a regular cadence, and soon I could breathe normally again. The odor in the room was foul; I was sure it came from my festering body. Every part of me hurt, especially my back where I had been viciously beaten. She soothed me, and told me she would be right back. I saw her go into the bathroom, and she began to run a bath for me. I had no idea how I would even get up, but she took a hold of me, swung my legs over the bed and pulled my body upright, which made me cry out. "You're alright," she said. "Come, hold me, and I'll take you and clean you up."

Somehow I managed to get into the tub, leaving bloody footprints behind me. She held me tight and carefully seated me in the tub, taking the shower head down, soaping me up and rinsing me off. I watched the tub turn a foul reddish-brown color. When she finished rinsing my upper half and washing my hair, she managed to pull me up again, and got me to hold onto a bar in the shower. She then cleaned my backside and legs, and then drained the tub, finally washing my feet. She had me stand on a mat outside the tub, still holding on to the bar, and she dried me off, wrapping me in a large towel. She guided me to the toilet, and had me sit on the closed toilet seat as she finished cleaning my feet. She had brought in my toiletries, and proceeded to lather my face and give me a shave. When this was done, she got me to the sink to brush my teeth, holding me from behind so I didn't lose my balance. I was still in agony, but was glad to be clean again.

She brought me clothes from my bag, and dressed me. I was very glad that I didn't bring anything restrictive to wear, as I now saw why this was important. She brought me a three-footed cane, and let me use that to walk with as she guided me to her bedroom. I felt better overall, but my back and legs were in excruciating pain. I passed an area where two mirrors faced each other, and got a look at my back. I wished I hadn't. "Don't worry about that," said Layla. "That's the worst of everything, and it will get better. You have no internal bleeding, no concussion, and no broken bones. Everything else is just ugly now, will heal up later."

"I'll trust you on that."

She sat me on a comfortable chair in her room, though it hurt to put my back against anything. She brought me another liquid concoction—this seemed more like a protein drink. I drank it quickly, and she then brought me some soup to drink. "Start small, don't shock your insides," she said. "You will get some rest, and then you can have some solid food when you get up."

She rubbed an ointment on my hands, and I realised that the Druid tattoos were visible there; I had brought them back to my physical body. I also saw the robe and other tools that Gwydion gave me piled neatly on another chair in the room. The whole thing had been real. I wanted to process it all, but was too tired and in too much pain to think too hard.

She carefully laid me on her bed, on my stomach, propping me with pillows to make it more comfortable. She then began to rub a salve on my naked back, and the effect was cooling. I began to feel more comfortable, and was soon asleep.

*****

Mila's Vision

Malcolm's plane landed at Heathrow that same afternoon. His girlfriend wasn't able to join him right away, so she was coming back to stay with them in Esher at the end of the month. It was only a temporary trip, as he wanted to get some things sorted at home and to get back to work as soon as possible.

The first thing he noticed was that Steve's car was in the driveway. He stared at it, stunned. Why was he here alone with Layla? He had never pressed the issue of what was going on; now he was going to press it.

He walked into the house; he was going to call out to Layla, but again something stopped him. The house was clean and in order, so he made his way down the hall and upstairs. He heard her singing to herself in the very upstairs room of the house. He climbed the stairs and entered the room. What he saw drained the colour from his face.

Layla was cleaning up the room—there were bloody footprints on the floor, and she was re-making the bed, with a pile of bloody sheets put aside for the wash. The footprints went toward the bathroom. She looked up at him very casually as he came in. "Oh you're home. I didn't hear you come in. Did you enjoy your trip?"

He stared at her incredulously. "Layla—what the hell happened in here??"

She continued making the bed. "There was an initiation."

"A what??"

"An initiation."

"I don't know what you mean by that."

She turned her attention to cleaning and straightening up. "An initiation into Druidism. It can't happen here, so the initiate has to move to my other-dimensional home to get to where there are actual Druids. That is accomplished partially through a drug, and partially through physical torture. Shamanic, if you will."

Malcolm was speechless. "Who..." though he was sure he knew the answer.

"Steve Abbott, of course."

"What...why..."

"Hush!" said Layla. "He is resting right now, and has been through a lot. I don't want to wake him, he needs sleep."

"Where is he?"

"In my bedroom. I can't leave him in here right now, I need to clean."

"I want to see him."

She turned. "You can see him, but don't try to wake him! I will go with you. Let me put these sheets in the wash first." She went to the laundry room down the hall, and put the sheets in with a solution to take out the blood. Then she motioned for her father to come, opening the door carefully.

Malcolm walked into the room, and saw Steve laying on Layla's bed, face down. He was breathing, and did not appear to be in distress. He saw Steve's arms, which he had over his head, and saw the tattoos, his eyes widening. His face looked placid, and he didn't appear hurt in any way. However, Layla carefully lifted the bedsheet that was over him, and Malcolm saw his back. He had to cover his mouth to keep from crying out. Layla carefully covered Steve again and ushered Malcolm out of the room quickly.

"Layla…I can't believe this…did he know this was going to happen?"

"Yes he did. He came and discussed it with me after his nephew's funeral."

"Is that what he wanted to talk to you about??"

"Sort of. He wanted to know how to remove the curse from his family. So, I told him—he had to renounce Christianity, renew his ancestor's vows to me—and in this case, because there are no more Irish kings and he's not royalty anyway—he has to commit to Druidism."

"Are you saying—he did all that?"

"Indeed he did. He is much better off for it, in spite of the suffering. He knows it, too."

Malcolm sunk into a chair in the living room, running his hands through his fingers. "I...there's more to this than I'm understanding ... I need the whole story. This is madness. And fuck, his back looks terrible!"

"No, you certainly don't understand," said Layla drily, "even though you've already been told almost everything already. You're not connecting what I've told you in the past—and what's happened in the past—with what happened in the last few days."

"What have you told me? I don't know anything."

"Yes, you do know. And when Steve wakes up, I need to give him some solid food—he hasn't had that in a few days—and then we will talk about it together. For now, stop fretting about it."

"Stop fretting? Layla, you've beaten the living shit out of him!"

"Oh, stop it. He wasn't randomly beaten; every stroke has a meaning. And he has no concussion, no broken bones, and no internal bleeding. It's mainly bad bruising and soreness. He will need some help getting around for a week or ten days, but then he'll be fine to go back home."

"What about his wife?"

"She's abroad with the kids."

"Layla...I'm sorry, but I'm really freaked out by this. You've never done anything like this before."

She sniffed. "How do you know?"

Malcolm looked at her wide-eyed. "Please don't say you have…"

"Well, I haven't initiated anyone else. I've done things you'd probably think are much worse."

"Like what?"

"Oh, quit asking. You know you don't really want to know. Go get yourself a whiskey and sit down and get a hold of yourself. It won't be long before he's up, and we can talk about it all." She then headed back upstairs to finish cleaning the room and the bathroom.

Malcolm gave a deep frustrated sigh. He finally did as she said, going to the cabinet to get a fifth of Jack Daniels. He downed it, sat on the sofa in the living room and turned on the telly. He had just arrived home, and was too disordered in his mind to do anything.

In the meantime, Layla finished cleaning the room, and it looked as though nothing had happened. She checked on Steve, who began to stir, and finally he woke up. She sat on the bed beside him, stroking his hair.

"How are you feeling, love?"

"OK, I think. I haven't moved yet, so I shouldn't speak too soon." He laughed.

She also laughed. "Mentally, how are you?"

"I've never felt happier. Isn't it strange?"

She laughed again. "Not really. Your whole body and psyche knows the magnitude of what you've just done, and such heroics are always rewarded. Right now, though, my father has come home, and noticed that something has gone on. He's a tad freaked out."

"Oh shit—he didn't see the room did he?"

"Yeah…not the worst of it, but the tail end."

He laughed. "That gives me a little trepidation. He's going to want the whole story and…we'll have to go back to when you were three…"

Layla sighed. "Yeah, this is going to be the time to tell him, I'm afraid. It will upset him temporarily, but he will get over it. It may make him feel less bad about your wounds, though."

Steve laughed, probably harder than he should have. "OK, now THAT hurts…"

"It will all be fine. Here, let me get you up. You need to eat something first, and then we'll talk."

Layla pulled away the pillows and rolled him onto his back. He let out a yelp. "You're alright. Steve, just hang in." She carefully turned him so that his legs hung over the side of the bed. Then she climbed onto the bed and carefully lifted him up, putting her hand on his lower back rather than grabbing the top. He managed to sit up, and then she got him into a standing posture. She had him grab onto the windowsill as she got a button-down shirt and put it on him before he went downstairs. Steve was trying to gauge how he felt; he was really sore and every move hurt, but it wasn't unbearable, just uncomfortable. She handed him the cane and he carefully walked out of the room, toward the stairs, Layla standing near him to steady him if necessary. He grabbed the railing and made his way down the stairs. Malcolm heard them coming, and turned off the telly,

169

standing up. They made eye contact, and Steve could see the confusion and bewilderment in Malcolm's face.

Steve smiled. "Hello, Mal. I know you didn't expect to meet me like this."

"No, I didn't. Layla explained some of it, but I really don't understand what the hell is going on."

Steve nodded. "I wouldn't think that you would. It's a long story."

"Well I want to hear it."

And thus Steve and Layla recounted their long relationship. Malcolm was visibly upset when he learned that Steve was the one who had taken Layla's virginity at the age of three. But Layla checked him, reminding him that if he was going to apply human ethics, he was just as guilty as Steve. Steve looked at her quizzically, and then at Malcolm. "Malcolm you didn't..."

He put his head in his hands, and ran his fingers through his hair. "It was a moment of weakness. Well, okay—several moments."

Layla broke in—"I didn't get involved with either one of you without a good reason. Now stop with all this nonsense. You are continuing to make the same mistake—I am your goddess, not your child, in spite of how I was born."

Steve broke in: "How exactly were you born?"

Layla looked at Malcolm, who looked uncomfortable. "Tell him."

Reluctantly, Malcolm pulled up his shirt and unbuttoned his trousers. He showed Steve a scar on his lower abdomen. Steve stared at it wide-eyed, with realisation.

"Holy shit! How did you keep people from finding out about that?"

"I told them I'd been up in Scotland and had to have an emergency appendectomy."

"But how…did that happen in the first place?"

Layla laughed. "It happened because my father may be a fine guitarist, but he is a poor magician."

"I don't understand."

Malcolm cut in: "I was dabbling in magic then, and attempted an evocation that I really knew very little about. As it turns out, it opened me up to a lot of possible experiences. I would have never expected this in a million years."

"I was looking for a way in," explained Layla. "My father was ideal, because he was in good proximity to where I needed to do my work—and to you," she added, nodding at Steve. "The fact that he practiced magic—even if poorly—would make my presence easier to accept. And he made himself an easy target."

"But that shouldn't be physically possible!"

"And everything else you've seen me do—and everything you've seen through my eyes—was that not possible?"

"Well…OK…touché…"

30

Steve Abbott's Diary

A few weeks had gone by since the initiation, and I was slowly regaining my strength. Much of the bruising that I had on my back had gone away, but it was still a bit of a challenge to get up and down when sitting. Still, my mental state was better than it had been in years, so the physical part did not bother me so much.

It was summertime, and my wife was still away with the kids; she did call a couple of times a week, but other than that I was free to be away from the house. Layla and I were sitting on the patio in her backyard, and I could tell by the look on her face that she was deep in thought about something. I asked her what was on her mind.

"I keep feeling like we need to hurry along; time here is moving along faster than I would like."

"Moving towards what?"

She sat back looking serious. "Towards war."

"War with whom?"

"War on a couple of fronts. For one, I have the internal war with the dark elves; it's clear to me that Duncluan has been manipulating things behind the scenes. He wouldn't dare oppose me directly; he knows he can't win that way."

"What has he done?"

"Well, he manipulated you for one, before I was able to break you out of that mental hold. He definitely manipulates your Gran; she acts as a mouthpiece for him."

"Gwydion said something about that. So, all of her angry Morrigan curse stuff..."

"Make no mistake, there was a curse. You've just lifted it. In fact, the son your sister just lost will be returned to her soon."

"How?"

"She'll be pregnant again. It is the same child. She will realise that soon enough." She paused. "Duncluan knows how important it is for you to be on my side; your Gran was already entrenched in religious orthodoxy, so she was a perfect target to manipulate in order to intimidate you, and to make you think something awful would happen by reconciling with me."

"Well, he's obviously lost that battle."

"Yes, he has. I won't lie to you—I was worried about leaving your body, if he found out what you'd done. He did eventually find out, but it was too late; I was successful at keeping it a secret from him until you'd returned to your body. If he knew in advance, he may have tried to attack your body, and you may not have been able to return from the Otherworld."

This was unnerving to hear, and I was glad she'd not mentioned it in advance. I would have probably been too scared to proceed. She continued, "But that's not all."

"What else?"

"When I showed you the world through my eyes, you could see that there are multiple dimensions and timelines. In this timeline, Duncluan hasn't really been able to touch me; however, in another one, he is wreaking havoc."

"What is happening?"

She looked grim. "In another timeline, he has manipulated my father. And that has led to disastrous results for me. In that timeline I will eventually handle him myself. But in this one..." she trailed off.

I leaned forward. "What can I do to help?"

She now turned to me with a smile. "I like your attitude. You and I have a project."

"Anything. Whatever you need me to do."

At this moment, Malcolm came out and joined us. Layla turned to him. "Daddy, we still own the house in Scotland, near the western coast, yes?"

Malcolm raised his eyebrows. "Uh, yeah, we do. I was thinking of selling it, but haven't gotten around to it yet. Why do you ask?"

"Steve and I need to go there."

"For what?"

She smiled and looked at me. "Steve needs to manipulate someone into going there...and we need to be there to meet him."

"Wait, what? I'm confused. Who?" said Malcolm.

"Aaron Langley."

"Layla…" he paused. "Does this have something to do with that thing you said to him when you were a child…?"

"When I asked him if he liked war?"

"Yes."

"Of course it does."

Just then I remembered what Gwyddion said about the Dagdachoris. And then I understood what Layla was doing.

"You know best," I told her. "But is there any way he'd come voluntarily?"

She roared with laughter. "Him? Voluntarily? You are very funny. You know what an arrogant bastard he is. There is no WAY he'd come unless he was tricked into it."

I thought about Aaron. He was extremely tall, and very strong. While he always claimed to be for peace, he had a nasty disposition that could be easily channeled into fighting. "But," I said, "doesn't he have to do battle to prove himself?"

She nodded. "Yes, that's the difficult part. I haven't sorted that yet. But I have a feeling something will come together once he's there."

"Very well, then. Let's make a plan."

Malcolm looked at me in a way I couldn't quite decipher; I think he wasn't entirely sure that I hadn't gone mad. But he just said. "Right, well…I can give you the keys. How are you getting up there?"

"Steve will bring us up there. No one else should go."

***

Aaron Langley's Account

(Taken from his remarks after the battle)

I don't know why I chose to head up to Scotland that weekend.

My girlfriend and I had plans to head down to the French Riviera. I was looking forward to relaxing on the beach, in the warm weather. But her plans suddenly changed, and we were going to have to postpone. I got it into my head that I'd like to go hiking instead. It was a bit of a last minute decision, and I didn't tell anyone where I was going. In retrospect, it was a bizarre thing for me to even think of doing; however, at the time it felt right.

I'd stopped off for a pint on the way up, near the area where I'd planned to hike. The locals were a bit surly; I don't think they cared to have someone from the South of England up in their territory, especially not someone who obviously came across to them as "posh". I planned to get out of there as soon as possible, but then I had another surprise. I heard a voice, more Irish than Scottish, speak my name. When I turned around, I saw Steve Abbott. I had met him once or twice, but didn't know him very well. Even so, it was something of a relief to see a familiar face.

"What brings you to Scotland?" he asked me.

I told him why I was there. "I'd wonder the same thing about you," I returned.

"Oh, I'm helping a friend open up their cottage up here—more of a holiday home."

"This is a strange place to have a holiday."

"Mm, yes, not the French Riviera certainly, but it has its charm."

I stared at him. How did he know I was planning to go there? Or was it just a coincidence that he mentioned it? I decided not to say anything.

We exchanged a few more pleasantries, and I suddenly felt I needed to go use the loo. I'd brought a notebook in with me, and really didn't want to take it into the toilets with me; I asked if he wouldn't mind watching it for a moment. "Not at all! Take your time." I felt him watching me as I headed to the stairs. I shook myself and just decided that I was in a weird place, the whole thing felt weird, and I was psyching myself up over nothing.

When I returned, Steve had just finished his own pint, and was standing up. "I do have to run now," he said. "Enjoy your hike! Hope the weather holds." It had been surprisingly sunny that afternoon, in an area that was usually quite gloomy.

I headed out to my car, and put my notebook on the seat. As I did, I noticed an extra sheet of paper that seemed to be inserted with the others. I opened to the loose page; it had a very strange drawing on it, and I suddenly found myself reminded of the drawing given to me by Layla Black years ago. God, I hadn't thought about that in a long time! I was pretty sure it wasn't the same image, but it had a similar quality. How did this get in my notebook? The only possibly answer was that Steve put it there—but why?

I slammed the notebook shut, turned the car on, and got back onto the road. I was going to do what I'd set out to do, and then head back to the closest town to spend the night. Something just didn't feel right to me the whole time...but I was determined to conquer whatever it was and keep moving ahead.

Unfortunately Steve's wish for good weather did not hold, and I found myself in quite the storm. The rain was coming down so hard that I couldn't see the road in front of me. I inched along, until the rain started to let up. I could see menacing black clouds in front of me; I swore out loud, as my prospects for a hike were likely to be washed out up ahead. Then I glanced in the rearview mirror, and got the shock of my life.

There was someone—or some THING—standing behind my car. Not just one, but several. They were dark figures; I could not make out any features initially, but then I saw that one of them had glowing red eyes. This was enough for me. I slammed the car into gear and took off. I didn't look back for a couple of miles, and I was driving way too fast for these roads. When I looked into the rearview mirror, I almost shit myself—the figures were FOLLOWING, and following fast.

How the hell can they do that? After I had the thought, I realised that I didn't want to think about the answer. To make matters worse, the rain picked up again. I found myself zig-zagging, going on gravel side roads, just trying to go anywhere to get away from what was behind me. Finally, after what seemed like an eternity, I no longer saw them. But the rain was still coming down, and now it was starting to get dark. I didn't know how much of a reprieve I would have.

I resolved to turn around and get back to town, but I suddenly realised that I was completely and utterly lost. I was

reluctant to go back the way I came, in case I ran into those…
those things. I didn't know if I wanted to cry, to punch someone,
or maybe both. There was nothing to do but to try to push on in
this desolate area. And then up ahead, I saw it.

It was a house—the only one in this area—and there was a
light on in the window, and a car in the driveway. I hesitated; the
locals tended to detest anyone from England, and I was not sure
about the reception I was going to get if I knocked on the door.
But I had no other choices at the moment. I reluctantly got out of
the car, and made my way to the front door. I took a deep breath
and gave a forceful knock.

It was only a few seconds before I heard footsteps;
someone peered out the window, and then the door opened.

It was Steve Abbott.

Needless to say, I was stunned. What were the odds that I
was going to end up at the same cottage he said he was going
to, to help someone open up? At the moment, I was so relieved
to see a familiar face, I'd forgotten all about the drawing left in
my notebook; that should have given me pause.

"Aaron! How did you end up over here?" He beckoned
for me to come in. It was a stone cottage, but he had a fire
going, and the warmth inside was inviting. I knew the torrential
rain would be back, so I stepped inside without hesitation. I
explained to him what had happened on the way over.

"Well, that's very strange! I've heard that there were…
well, that there are strange things that walk in this area. But I
assumed all that was just folk tales."

"Strange things?"

"Yes—there are all kinds of tales about fairies and other kinds of creatures that are supposed to live in this area. But never mind, you've had quite an ordeal; can I get you a drink? Perhaps a shot of whiskey?"

I was grateful for the suggestion, as I needed something to calm my nerves. I heard Steve humming to himself, as he went into the kitchen, and I heard him pouring something from a bottle. He then returned with two short glasses of whiskey, and handed one to me. I downed it quickly, and began to feel suddenly languid. Steve suggested that I crash in the spare room.

"You're not going to be able to find your way out of here in the dark, and it doesn't sound like it's safe. Have a rest, and then push on in the morning." I was in no condition to disagree with him. He led me to a back bedroom, and as soon as I pulled back the covers I fell asleep.

31

Mila's Vision

Aaron awoke shortly after this. He looked up, and saw he was in a room in what appeared to be a castle. He was laying on a bed. Looking around the room, it was furnished with dark wood—it had a rather medieval look to it. *Where the hell am I?*

He looked around the room. There was a heavy wooden door. When he tugged at it, he realised it was locked. Walking around, he saw there was no other exit. There was a very narrow window. Looking out the window, he saw that he was way up on the top of a hill, or at least towards the top of this building. Even if he had been able to squeeze himself through that narrow window, he would surely fall to his death.

When he looked down, he saw the townspeople moving about. But this was not any ordinary town—the denizens were all of a strange size and shape, and the buildings were also oddly constructed. The scene was familiar—where had he seen this before?

He tried to think—he was in shock, and not entirely sure if he was awake or dreaming. He then realised that the buildings and the people were familiar from dreams he had long ago. Was he having a dream? Everything seemed far too realistic.

He thought about the events of the day, and now understood that he had walked into a trap. Steve had somehow diverted him to that house; he thought of the drawing in his notebook. Was it some kind of weird spell? And he had been tired, but the whiskey shot put him out much more quickly than it should have. He didn't see Steve pour it, and now he felt certain he had been drugged. But he still didn't know what any of this was about, or how he got here. He felt his anxiety increasing, his blood pounding in his veins.

Suddenly the door to his room opened. Layla appeared in the door, flanked by two faerie servants and Steve. She also looked different—she was longer, more willowy, and somehow less human. Steve also had lost about twenty years; he wore what appeared to be the garb of a priest—maybe a Druid? His hair was long and flowing, and his eyes were a steely blue, but his face was amiable. When they entered the room, the servants shut the door behind them. Aaron stared at her. She noted the look on his face and in his eyes. "Sit down, Aaron."

He looked at her—there was some defiance, but also fear. "What is this place? What do you want from me?"

"Ah, you do not know this place from your dreams?" She laughed and it made him uncomfortable. "This is Tir na nOg. It is where I come from, and we don't tend to go to the human world unless we have a reason. At one time we were part of the human world, but out of necessity we retreated, closing up the doors to the island into another dimension. Still, things that happen in the human world do affect us."

"But what does that have to do with me? I don't understand."

"You are extremely important to us. But I'm not going to say why yet—if you know too much, it might be a problem for you. Things have to happen naturally."

"But I don't want to be here—I want to go home."

182

"Of course you do. I wouldn't have had to bring you here in the manner that I did if you were willing. If you understood, you might have been more willing. But judging from your reactions, telling you would have made you resistant. In any case, you're not going home, there's no way back once you're here if you're human, unless there is a reason to open that gateway.

Aaron glowered at her, his brain reeling. "This has to do with what you kept asking me about war, doesn't it? That has to be it." He could feel his face getting hot.

She smiled. "That's very likely, yes. But don't assume too much; you don't know anything yet."

Aaron now felt weak in the knees. He sunk down onto one of the benches, pale. He could not imagine in a million years that he would be caught up in something like this. He couldn't even process his emotions; he didn't know if he was angry, in despair, or just in shock. Or all of the above.

"Oh, don't be so grim," she said, reading his thoughts. "You'll get over your shock. In the meantime, you need to get used to this place slowly. You need some time to get adjusted. Once that's settled a bit, you can venture outside—though I will advise you to stay out of the town proper. I will show you where it is safe for you to go. You do not speak the language of the local tribes, and they do not know what English is. Eventually you will learn the language too—but it's best to wait on that for now."

Aaron just stared at her, not knowing what to say. He was dizzy, overwhelmed. He wanted to run from the room and lie down on the bed at the same time. In the end, he went over to the bed and lay there.

183

Layla rose from her seat. "Yes, rest is the best thing for you," she said. "Your curiosity will wake you up soon enough." She then left without waiting for him to respond.

***

The news media was abuzz with Aaron Langley's disappearance. His car was found near the Scottish coast, and there had been a notebook inside the car with some of his jottings and a Celtic-looking drawing. They also found his wallet, and the standard documents in the glove box of the car. A suitcase was in the trunk with just a few items; it seemed he was going somewhere, but it was not clear where that was; no local accommodations had any reservations for him. The men at the pub did remember seeing him, but they did not remember him speaking to anyone. The trail went cold very quickly, and there were far more questions than answers.

32

Mila's Vision

For several days, Aaron alternated between thinking about how he could escape and breaking down in despair at the hopelessness of his situation. Layla was clearly some kind of queen here, and they referred to her as Macha. Aaron did not know anything about the Morrigan, or any of the history of the place, and no one enlightened him, leaving him with more questions than answers. His mental anxiety and continued rehashing and analysing of the situation left him drained most of the time. One day though, he started to feel restless, and wanted to know what was beyond the castle walls. Sensing his readiness, Layla finally visited him with a map of the island. She showed him the beach areas on the outskirts of the town. Aaron would want to avoid the Unseelie territory, and stay near the shoreline closer to the town. The townspeople had been put on notice that he would be about, but that they should not speak to him until her approval was given.

With violently mixed feelings, Aaron went out of the castle. It was difficult not to feel weighted down by the weirdness of the place. Part of him wanted to defy her and run now that he was no longer confined, but where could he go? He glanced over at the town, and could see the bustling non-human activity, and this immediately made up his mind; he'd better just do what he was told for now. Following her instructions, he walked along the shore line. It was quite peaceful there, and he walked for what seemed like a long time. As he walked towards what appeared to be the Southern tip of the island, Aaron noted a small grove of trees. There were other groves along the path, but he felt drawn to this one. He stepped in and sat on the ground. A very peaceful feeling enveloped him. He could hear the lapping of the water, and felt the cooling breeze of the afternoon. Amongst the trees, he lay down on the ground, which was soft and sandy, and fell asleep.

Not long after, a young fey named Allette was traipsing towards the woods with a basket of seeds and nuts. She was going to build a little altar in her grove. It was customary for the faerie girls, upon reaching marriageable age, to set up these little altars for the love goddess, in the hopes that the right partner would come to her. Allette was a beautiful girl; she was willowy with sinuous limbs, and had beautiful long dark hair and dark almond-shaped eyes with just a hint of green. Her family was an elite one ancestrally, and very old. There had been human blood in the family, which is why the line lasted so long. Human bloodlines mixed with faerie ones was a very healthy combination, in spite of what one might think. Allette almost looked like she could have been human, more so than many of her friends.

Allette wore a trinket around her neck, like most girls her age. Carved on it was the symbols for her family heritage, and a symbol representing her name. The idea was that at a marriageable age, the girl was supposed to give her trinket away to the man whom she chose to be her husband. The girl did not automatically get to marry that man, though families tried hard to accommodate. On an appointed day, the girl would be brought into the village square, and be put through a process much like auctioning. Men would come offering their bids on a dowry for the girl's hand. Naturally her chosen suitor was expected to be there, and the fact that he was chosen would give his bid a little more weight. But if he was seriously outbid by another, then the girl was married to the higher bidder. Girls did have the choice of becoming priestesses. But most families did not want their daughters to become priestesses—they wanted gold.

This was the position Allette was in as she walked towards her grove. She did not really like anyone well enough to hand over her trinket to them. She saw the way faerie men treated their wives, and was not sure that she wanted anything to do with that. Yet, she did want a family and children. She hated having to make a decision so quickly. Why couldn't she have more time?

Just as she reached the grove, she felt suddenly that she was not alone. She looked around, then down, and gasped.

The mortal man who had come to the island was sleeping in her grove! She almost dropped the basket she was carrying. Why was he here? What did it mean?

Allette carefully set down her basket at the edge of the grove. Then she quietly tiptoed over to where the man slept. She circled him, peering at his features. He was very tall and clearly very strong. He gave off a kind of warmth that she liked. She stood looking at him for quite a while. Suddenly he stirred. Frightened, Allette quickly hid behind a tree. He only turned over and returned to a deep sleep.

Allette was full of mixed feelings. He was so beautiful that she instantly fell in love with him. But she remembered that Macha had instructed them to stay away from him. But here he was in her grove. Should she consider him a gift from the gods? She shouldn't refuse a gift from the gods.

Seeing him lying on the ground, Allette cautiously moved

forward. She took a cloth that she was going to use as an altar cover, folded it, and placed it carefully under his head. She took another one and carefully covered him to keep him warm. She then took a cup, filled it with water, and placed it on a nearby rock. She then took another cup and filled it with some berries and nuts. Then, removing herself and her basket, she climbed up a tree to watch him for a while, to see if he awoke, and what he would do.

Not long after, Aaron did wake up. He was a bit dazed and groggy. As he became conscious, he was aware that something was different. Looking around, he noticed the blanket that covered him, the small pillow under his head, and the food and drink left for him nearby. His reaction was one of amazement; he looked around carefully to see who might have left this hospitality for him. He did not see Allette hiding, watching him from the tree.

Since he did not see anyone around, Aaron went and sat down again. He was quite hungry and thirsty at this point, so he took the hospitality left for him, much to Allette's delight. He stood up afterwards and stretched. Allette marveled at his physique. She wished she could approach him.

Aaron looked around one last time. He then carefully folded the blanket, stacked it with the smaller cloth, and neatly placed them near the cups left for him. He then turned and started to walk back towards the castle. He thought about the queer experience he had in the grove. Someone had to leave those things for him. In any event, Aaron did not interpret the act as hostile—it was as though someone was trying to welcome him. It made him feel a little better in this strange place. But he wondered who did it, and why.

33

Mila's Vision

Aaron returned to his room in the castle. He did not tell anyone there of his experience in the grove. But he found himself going there every day and taking an afternoon nap. It had an air of familiarity in an unfamiliar place, and was weirdly comforting. Allette interpreted his continual returns as a good omen, and continued to leave things for him.

In the meantime, Allette was being pressured at home to make her marital choice. She asked her mother for advice. Her mother replied, "Use your best judgment, my dear. Whatever feels like the honest choice, make it."

Whatever feels like the honest choice. Allette decided that reasoning out the person her parents would want her to marry was not the thing to do—and there was no one she really wanted in the village at any rate. So, she made what was the honest choice. Upon returning to her grove, she saw Aaron there. Taking the trinket from around her neck, she carefully hung it around his neck. She was trembling as she did so, fearful he would wake up and be upset. But she did not wake him in the end. She desperately wanted to see his reaction, but she was also afraid to hang around. Deciding that she had some time, she climbed her tree and watched him.

This time when Aaron awoke, he sat up, took the food and drink as usual, and then prepared to stand up. But as he bent down, he noticed something swinging from around his neck. He stopped and looked at it. It was a small golden trinket with strange carvings on it. Where the heck did this come from?, he wondered. He was puzzled by it, but kept it with him. After straightening up the area, he walked back to the castle as usual.

He was not prepared for the reaction when he returned to his room.

One of the priestesses waiting on him almost screamed when she saw the trinket around his neck. She called another priestess, and they both started jabbering, pointing at the trinket, wide-eyed. Aaron stared at them aghast, and with some annoyance; were they crazy? What the hell was wrong with them? He looked down at the trinket—what was it?

Presently the Morrigan came to see what the commotion was about. She took one look at the trinket around Aaron's neck and laughed out loud. "Oh Allette! I would not have thought of that but yes...yes." She laughed again. "Oh, if only she knew how you got on in the human world!" She was laughing so hard, tears came to her eyes.

Aaron was perplexed, and not just a little irritated. What in the world was she talking about? Noticing his look, she managed to control her laughter, and said, "Aaron, come with me. We must talk about this."

Now sitting in one of her private chambers, the Morrigan asked him, "Where did you get that trinket?"

"I don't have any idea. I go out every day, and walk around, sticking to the areas you tell me to stay in. Towards the end of the island is a peaceful little grove of trees. When I'm tired I lie down there, and usually someone has left food and water when I wake up. I've never seen anyone there."

"You mean the grove just to the south of the beach?"

"Yes, that one."

The Morrigan nodded. "That explains everything. You see, Aaron, you have walked into the sacred grove of one of the young fey girls with a rather high pedigree, as far as faerie families go. The girls all have a little grove, and often they go there when they are reaching marriageable age, to leave offerings for the love goddess. In this case, you laid down by the altar, and the fey girl, whose name is Allette, found you there."

"How do you know her name?"

The Morrigan took a hold of the trinket, and pointed to a certain symbol. "That is the symbol for her name. All fey girls get these trinkets made at birth, for when they reach marriageable age."

"What does marriage have to do with the trinket?"

"Well, it works like this. The fey girls are expected to choose a preferred spouse. The way they show their favor is by giving their beloved this trinket."

"What!? But the girl doesn't even know anything about me."

"It doesn't matter. You are a human, you are tall and imposing, and most importantly, you were asleep at her altar when she was leaving offerings for the love goddess. So, she sees you as her gift."

"Oh dear God," muttered Aaron.

"Allette is a very strong-willed but sweet girl. She is not willing to settle for many of the faerie men—many are very abusive to their wives. I am sure she chose you because she has fallen in love with you."

"But that's insane! She doesn't even know me!"

"Is it? People fall in love based on images all the time. And frankly, compared to her other choices, you might as well be a god yourself, at least in her eyes. Now the trouble is—what her family will say and how the auction will go. Even though the trinket has gone to you, Allette will be married to the highest bidder."

"I beg your pardon?"

"The highest bidder. The girls are auctioned for their dowry. Preference is of course given to whomever wears the trinket, but they can be outbid, and the girl married to someone else. Like many human marriages in earlier times, it's about money for the family, not the girl's happiness."

"Well, that's just atrocious."

"Perhaps. But it is their custom."

"Well, what happens now? It's not like I can marry her."

The shadow of a smile on the Morrigan's face spread into a mischievous smile. "Oh? Can't you?"

Aaron looked up at her, his eyes widening again. "What are you suggesting?"

The Morrigan stood up. "It's easy, Aaron. I have brought you here with a purpose. The first step will be to integrate you into society here. If you have a high-ranking spouse, that will make it that much easier. As to your purpose here..." she paused thoughtfully, "I have a feeling that this scenario will play out in such a way that you will be on your way to that as well."

"What 'purpose' are you talking about? Why are you being so cryptic with me, if you want me to do something? It's not like I can run away from you."

She shook her head. "I can't tell you yet. But you will find out soon enough. First though, you need to speak the local language. I have waited long enough for that."

With that, she grabbed a hold of Aaron's tongue, and pinched it hard. When she let go, she began speaking to him in the faerie tongue, and to his surprise, he immediately understood her and could answer her.

"I still don't know what I'm supposed to do."

"Don't worry about that—I will guide you on that part. In the meantime, rest up, you are going to have a rather exciting life in a short time." With that, the Morrigan stood up to leave, but Aaron stopped her.

"Wait," he said. "Who is this girl? Can you point her out to me?"

The Morrigan motioned for him to come with her. They went to a balcony that looked over the town, and stood near a tree so they would not be easily seen. Peering down through the branches, the Morrigan saw Allette walking with a basket on her shoulder, and pointed her out to Aaron. She stopped and put it down nearby, and was sorting through something in it. She happened to look up at the castle; she did not see Aaron or the Morrigan, but Aaron got a good look at her.

The girl was willowy with long arms and legs, and a gracefully long torso, even though he didn't think she was that tall—not as tall as he, certainly. None of the fairies were tall; Aaron towered over them. It was the elvish race that seemed the tallest, and Allette seemed like one of them, although she had some exotic human characteristics as well. Her long dark hair hung down her back, and he could see the glint of green in her dark, almond-shaped eyes. He thought she looked a bit troubled as she looked up; she had the pensive look of someone who had a lot on her mind. She finished her task, and stood up and walked towards the little houses in town, disappearing into the crowds.

The Morrigan looked at Aaron inquisitively. His brow was furrowed, but he looked thoughtful rather than upset. They walked back inside, and the Morrigan closed the balcony windows behind her. As they made their way back to Aaron's room, she said, "Well? What do you think of the young lady?"

Still looking pensive, Aaron responded without looking at her. "She's lovely..." he said. "But she looks so fragile. If what you're saying is true about this whole thing, I'm worried about what her family is going to think, and how they might respond."

The Morrigan was surprised that Aaron took to the idea so quickly. "Yes, they might not be happy if she tells them. But I get the sense she hasn't told anyone. She will be pressured to do so. And because she has not spoken to you and does not know your response, the girl will be very stressed, I daresay."

Aaron's frown deepened. Reading his thoughts, the Morrigan said, "I'm sure you want to speak to her, but it's better if you don't—she might be accused of impropriety, and that could make things worse. If she seems over the edge with fear I will send Steve to speak to her. In the meantime, I'd stay here—there are only a few more days. Things might be found out if you go to the grove, and this needs to be a secret."

As they entered Aaron's room, the Morrigan turned to him, her face serious. "There is one more thing I haven't told you. I told you about the Unseelie part of the island. One of the higher class beings there is a dark elf, Duncluan. He is vicious and nasty, and feared by most of the townsfolk. He has his eye on Allette, and I know he intends to make a high bid for her. The family will do anything to prevent him from taking her—they do not want him to get their daughter, no matter how much gold he has. But if he is the highest bidder, there is nothing they can do. You can outbid him easily with your wealth, but he will not leave without trouble, you can be sure. Allette has other men from the village interested in her, she will likely get lots of bids, but they would not challenge you."

"If all of my money is back in England," said Aaron, "how can I bid on her at all?"

"When all is done and ready, we will go back together and get your money and earthly affairs sorted out. But not until something else happens first. I will be there to tell you what to bid, which will be a mere pittance of your wealth, and to guarantee that the dowry will be received."

Aaron went back to his room feeling very troubled, and did not sleep well. This was all leading somewhere, and he was sure there was going to be a crisis before it was all over. Exactly what it was he didn't know, it just hung over him like a threatening storm. He did not like the fact that he wasn't in control of the situation. But there was nothing he could do.

As for Allette, her panic increased when Aaron failed to show up in her grove the next day. Was he going to reject her? Did Macha stop him from coming? Was she angry? She had no idea what was going on, and she was afraid.

Allette lay in her room that night, her face tear-stained, as it had been for the last several days. Aaron had not returned to the grove since she gave him her trinket. The Morrigan had said nothing to her, so she didn't know if she was displeased or not—surely if she'd done something terribly wrong, she would have been punished. But she was punished enough already by her own family. They saw that she had finally given the trinket away, but no one could tell who she'd given it to, as Aaron did not yet enter the faerie village. She was afraid to tell them her choice, because she would have been accused of indiscretion and of violating a taboo. But not telling got her several beatings and no food for several days. The situation had become a scandal in the village almost overnight.

The next day was her "day," and she was sick almost to the point of vomiting. She had no idea if Aaron would show up, or what would happen if he did. She did not have much hope that he would. An even bigger concern was that she would be married off to Duncluan on the Unseelie part of the island, regardless of who wore her trinket. That just wasn't acceptable; she would prefer to die than to meet that fate.

Unable to sleep, she sat up and looked out the window. The peaceful village she loved now looked menacing. She looked out to the forest beyond the village, where a full moon shone on a meadow just to the right of the forest entrance. It was a moon garden, full of flowers and other shrubs that were

dedicated to the moon and the underworld goddesses–
gardenias, lilies, poppies, and deadly nightshade.

Nightshade. Allette suddenly had an inspiration. If she
could manage to sneak out and gather some of the nightshade,
it probably wouldn't take long for her to make it into a potion
that could be drank. She knew that there were some small
bottles outside her house, in the back. But it would have to be a
small bottle, and a small amount. She wanted to carry it with her
tomorrow, and it couldn't be detected or there would be even
more trouble.

She winced with pain as she got up, but now she had
new strength and determination. She did not want to die; she
had her whole long life ahead of her. But the odds of things
going well for her tomorrow were not good, and she felt it was
the only other real choice that she had. She would go, and see
how things went. If things went as expected, she would drink the
poison, and let it take her. She still had a shred of hope in the
fact that she had not been upbraided by the Morrigan for her
choice. Maybe things would work out. But she did not want to be
trapped in a bad marriage, or be disgraced because her chosen
one rejected her.

Everyone else in the household was asleep, so Allette
slipped out quietly through the back window. She found a small
bottle that was suitable, and quietly stole away to the meadow,
staying in the shadows and avoiding any remaining light in the
town. The meadow was not far from her house, so it took very
little time for her get the parts of the plant that she needed. She
looked around nervously; was there anyone around? Was she
being watched at all?

Suddenly she felt someone touch her shoulder. She had to stifle a scream, and she turned around quickly, her heart pounding. She was looking at Steve Abbott.

"Hush!" said Steve. "I know what you are doing—and I'm telling you not to do it. I know you're frightened, and you've been through a lot already, and I don't blame you for wanting another way out. But I will tell you—the Morrigan is very pleased with your choice, and you will get the outcome you want. Go home and try not to worry."

With that he looked around, and carefully guided her back to her house, so that she would remain unseen. With a lighter heart, Allette found her way back into the room. Steve was the closest official to the Morrigan, or at least one of the closest, and he had a reputation for honesty—she didn't know anyone who didn't like him. She knew he would not lie to her; she just hoped that nothing else happened to interfere with that outcome.

34

Mila's Vision

The next morning came, and Allette's mother and sisters came to bathe and dress her for the auction day. Everyone was grimly silent and tense. Allette did not resist efforts to get her ready, but she never looked any of them in the face. She was still very nervous, but she clung to Steve Abbott's words like a rock in a hurricane. It was all she had to give her any hope. At her father's sharp call, she immediately went to the town square where the bidding was to take place.

She rose to the platform with her family, and took a seat on a bench placed there for that purpose. She glanced out at the sea of faces looking at her. Aaron was not among them. A sort of calm came over her, as if she was entering an altered state of consciousness. She had let go of her control of the outcome, and silently prayed to the Morrigan. She tuned out the gossipy and insulting comments of some of the women.

Her father was to start the bidding, but first he looked at her. "Where is your chosen? They should be the one to start the bidding."

Allette did not know what to say. "I expect that he is late. Go ahead and start, and see what comes of it."

Her father was not happy with this response, especially as he could see that Duncluan was in the audience, and prepared to make a bid. So, he allowed the bidding to start. As expected, the numbers went up, and towards the end, Duncluan made the highest bid.

Her father was now feverishly anxious. "Allette, where is your chosen one? They have to make a bid."

At that moment, the voice of the Morrigan was heard in the crowd. "He is here."

Allette's head shot up, her eyes wide. Everyone there turned around and gasped. It was the mortal man who had come to the island. He looked tall and imposing, and they were almost a little afraid of him. The Morrigan stood with him, looking rather pleased.

Her father looked at her alarmed. "How did he come to have your trinket? He was taboo!"

The Morrigan stepped forward before Allette could answer. "Don't pick on her; she has committed no indiscretion. She never spoke to him; she found him asleep in her grove, which is on the far side of the island, away from the town. Seeing him there when she was praying to the love goddess, she naturally assumed he was a gift. That is right, isn't it, Allette?"

Allette could barely speak, but she nodded vigorously. The Morrigan continued: "She put her trinket around his neck while he slept. He had no idea what it was, or where it came from; he had never even seen Allette until I pointed her out to him. And I kept him from returning to the grove after that, so that there would be no accusations of indiscretion."

There was a murmur among the townspeople. Duncluan glared at Aaron hatefully, and spoke up. "Enough of this! Let him make his bid, and make this final." It was clear that the dark elf expected to be the winner.

Aaron looked over at him and glared. He already hated him on sight. The Morrigan had told him how much to bid: ten thousand gold pieces. Again, everyone gasped—that was more than ten times what Duncluan offered.

Allette's father was stunned. "He has that much wealth?"

The Morrigan replied, "That is only a fraction of his earthly wealth—a small fraction. He will have to leave some of that behind for those he has left behind in the human world. But you have my absolute guarantee that he has the money, and that you will get that amount."

Allette's father now began to feel some guilt about beating his daughter. And the dowry amount—he was terribly pleased about the amount, and clearly from Duncluan's reaction, he could not beat that bid. However, for formal purposes, he asked if anyone could challenge that bid. There was silence. Aaron was then declared the winner, and Allette's eyes lit up and she broke out in a smile. She wanted to weep with relief.

Duncluan, however, was not going down without a fight. "I intend to be the winner," he hissed, and he moved forward to grab Allette from her bench. Aaron, who did not need an excuse to go after the dark elf, moved forward and grabbed him forcefully, pulling him away from her. The Morrigan stood back and just watched, holding up her hand to keep the nearby Dagdachoris members back. A fight broke out between the two of them. Aaron was taller and stronger, but Duncluan was smaller and moved like a snake. He was also armed, which Aaron was not, but this didn't deter Aaron at all. He knocked Duncluan to the ground with intense force, and put his hand around his throat in a lock, choking the life out of him. There was a bit of wrestling, and Duncluan almost got to his weapon, but Aaron knocked it out of his hand. In the end, Aaron killed him with his bare hands.

When it was over, Aaron stood up, and dusted himself off. The townsfolk were silent and aghast. The Morrigan turned to the retiring captain of the Dagdachoris and smiled. "Well?" she said. "What do you think?"

He himself looked astonished, and he gave the Morrigan a single nod of approval. With that, she stepped forward, beaming.

"Now, Aaron, I can tell you why you were brought here, and everyone else might as well know. Olaf has been the captain of the Dagdachoris for many years, but he is well beyond retirement. I have needed a human warrior to fill that position. You, in spite of your pleas otherwise, are the person I need. I needed to prove it to you, and to the Dagdachoris, and that could only be done by testing you. The dark elf you have just killed has been a difficult menace to this side of the island, and no one has been able to kill him. You did it without any weapons. So, I declare that you are fit to take over as captain of the Dagdachoris. And you will marry Allette as soon as that initiation is complete."

There was a rousing cheer in the crowd, and Aaron did not see anyone who looked ill-disposed towards him. The whole thing happened so fast, and was quite overwhelming. Even more astonishing, he found that he had no remorse in killing the dark elf, nor was he concerned about the fate the Morrigan had in store for him. For once he felt like he was on the right track.

He did, however, have one more concern. He whispered to the Morrigan—"Well, what do I do now? What is the proper protocol? Can I speak to her? Touch her at all?"

The Morrigan laughed. "Come—you will come up and take her hand. There will be a celebration afterward, and you can speak with her then." So, Aaron stood on the platform, and the faerie folk marveled at his chiseled features, and his powerful physique. Allette looked so small and delicate next to him. But she took his hands, and was overjoyed when he smiled back at her. The women of the town were still stunned by this beautiful man, and many were not just a little jealous that Allette had made this choice. Yesterday they were ready to mock her for being rejected by her choice person, but now they were put to silence by how unbelievably clever she had been. And the Morrigan said there was no indiscretion, so that laid those rumours to rest.

Aaron met Allette's parents, who were extremely deferential to him. Her father could not believe his luck, as ten thousand gold pieces would make him a wealthy man for eons. And for her to marry the captain of the Dagdachoris—well, his family was already of a high class, but this just made them more prestigious.

Aaron had some time alone to talk to Allette as the celebration was being prepared. She blushed as she looked at him, and felt very shy. He asked her many questions about herself, and about the whole marriage process. She explained the tradition to him. "What do humans do when they get married?" she asked.

"Well, we choose to marry or not marry. I suppose there are some cultures that arrange marriages still, but that's hardly

203

the norm. Even the ones who do make arrangements usually allow the two people to decide if they like each other before accepting. But in most of the world, men and women can choose to be married or not."

"Really? That sounds wonderful. We don't have much choice here. I am so glad that you came along, and that you've agreed to marry me. I had just about lost hope."

"Considering that Duncluan was likely to be the winner if I hadn't come…"

Allette shuddered. "Please don't speak of him. I am very glad you got rid of him. Everyone is; you just have no idea. I am certain he wanted to overthrow the Morrigan, along with a few of his kind, but no one else wants it."

"But what if I wasn't there, and he had won? What would you do?"

"Oh. I would have poisoned myself. In fact, I intended to get some poison just in case. But I was stopped."

Aaron scowled. "What do you mean?"

So, Allette explained her midnight sojourn, avoiding the story of her beating beforehand. Now Aaron looked angry. "I'm very glad that Steve was there to stop you," he said. "But I don't like the idea that you felt that was your only other choice."

Allette became momentarily alarmed. "Oh, I've upset you, haven't I?"

"I'm not upset with you; I'm upset that you've been put through this idiotic system to begin with." There was a bitterness in his voice. But seeing that she was a bit intimidated, he put his arms around her and kissed her forehead. "Don't worry yourself, I'm not going to start a revolution. I just don't want anything to happen to you." Allette immediately brightened up again, warming under his touch. But she then ventured to ask: "Are you married in the human world?"

Aaron now thought about Deborah, who had been miles from his thoughts. "No," he said. "I was married before–twice– but both ended in...." he did not have a word for "divorce."

Allette looked puzzled. "Ended in what?"

"Hm, you don't have a word for it. It's when the couple decides to get un-married, if that makes sense."

Now she looked surprised. "How does one do that?"

"It's a legal arrangement."

"But what about dowries?"

"There are none."

"None??"

"No–again, that's a practice in certain cultures, but they're not mainstream at all. People tend to marry for love, though if you have a lot of money, you may have a legal agreement in advance in case the marriage does end."

This was an incredible idea to Allette. "Well–this must all be strange to you, then!"

Aaron laughed for the first time. "Yes, my dear. It is very strange."

Allette had pushed up her sleeves with the increasing heat of the day, and for the first time Aaron noticed red marks on her skin.

"What are those?" he asked.

She hung her head. "Those are from a beating. Well, more than one."

His eyes darkened. "Who beat you?"

"My father and my uncles."

"Why?"

"Because I would not tell them that I gave my trinket to you. You see, we were told that talking to you or otherwise dealing with you was taboo, until the Morrigan said otherwise. I didn't dare tell them, or I would have been killed for violating a taboo. I had no intention of violating it—and really, I didn't, as we didn't really interact or speak. But I would not have been believed. So, it was better to take the beating for disobedience than to tell the truth."

Allette could see that Aaron was angry again. "I'm sorry—I think I've upset you again."

"My dear, don't apologise! I'm just—utterly amazed at how a man could beat his own child. I find it disgusting."

"Oh, it's very common."

Aaron grunted.

"That is why I didn't really want a faerie husband from any race—they always beat their wives. I didn't want that—I would have been happy being a priestess in the De Daanan court. But most fathers don't allow that—they want their gold."

Aaron gave a deep sigh. He was angry, but he was going to have to swallow it for now. "Well, I'll tell you one thing—no one had better dare to lay a hand on you from now on, because they will have to deal with me, and it won't be pleasant."

Allette was deeply touched by this. She thought he was beautiful and strong, but now she also found he was kind and respectful. She would have hardly guessed how much trouble he had with relationships in the human world.

It was a very strange gathering, and it reminded Aaron of things conjectured about Neolithic culture. Olaf, the captain that Aaron was to replace, spoke to him for a long time during the celebration, asking about things in the human world. They recently had a rare Fomorian/human hybrid called Judas come to provide some leadership to the Fomorian forces, though these were much more disorganized than the Dagdachoris. Olaf told him that Tir na nOg closed its doors to humans sometime in what Aaron reckoned was the 400s A.D., with the coming of Christianity in the part of Europe where they lived—about the time that Steve's ancestor committed treason, laying a curse on his family. They still had some contact after that, but humans and faeries really did not live side by side—they were considered the devils of the new religion, and retreated in the face of this change in consciousness. Many faeries were not willing to leave the old world entirely, and indeed many still inhabited glades and woodlands—they kept in regular contact with Tir na nOg, but they were virtually invisible to humans. He had not heard good reports from them about the current human civilisation, and

Aaron could only confirm those reports with his description of how things were.

After the festivities, Aaron and Olaf returned to the Morrigan's castle to talk some more, and then he was made ready for his initiation, which would take three full days.

35

Mila's Vision

Dagdachoris initiations were very much secret, so Allette had no idea what her husband-to-be went through in his three-day ordeal, and she knew he would not speak of it. At the end, however, he was officially made Captain by the Morrigan. He looked quite different from the way he did when he arrived—he now dressed the way the others did, in sheepskin and leather. His arms were tattooed with the symbol of the Dagdachoris, the one that had plagued him in Layla's drawing of earlier years. He was younger now, with the blonde hair of his youth, and it was cut in the same style of the rest of the Dagda—his hair was growing fairly long, but the side was cut, and three braids were made on the side. He was given the Captain's ring, and he had an array of weapons—a broadsword, an axe, a mace, and a bow and arrow, as well as a shorter hunting knife. He looked extremely impressive at the ceremony; no one had any question that he would be a formidable leader for the Dagda.

For once in his life, Aaron got on well with everyone around him, which probably surprised no one more than himself. He had fought against Layla's assessment of him as a warrior, but she could see him as he was not able to see himself. Life was so much different on the island, and so much simpler; he now dreaded the thought of going back to the human world.

But go back for a short time he must, and after his wedding to Allette, he set off with Layla just days after his marriage, to finalise his affairs, and secure the dowry that was to be paid to her father. They passed through the aether, and back to the Scottish shore where he had originally been brought across. Aaron wore the same clothes that he had when he left, but he still had the distinctive tattoos and hairstyle, though his hair looked a bit whiter when he re-entered the human realm. Indeed, everything seemed quite thick to him; the English air was polluted and dense. He felt like he was walking around with leaden weights on his legs; it was awful.

His return caused a sensation. He and Layla were careful not to associate with each other, to avoid arousing suspicion. The first thing he did was access his bank accounts, and purchased the requisite amount of gold coinage; he doubled it so that he would have money for his life with Allette. This did not amount to much of his fortune, and he ended up giving the rest of it away to the children he'd had in his first marriage. He arranged for royalty payments on his songs to be given to family.

His lawyer was in disbelief. "Aaron, what has happened to you? What are you doing?"

Aaron was now very soft-spoken, and English was not his first language anymore, so he had to remember to speak it. "I've made a new life elsewhere. I have no need of any of this anymore. I'm taking what I need, and will live simply."

"Aaron, this is so unlike you—it makes me wonder, if you'll pardon me saying so, if you're of sound mind? Or perhaps that you're being impulsive?"

Aaron's face was serious, though he managed to crack a smile. "Mike, I'm more sane than I've been in my entire life." The calm look in Aaron's eyes unnerved him a bit. "Well, very well—if that's what you want to do."

"It is. And the sooner it happens, the better. I need to get back home."

Everyone who saw him was shocked; what happened to him? Did he join some weird cult? He was so different—and yet it was so obviously him—no one knew what to make of it.

Deborah, of course, was the most alarmed by the change in Aaron. He felt obliged to visit her and to say goodbye. When he told her this, she flew into a despairing rage.

"Aaron, what the hell is wrong with you? What has happened? You've lost your mind!"

Aaron just closed his eyes and shook his head. He knew that Deborah would not understand, and he anticipated an unpleasant break-up. "I haven't lost my mind at all. I've found my life, and now that I have, I can do nothing but that. And that means I'm leaving here for good."

"Well, wherever you move shouldn't be an issue."

"Oh yes—yes, it is. It's not a place where anyone can follow me. Not too many people, anyway."

Deborah was staring at his hair, and then at the tattoos. The tattoos looked familiar. Where had she seen them before?

As Aaron turned to leave, she suddenly remembered where she had seen them—they were on the drawing that Layla Black had given him. He only spoke of it once, but it had been clear that it plagued him throughout his life. "Aaron!" she called out sharply.

He turned and looked at her.

"Those—things on your arms—they're like that drawing..."

Aaron put his hand up. "Say no more about them."

"Does Layla Black have anything to do with this?"

"No," said Aaron. "Nothing at all. Good-bye, and best of luck to you."

Aaron's financial transactions elicited a lot of suspicion, and as he expected, he was getting phone calls from government agencies after buying his gold. Steve met him in secret, and loaded the gold into his car. He drove him back to Scotland and to the place where they would meet the ferry. They successfully reached the boarding place, and he got him back on board and back to the island without incident.

Upon his return, Aaron was greeted by four priestesses who helped him bring his gold back to the Keep. He brought the requisite ten thousand gold pieces to Allette's father, with the suggestion that he take some of it and lock up the rest of it in the Keep, where he would have full access to it—he should not risk having it stolen by leaving it around the house. Aaron was aware that there was nothing like a banking system among the faerie lot, and that they also didn't tend to have this much gold. Allette's father thought this was a wise idea, and followed through accordingly. All that remained was for Aaron to store his own gold, and to return to Allette. She greeted him joyfully, and announced that she was already with child. Aaron kissed her, and held her tight to him. It was as if life had started over for him, and now he had a chance to be happy, instead of the miserable wretch he had been in the human world. He now could no longer imagine what happiness that world could hold for anyone. But he was also realistic enough to know that his life here was going to have its challenges. The Morrigan expected a war, and when that occurred, he had to be the one to lead the charge.

***

Steve Abbott's Diary

Summer was almost over, and my wife would be home again soon. I spent my last weekend before heading home with Malcolm and Layla. The air was already starting to turn cooler; England did not get particularly hot during the summer, but you could tell that the sun was on the decline, and it was inching its way into autumn.

We were all silent for some time; I wondered what the future was going to hold. I had no idea what I was going to tell my wife about this summer, and my intuition told me that our marriage was probably not going to last much longer. True to Layla's word, my sister was pregnant again, but I rarely heard from my family. While there were no actual arguments, it seemed pretty clear that they were done with me after I left the funeral. I had mixed feelings about this; I was sad to be losing my family, and also a bit angry. I'd gone through a lot to remove the curse, and they had no gratitude whatsoever. Maybe one day we would speak again, and things would get better. But it didn't seem likely in the near future.

At the same time, I felt very calm about everything. Everything was as it was supposed to be, and loss is as much a part of life as its gifts. In a way, with my new role, it was better not to be burdened by past entanglements. I was sure my career would continue as it had, but now I had new responsibilities. I was Layla's Arch-Priest, but my job was to help her in this world.

And that ended up being my remaining question to Layla: what lay ahead?

Layla was lounging out on long chair on the patio. She sat up when I asked my question, putting her legs over the side, her face serious.

"I—we—have accomplished a lot this summer. I feel good about that. But I don't feel good about what's coming. It may take a few years."

"You said there would be a war. But Duncluan is dead..."

"Yes, that has been solved in this timeline, and will be solved differently in another, as I told you. He's not the particular problem. For one, he does have other dark elves who will want revenge, and who will likely still try to interfere with my goals. The other problem is humanity itself."

"Hasn't humanity always been a problem?"

"Yes, but it's going to get out of hand. They're driving themselves to extinction through greed, and the idea that they somehow dominate everything, that they are the gods over nature, and that nature is to be used and then discarded. Things are moving decidedly out of balance, and it's creating...well, things that have never been before."

"Such as?"

"Well, for one—those creatures that I saw the day I encountered Judas, the half-Fomorian."

"I seem to remember something about that..."

"I don't," Malcolm put in. He was now leaning forward; he'd been listening to the conversation thus far, and was still trying to absorb it.

"Judas and I fought that night, but not with each other— with these things that seem to be proliferating in dark places: underground tunnels, sewers, and even caves. They are tall, white, with spindly limbs and horrible faces. They only live to devour."

"Where do they come from?"

"Good question. They seem to arise out of human consciousness."

"How is that possible?"

"Consciousness is more than just your thoughts, you know. Human consciousness is limited on the surface, but does go deep—the brain filters out most of what goes on behind the scenes. You know this, Steve, because I showed it to you."

"Yes, you certainly did."

"In any case, thoughts are things, and can create things. And the things they are creating are going to destroy them. Now, I might not care if it had no affect on the Otherworld, but unfortunately it does; we're all tangled in a web together, this world, the Otherworld, and all the copies thereof in various universes. What I predict is that at the breaking point, at least two of these universes will collide, the timelines will meet. That is both good and bad."

"What's good about it?"

215

"I will be able to combine with other versions of myself, and that will give me a lot more power to deal with the threat. But the collision of timelines is permanent; two universes will fuse together. And I'm not sure how that's going to affect the earth. I *think* the result will be better. But we just have to see."

PART II: INWARD SPIRAL

1

Chris Wood's Reflections

Full-time faculty positions are harder to come by these days, even in the sciences. We'd done quite well at getting funding for ourselves, and found that we needed someone else to help with research. As expected, we received a massive number of applications; trying to weed through them all took far more effort than I wanted, and I'm not the most patient person. We did things in stages, first weeding out those who clearly didn't have the credentials, then weeding out those who were inexperienced.

When we got to the last batch of applications, one really stood out: Layla Black. She'd graduated from Oxford, only slightly unusual for the Physics field, as there seemed to be a lot more Cambridge graduates. She'd worked on various projects around the world, and wrote quite a few impressive papers. But what really got me was her reference list. She listed Mark Gordon as a reference. This was absolutely unheard of, as I know the man does not give references. I was ready to toss her application as fraudulent on that basis, but I decided to call him just to see if it was legitimate.

To my utter surprise, it was totally legitimate.

"Listen to me, Chris," said Mark. "If you don't hire that girl you are insane. I was on her thesis committee, and her understanding of Physics and Maths is genius-level. You know that I don't recommend students as a rule, but she is nothing like any student I've ever had. I'm already furious at Oxford, as we could have hired her back, but the salary they offered her was a pittance. She was absolutely right to reject it; it was insulting. Not only should you hire her, you should give her whatever pay she wants. If anyone is going to be able to solve the puzzles of quantum mechanics, it's her—I'd swear she's solved it already, she's just trying to prove it. You will not regret it, you will be paid back, I guarantee it."

I hung up the phone in amazement, and I wasn't just a little intimidated, truth be told. Did I really want to hire someone who I knew was going to outshine me in my own field? But this wasn't about me, I chided myself. This is about the university, about the field, about making advances, having our name out there, getting funding...

I called her up and asked her to come in for an interview. She showed up exactly on time, and dressed in the rather stiff manner I've come to expect from her. But I was not prepared for how young she looked—could she really be that experienced? She would have been thirty years old, but she looked like she was half that. Still, I resolved to stop making judgments that were not based on facts; I was a scientist, after all. I wanted to hear what she had to say in the interviews, and I wanted to test her a little bit.

Her temperament was very even; she did not seem nervous, but she was also not particularly extroverted. She was very—well—English in her presentation. I don't know why I was surprised.

Then I gave her a math problem to solve—I'd already written out the steps, and deliberately put in an error. She looked at it for all of five seconds, picked out my error, and to my embarrassment, picked out two others. But she was able to calculate the result in her head, and this was not a simple equation. I checked her work on my calculator; she was correct. It didn't take long for the committee to decide to hire her, and we were all unanimous in our thinking about her. She was clearly brilliant and not just a little intimidating as a result. But there was nothing arrogant or bombastic in her personality; she was straightforward and about the facts. And isn't that what we were looking for?

I had to admit, I was looking at her for other things too, and probably every man at the table thought the same way. I reflected on the irony of this later; people always stereotype women as focusing on foolish or superficial things. But this certainly wasn't the case here, and we wondered what she would be like as a colleague. Certainly she seemed like someone willing to work hard and to accept the academic grind.

The salary she asked for, as Mark implied, was quite high. Fortunately our Chairperson felt the same way Mark did, and gave her what she asked. And—as Mark also said—she proved that she would pay us back over and over again.

2

Mila's Vision

It was a crisp October evening, and the days were getting shorter. Layla had a studio flat just outside the center of Manchester. It was cheaper to rent outside the city, and she didn't need a lot of space. She hardly owned anything.

Everything in her flat suggested "one": the twin bed, the small bureau, the noticeable lack of crockery and cutlery in the kitchen. There were not many furnishings; she was always nomadic, moving from job to job until now. Even the kitchen table only had one chair. She had never needed any more than that in her adult life—or her adolescent life, for that matter. This wasn't always the case, and she didn't care to be reminded.

She put away the few groceries she had picked up on the way home, and sat down to continue working on her project throughout the night. She worked until 5:00 in the morning; she always knew the time, even without looking at the clock. Rising from her desk, she saved her work and closed her laptop. She took a five-minute shower, chose her "Tuesday" outfit for work, and quickly brushed her long hair. Some women spent an eternity on their personal toilet, but Layla did not need to; she had never worn makeup in her life, and smelled like roses regardless of the state of her. After putting on her stockings and shoes, she carefully made the bed, and went to the kitchen to put on the teakettle and make a piece of toast. Everything was timed, and she knew she would be out of the flat by 5:36 AM, before the morning traffic, pulling into the university parking garage at 5:55, and at her desk by 6:00. Her daily routine kept her in check, and did not allow her to think about the loud echo of her footsteps on the floor, or the hollow sound of the door as it closed behind her into silence.

3

Laura Wood's Reflections

I liked to bake on Saturday mornings. A variety of muffins, cakes, and scones would appear in our household, which was appreciated by Chris, though he remarked that he'd easily put on a stone if he continued to eat them at the rate I produced them. So, some of these goods went to friends and neighbours. One morning I decided she was going to stop by Layla's flat, and bring her some of the fresh bread I'd just baked.

I didn't tell Chris that I was going to visit her; while Layla had been to our house for dinner a few times, and occasionally met us after work, she seemed to prefer keeping to herself. Chris wrote it off as a personality quirk, but I found myself feeling concerned and a bit motherly toward Layla. It was a bit awkward going to her flat, as she never invited anyone over, but I figured it couldn't hurt. The worst that could happen was that Layla would not be home, or I could just give her the package and leave.

I arrived at the flat, using the address on the Physics Department staff list. I rang the bell, and waited. After a moment I heard footsteps coming toward the door. I heard the deadbolt unlatch from the inside, and the door swung open. Layla looked at me with surprise and curiosity.

"Oh! Hello Laura. My apologies, I hadn't been expecting anyone."

"Oh, no, I apologise—I don't usually just drop in, but I did some baking this morning, and thought I'd bring you some."

"That's very thoughtful," Layla paused. "Um, would you like to come in?"

"Oh, thank you—I won't stay long if you're busy."

We entered the flat, and I got a good look at it for the first time. I was shocked by how small it was, and how little was in it. There were no photos, no paintings, nothing on the walls to brighten the place up or to make it look like home. She did have a chair in what I supposed was the living room area, and a small folding table. The kitchen was the same way, with one chair, and a card table acting as the kitchen table. There was a narrow bed in the corner that didn't even look like a proper bed—there was no boxspring. Layla's laptop sat on the table, and there was a small dresser and a small closet which seemed to contain her clothes and anything else. I couldn't keep from commenting on it.

"Is this everything you own?"

Layla nodded.

"My God, it feels so—transitional. Like you're just staying here temporarily."

Layla shrugged. "No place feels like home, and I don't want to be saddled with a lot of stuff in case I do want to move on."

"Why is that Layla? I won't lie to you, it bothers me that you seem to be so alone all the time."

She did not look me in the eye, and took her time about answering. "I lost my family a long time ago, and a lot happened after that—I just don't trust anyone, and I don't know how to relate to anyone."

"What happened to your family? Did your parents die?"

"No. They're still alive."

"Oh—but—how could that be?"

Layla gave a long sigh. "I can tell you about it if you want. But I usually don't tell anyone."

"Is it a secret?"

"Not necessarily. But I've learned that no one really wants to know. I don't want to tell my story to strangers, and if I'm meeting someone for the first time, the last thing they need is all my baggage dumped on them. It's not anyone else's problem."

"Tell me. I'll go get a bottle of wine if necessary."

Layla went to the kitchen and opened the cabinet. I was stunned to see a cabinet full of wine and scotch. "I've got it covered."

"Do you drink a lot?"

"All the time. Not when I'm at work, though."

"That can't be good for you."

"It doesn't matter. I don't sleep much, but if I want to sleep at all, it's the only way I can get tired enough not to dream."

"Layla, have you ever talked to a therapist?"

"Oh no, absolutely not."

"Why not?"

"Because…" she paused. "There are things I cannot tell a therapist. Things that would not be believed."

"But if you've been victimised…"

"I have. But those are not the things I can't tell."

I was going to ask another question, but then paused. "All right, let me stop asking so many questions. I'll let you talk."

So, Layla pulled up the only other chair in the living room, found two glasses, and poured us some wine. Then she began to tell me her story.

4

Layla's Reflections, as told to Laura Wood

It was a late August afternoon in 1985 when I came into the house from a walk by the river near my house. My father was in the living room, and greeted me enthusiastically. He was giggling, smiling, cracking jokes—after months of being rather distant, it was bizarre to watch. But his face seemed to convey relief. He'd been a bit distant and nervous with me over the last few months, and would not tell me what was wrong. He implied that it wasn't personal, but I noticed that he didn't treat my sister the same way, or anyone else. All he said to me when I confronted him was that he was "working through a problem" and I shouldn't worry. Given his strange attitude over the previous months, I deduced that his relief must somehow be connected to his problem. It was weird, but I didn't care—I was just happy that he was not so distant. Surely this would calm down.

We sat down to dinner. As I ate, I noticed my father watching me intently. I stopped eating and looked at him quizzically. He seemed to become aware of himself, stopped staring, and began asking me about what I did that day, where I went, in a normal conversational tone. After dinner, I settled down next to him in the living room to watch telly, but I started to get very sleepy. I found myself fighting to stay awake.

My father noticed my sleepiness, and suggested that I go to bed. I was apologetic–I really wanted to stay up with him. He laughed. "No apologies necessary my dear–you're exhausted and should get some sleep."

So I made my way upstairs, changed into my pajamas, brushed my teeth, and was asleep within seconds after hitting the pillow.

The following morning, I woke up realising something wasn't right.

My body hurts. My legs. My stomach. My back. I went to the bathroom. A small amount of blood trickled into the toilet. Oh, I thought. Must be my periods. I'd heard something about bleeding, though I hadn't had it before–and didn't usually bleed anyway. But something still isn't right.

I came out of the bathroom to find my father's assistant packing things for me.

"What's going on?"

"Your father is sending you away to school."

"What??? Why???" The pain changed into a icy cold that swept over me. I felt faint.

"I don't know. I've just been told to get your things together."

Straightaway I left the room and looked for my father. When I found him, I was in for a shock. His face and eyes were stone cold.

228

"Get dressed. You're leaving soon."

"Daddy, what is this all about? Why are you doing this?" My breathing was more laboured, and I felt tears stinging my face.

He turned his face away. "Don't ask me. Just do as your told and get out of here."

"But.."

"Now!"

Horrified, I stepped back and retreated to her room. I was sobbing as I got dressed—my arms felt like lead, I felt like I couldn't breathe. *What have I done to make him do this?* My mind worked frantically, but I was too stunned to come up with anything.

He did not even say goodbye to me as I left. Throughout the car ride, I stared out the window. The tears did not stop.

It was like a horrible nightmare. I was now waiting to wake up, but it wasn't happening. *It doesn't make sense, doesn't make sense, doesn't make sense...*

Arriving at the school, I was taken to the headmistress. I looked at the woman, who stared at me with a contemptuous expression on her face. I was still too naïve to recognise the look as one of jealousy.

I was shown to my room, and shown around the school grounds. It was a single room, so at least I didn't have to share with anyone. I was given my schedule of classes, and had to start in a couple of days with the other students, who were also arriving at that time. Other details were worked out between the assistant and the headmistress. The headmistress was very brusque and dismissive, looking to be done with me as soon as possible. The assistant said, "She's rather traumatised right now. I hope it's not a lot of trouble."

"Oh, don't worry. Students always go through this when they're away from home the first time. She'll get over it."

No I won't, I thought.

***

I stared out of the window of the dismal little room. I had been crying since that morning, and somehow could not stop. My stomach felt awful, my head pounded. I forgot about the pains I had that morning.

I was going over the events of the last two days in my mind. What could I have possibly done to cause such a sudden and violent change in my father?
It was like he was possessed by another being. It just wasn't him at all.
This can't be. I just have to give it time.
Things will be better when I go home for Christmas holiday.
He's having some sort of relapse of whatever was wrong. This makes no sense.
Maybe I shouldn't have gone to sleep so early?
Maybe he really wanted me to stay up?

*That makes no sense. Even if he was annoyed at
something, that doesn't warrant sending me away.*
  Maybe I shouldn't have stayed away all those months?
  Maybe he sees me as distant?
  That's silly. Of course I'm not. He wanted me to stay away.
  He didn't ask my sister to stay away.
  This has to be about me.
  It's personal.
  But what did I do?

The loop of thoughts went on, and on...
I finally fell into a fitful sleep.

***

The boarding school was very far away; it was the Cedrig
School in Wales, in the Southwest. It was a co-educational
school, and it was the first time I'd ever attended a school; most
of my education had been at home with tutors. Needless to say I
was still hysterical and very much in despair when I arrived. I was
greeted by the headmistress of the school, and I could tell
instantly that I was disliked. She had no sympathy for me
whatsoever. I was fortunate enough to have a private room,
rather than sharing with other girls, but this wasn't much
consolation. I had no answers, and I just had no idea what was
going on.

Well, I think I spent the rest of the day crying. I unpacked
my things, and just lay in bed, feeling sick. School was not going
to officially start for another week—this was in late August. I felt
like I'd been abandoned, dropped in the middle of nowhere,
with no one to call. And in fact, I was not being dramatic; that
was the case. That first term was absolutely miserable. I did not

fit in at all with the other girls there, and I think I was universally hated and bullied. I'm also pretty sure that the headmistress encouraged the bullying; she very much had something against me, and I had no idea what it was; even as I realise now that she probably was jealous, it was still excessive. I started to feel like I was an awful person. I never thought I was so awful, but now I'd been turned out from my family, and I was hated by my peers and superiors. It's hard not to be affected by that.

I wrote to my father often, but got no replies. When Christmas holiday came, I was anxious to go home—I hated the school, and I hoped that he would be reasonable. Unfortunately, going home was the worst thing I ever could have done.

5

First Term and Christmas 1985

Layla's Reflections as told to Laura Wood

My first term at Cedrig was awful. I was already shaken up at having been sent away with no warning, and for no apparent reason. I normally didn't have any problem socialising, but I was absolutely grief-stricken at this time. You might assume that such schools have a means for coping with student mental health issues, and that there would be at least one person who would reach out and be helpful in such a situation. You would have assumed incorrectly.

The girls had already known each other for years, and when I came into the picture, I was viewed with a kind of disdain and disgust. No one wanted to talk to me or sit by me at all, and if I was in class I heard nothing but whispered abuse from anyone who sat near me. They seemed to take great delight in trying to make my life more miserable.

Administration did not help. The Headmistress, as I have already said, hated me on sight—I felt it—and so she did absolutely nothing to be helpful at all. In fact, I got the sense from looking at the smirk on her face at times that she enjoyed watching the bullying. The girls would generally back off bullying someone if she spoke sharply to them; when they saw they had free rein with me, they took it.

So, this led to my habit of avoiding any common space other than the classroom. I stopped going to dining hall; I never had any appetite, anyway. When classes were done and students were running about with activities—sports and such—I would slip away through a back door and head over to the library. There would be a few students in there, but I always found a study carrel on the top floor, back in the stacks, away from everyone else. Rarely did anyone come over there, and when I could concentrate I would do my schoolwork. But concentration was difficult.

The teachers at the school were the only ones who seemed to have any sympathy, and would be the only ones to check the behaviour of other students in the class. I do know that on more than one occasion, different teachers had gone to the Headmistress with concerns about me—they were astute enough to realise that I wasn't eating, and was being neglected in general, and was depressed. But nothing ever came of it; in fact, in one case, the science teacher got into a huge row with her over it, and nearly lost his job. He was involved with the Board of Directors for the school, so that didn't happen. But pretty much every other teacher after that backed off; they were afraid of the consequences of speaking up.

My only communications with the Headmistress were negative ones. My father paid my tuition, but did not provide me with any money for essentials; thus, I didn't have basic things that I needed, and I always got yelled at for not making my father get them. But I could not talk to my father; when I tried to call, he'd hang up as soon as he realised it was me. The Headmistress did not believe me when I told her this, so I ended up losing both ways. I get the impression that she did have a conversation with my father that did not go very well; she would have liked to have had me expelled, even though I didn't really do anything, but he must have paid her off to leave him alone. In any case, none of that money ever reached me.

In that first term I was optimistic that I might be able to talk to my father when I went home for the Christmas break. I was relieved to be getting away, to hopefully get home and have a decent meal, and to at least see other members of my family who would be less hostile, and perhaps sympathetic enough to help me.

Once again, I was wrong. I knew and saw a lot of things, but now I was beginning to doubt myself. I seemed to get a lot of things wrong.

My father's chauffeur did come and pick me up, and I was brought back to the house. I had no gifts for anyone, because I'd had no money to buy anything, nor did I have any way of making anything for anyone. I was initially happy to see my house again, until I walked in the door.

When I entered the house, I greeted my sister, who gave me a tight smile, and put her head down. Everyone else in the room beat a retreat when I came in. I went to go look for my father, but he literally walked past me, looking very angry, like I wasn't even there. I could feel my heart sinking into my stomach. I slowly made my way to my bedroom, which was full of dust and clearly hadn't been touched since I left. I sat down on the bed, not knowing what to do. Why was everyone so angry with me?

When I came down later for supper, I found that a separate tray was left for me in the parlour; I was not wanted at the table. After being so hungry for so long, I found that I could barely eat. There was a Christmas tree up in the parlour, with gifts under it. I stared at them absently while dinner was going on, and found myself reading the tags. My name was not on a single one of them.

I finally pushed the tray away and went back upstairs. There was talking and some laughing downstairs, the general tones of celebration. I went out into the hallway to listen; they were carrying on like nothing was wrong, and like I wasn't there. The whole thing made no sense, and was terribly cruel.

On my way back to my room I saw my sister leaving her room. She looked up at me wide-eyed, and whispered, "What did you do? Daddy is so angry—he's threatened to throw out anyone who speaks to you."

I stared at her in disbelief. "I've done nothing. I have no idea what's going on."

Suddenly I heard my father call for my sister, and she hastily moved on, clearly afraid she would be in trouble. That was the only hint I got about the atmosphere that greeted me when I got home.

Christmas Eve and Christmas Day were one hundred times worse. I knew that there was nothing for me, and I was not wanted for any festivities. I did not come down for any meals. My father's assistant knocked on my door, and asked if I was going to eat anything—he could bring it up. I told him no. My stomach was just a burning pit of acid at this point. Relatives came over, and if I peeked around a corner at all, I got the same reception from them that I had from my sister when I came home. My father saw me and gave me an evil look. He did not say anything, but it was clear he wanted me to go away.

At this point I was beyond sad, and was feeling angry. If I had done something wrong, I had a right to know. However, I just stood there and gave him an even more evil look in return, for about ten minutes. Then I returned to my bedroom.

In the ensuing days before I had to return to the boarding school, I felt a shift in myself. All of the sadness, the guilt (for what?) began to be replaced by an icy cold in my soul. It was like watching fruit turn rotten before your eyes after a killing frost.

Everything shut off at that point. Everything was now a means to an end. I thought about my options; I could run away, but where would I go? I was thirteen-years-old, and not finished with schooling, it wasn't as though I could get a job and a flat somewhere. I had to finish school. I thought about what I was going to do moving forward. After some reflection, and thinking about the subjects I was studying, I was resolved to go into the sciences—into Physics in particular. I can see things that others can't; yes, I know it seems incredible, but time slips and multi-dimensionality have been part of my normal vision, and math unfolded before me like all languages; they were natural and required little effort on my part. However, trying to unravel and explain certain concepts mathematically and experimentally was something of a challenge, and these challenges served as a distraction for me. I had no friends or family that I could go to, so I was just going to go back to school and bury myself in my work. I had to make First Class grades if I wanted to get into university with the funding level I desired. My father certainly wasn't going to help me. In fact, I felt certain that this was the last time I'd ever be brought back home...

Correction. To my biological father's house.

This realisation sent me on a surreptitious scavenger hunt. I needed to find all my important papers from my father's office, and take them back with me. I heard him go out with my sister one afternoon, and it seemed everyone else had gone out, so I was alone. I wasted no time in going through his files, and finding all of my paperwork—my birth certificate, my medical papers…and then I thought about photos. Certain photos, particularly the ones from my birth. Where would he have these?

I rummaged through some storage closets, trying not to look at our family photos, as I did not want a single shred of emotion to return. I finally found what I was looking for, and smuggled the whole lot back to my room. I had a little time left, and decided to root around for some cash that might be stashed away; if he wouldn't give me spending money, then I'd take it from a place that he wouldn't notice right away. He kept a box of emergency cash in his bedroom; I ran into there and raided it, putting all but a few tens of pounds inside my folders of school work. I grabbed an extra suitcase and packed some more clothes, and looked around to see if there was anything I else I wanted from my room for the last time.

After I was finished, I put my bags near the door, being careful to keep the tote bag with the money under my bed. I looked at my watch; I couldn't remember when they left, but they'd likely be returning soon. I slipped down to the kitchen and got myself something to eat, grabbing some snacks and shoving them into a paper sack to take upstairs. I turned and saw the car pulling into the drive, so I ran back upstairs.

There were only a couple of days left until I had to leave again, and now I was anxious to get away. I spent my time making notes in a notebook I'd brought home—notes about future plans, about what options I wanted to investigate. Focusing on me and where I was going was the only thing that would keep me sane, and hopefully from lapsing into any kind of sentimentality.

When I finally left, I did not let my father's assistant take anything to the car; I did it myself, and would not speak to anyone on the way out. I am sure that my face was a mask of anger, and as I walked out the door, my eye caught a ceramic swan on a side table by the door, something that had been a family heirloom. I picked it up and smashed it on the floor. Then I walked out without looking back.

6

Layla's Reflections as told to Laura Wood

I returned to the school with a new mindset. I no longer cared what anyone had to say about me; I was just there to achieve my goal of getting into university, and making a career for myself. I shut everything else out. I still avoided common areas, but I would sneak around late at night and steal food from the kitchen next to the dining hall. Of course, this limited what I could have, as I couldn't cook in my room, but at least I was getting something. I now had some money, though I knew it wasn't going to last me for very long. In any case, I could solve at least some of my more pressing problems in the short term.

By Spring term it seemed that the girls had gotten bored with me, as they seemed occupied with other frivolities, and I was left alone for the most part. The only time I spoke with classmates was if it was necessary for class, and for me it was all business. I still preferred my routine of slipping away to the library and focusing on my studies for the evening. I didn't have anyone I could call a friend, and I knew I had no support from the higher ups, but now I expected it, and adjusted my own strategies accordingly. If I could keep my feelings out and just maintain this for the next few years…until I could do my A levels and move on…I was going to be fourteen soon, and schooling was really done by the time I was sixteen, then the A levels…

Deep down, there was a little seed of grief in me, of the loss that I never was able to properly process. But there was no time to process it now; it was a matter of survival. If I found myself slipping into thoughts of the past, I immediately went to reading some complicated work of science or philosophy to distract myself from giving in. In retrospect, this was a bit like being in a pressure cooker all the time, but it got me through the days.

Spring term ended, and now I had a new problem; I knew I wasn't going back to Esher. So, where was I going to go? I had no one to call, no friends that I could stay with, and I was definitely not going to let anyone at the school know my situation. I didn't trust anyone there, though the reality was that the staff never paid attention, except for the teachers as I'd mentioned. Someone was supposed to sign me out when I was leaving, but they never checked. I forged my father's assistant's name and walked out the door. I waited on the opposite side of the wall, just to see if anyone would actually come. No one did.

Soon everyone was gone, and I could see them finishing the last of the cleaning, and the staff packing themselves up to go home for the holiday. I did not want them to see me, so I made my way down a back road, toward a more rural part of the town. It was raining on and off—in Wales, it seems the rain never really stops—and I found myself dragging all my personal belongings down this rather challenging road, not having any idea where I would go.

I must have walked a couple of miles before I saw it. It appeared to be a farmhouse, but it was in a rather rickety condition. I walked over to it, leaving my bags outside, and walked around the circumference of the building. I then went inside, and looked around, to see if the place was still in use by someone. I couldn't be totally sure, but there were no animals in there, just some rusted farm equipment and some hay on the floor and in the lofts—none of it was put there recently.

I dragged my suitcases into the barn, and sat for a moment. Should I stay here? I didn't really think anyone was going to come around, but I tended to doubt all my impulses at that time. I sat on the rung of an old battered wooden ladder by the loft, getting my bearings.

All at once, it hit me. I had a surge from deep inside me, like a tsunami of feeling that came up out of nowhere. *Here I am*, I thought. *I no longer have a family, I have no friends.* And at that moment I realised that I was totally unloved—by anyone. People either hated me, or were indifferent—or just fearfully protecting their interests and "not getting involved." If I'd done something horrible, it would have made some sense. But I knew I hadn't.

I'd been pretty Stoic up to this point. But this was really hard to swallow. I found myself weeping, and it seemed like I had an endless supply of tears. I don't even know for how long I cried, but when I finally stopped, I didn't feel any better. I was exhausted and drained. There was nothing else to do but wait there, and see what to do next. I pulled my luggage up to the loft, pulled a blanket and pillow out of my suitcase, and lay down, trying to fall asleep.

I spent the summer sleeping in that loft, and foraging for food, mostly of the plant variety. I was depressed, but I managed to rouse my Stoicism again. No matter how cruel or neglectful the situation was, it wasn't going to change. I'd weighed all other options, and they would just lead to different problems, possibly worse. I reasoned that at least here, there was no one to give me dirty looks, no one to otherwise bother or harass me. No tense confrontations.

When I felt the days getting cooler and shorter, I would make my way into town to get a glimpse of a newspaper with a date on it. I knew what date I was supposed to return to school, and now I had to keep an eye out, so that I returned at the right time, and preferably before the other girls. For a moment I had a thought that chilled me—what if my father had just decided to stop paying my tuition? But I strongly felt that he wouldn't do that—he might only do the bare minimum, but he'd be in real trouble if it was discovered that he'd just abandoned me.

Sure enough, when I did return to school, I was enrolled. No one seemed to notice that I returned in the same clothes I'd left in. I hastened to my room and then to the showers, to clean up before the other girls returned. I had to wash my clothes, but I figured that could wait until the weekend, when most of them weren't around.

Soon enough I had settled back into the same routine as before, and I was adjusting. I grew accustomed to going to the abandoned barn on breaks, and this too became part of my routine. It seemed I was on my way to finishing and finally getting away.

However, as it turned out, things were not that simple.

7

Interview with Steffan Brown

It was an early summer day in 1986 that Joe, Tom, and I got together to talk about Layla.

Okay, that wasn't our only reason for getting together—it was more of a mutual catch-up time, as we'd all been busy. Malcolm had been invited, but was unable to come due to another commitment. However, he said we could stop by his place later that evening, if we wanted.

As we sat catching up on our personal and professional lives, the conversation had steered toward Malcolm.

"What is the matter with him these days? And where is his daughter? You know—the one he always used to go on tour with. Layla," said Tom.

"I asked him about that," Joe replied. "He got really odd about it—almost angry that I asked. He said he'd sent her to boarding school. Wouldn't say another word about her."

"Yeah, I had the same experience!" Tom exclaimed. We've all known her for so long—I always bring his girls a gift for Christmas—he said it was okay to bring one for Anika, but not for Layla. I asked why not, and he just said she wasn't coming home. I then asked if I could have an address to mail something to her, but he flat out refused."

Joe wagged his finger, "Yes—something is really wrong there. They were so close, he couldn't have her out of his sight, now she's at boarding school? And no one is allowed to know exactly where she is? And he's really belligerent about it. Sorry, he's hiding something. I don't know what or why, but it worries me."

What my mates said really echoed how I felt, and it really bothered me. Mal was generally a nice, soft-spoken, easygoing bloke. He got extremely defensive whenever anyone asked about Layla now. That's not something you do if there's nothing going on.

"Do you think he's murdered her?" asked Tom.

"Oh, for fuck's sake! Mal is acting strange, but I can't imagine he'd do that," said Joe.

"I don't know," I cut in. "There's no reason for him to do this, either. Yeah, I can't see Mal killing anyone, but then what the fuck is going on?"

"Has anyone talked to Anika, or anyone else in the family?"

"No, and that's another odd thing. I asked Anika about her sister, and she just said as far as she knew, she was fine. But she looked really upset, and she walked away—I realised later that she was crying."

"You are kidding."

"No I'm not. And unfortunately I didn't get another chance to ask her."

"Well, this is bullshit. Layla is like…well, I guess a niece to us. She's been as much a part of our lives as Mal has, we have a right to know where she is. I'm going to confront Mal about it when we go over there."

Tom and Joe both looked at each other, and at me, and the unspoken question was whether or not this was a good idea. But Tom just said, "I'll be interested to see how he reacts—or if he tells us."

"Listen—if Mal won't tell us, I'm calling the police. I want to see some evidence that she's at school and doing okay. I don't know why she's not coming home, unless something has happened."

There was a general murmur of agreement about this. It had been on all of our minds, but it was just too weird to know how to talk about it. Mal and I had worked together for years, and I realised I was not only risking a friendship, but a professional relationship. I didn't really care at that point.

We dropped by Mal's house around 5:00 that afternoon. He was his usual affable self, so it seemed awkward to bring up the subject. We spent a lot of time talking about other things. But finally, as the day drew on and I knew I would have to leave, I brought it up.

"So, has Layla come home from boarding school? It is summer break by now, I suppose."

His face darkened, and his pleasant mood changed. "No. She's not come home."

"She hasn't? Why not? Is there something wrong?"

He shrugged, but was glaring at me. "I'm sure she's fine."

"Is she staying with a friend?"

"Possibly."

"Possibly? You mean you don't know?"

"I mean I don't want to talk about it."

"Why not?"

"I just don't, that's all." This last bit was delivered with some decided hostility. Tom and Joe looked a bit nervous and awkward, but I wasn't having it.

"You know what, Mal? I think you've done something to that girl."

"I said I DON'T want to talk about it!!" he growled.

I was not giving up. "You're guilty of something. And you'd better say something, or I'm calling the cops. I've had enough of your evasive bullshit on this."

He stared at me open mouthed. "How dare you suggest…"

"Suggest what? That something has happened to her?"

"She's at boarding school!" he snarled. "I already told you that!"

"What school? Where?"

"None of your business!"

I could not believe how he was acting. He was like a man possessed.

I raised my voice. "Everyone here has been as involved with her life as you are. And we have a right to know where she is!"

"No you don't! I'm her father, it's my business, and my business only!"

I slammed my fist on the table and stood up. "Fine. I'm going home and calling the cops."

"You do that, and you'd better not ever speak to me again."

"This is your last chance to prove to me that she's okay. Otherwise, fuck you."

He stood up and stormed into the kitchen. He grabbed an envelope, opened it with shaking hands, and thrust the document into my face. It was obviously a report card—and Layla's name was on it. The grades were unbelievably good—all First Class. I wanted to take it out of his hands and get the name of the school—but he tore it away before I could.

"There" he said angrily. "There's your proof that she's in school and okay. I'm insulted that you would think anything would be going on. And I think it's best that you leave now."

I glared at him. He had indeed showed me proof—sort of—but I still wasn't buying that it was "okay."

"Fine. Thank you. That still doesn't explain why you've done it, or why you're acting like a perfect monster about it."

"I said you can leave now!"

I grabbed my things and walked out the door without another word.

It would be many years before Mal and I would speak again.

8

Layla's Reflections to Laura Wood

One of the required courses for graduation was a course in Ethics. The course had been taught by a local Anglican priest, Father O'Connor. However, when I was due to take the course, there was a new teacher. His name was Father Peter Walsh, but he was just called Father Peter around the school. Students who attend Christian schools have a moniker for clergy like Father Peter—he was a "Father What-a-Waste." With slightly long dark hair and piercing green eyes, the girls just dissolved at the sight of him. Needless to say, it was a rather good year for competitive piety among the girls. In class, they all became rigidly judgmental in their efforts to impress Father Peter with their piety. The school administration, which was largely female, was no better—they spoke of Father Peter as their "resident saint." He was adored universally—well, almost universally.

I despised him on sight. I had a very uneasy vibe about him; he was a bit too egotistical, soaking up all of this attention. When he spoke in our Ethics class, it was like listening to the glib bollocks of a used car salesman. He was a narcissist and hypocrite of the worst kind, and he was making all the girls in class just as bad as himself. He definitely craved drama, and it made my stomach turn.

But there was no way anyone was going to listen to me, or what I knew, so I chose to handle the situation by sitting in the back, doing my work, and minding my own business. I did not want to draw his attention to myself.

As for Father Peter, I could unfortunately read his thoughts. His desire to fuck me was uncomfortably apparent, and he was thoroughly miffed at the fact that I did not kowtow to him the way the other girls did, and that I went out of my way to avoid him. *The one girl I want, and she snubs me,* he thought. *Well, I can do as I please, and I will get my way.* His thoughts worried me, but again, I could not prove what he was thinking. He was a bad actor, but everyone else bought his act; I would be the one perceived as a problem.

I later discovered that Father Peter, through his influence, found his way into the files kept on me in the school. He had casually asked about me during a meeting with the Headmistress, feigning concern for my apparent shyness. The Headmistress, who had no shyness at all, was happy to tell him every detail of my personal problems, at least as far as she knew. Father Peter listened, and said that perhaps he would speak to me, to see if I needed any counseling. The Headmistress was quick to point out that I had very good grades, and to her this was an indication that I had adapted and was just fine. She did not really want Father Peter to pay any attention to me at all, and for probably the only time in my tenure there, she and I were in agreement.

Father Peter then said he would wait to speak to me, and they changed the subject. But he was very shrewd, and knew enough about my problems with my father to put two-and-two together. He knew that getting good grades and getting into university would be more important to me than anything else. And he clearly put some thought into what he would do.

As for me, I was feeling increasingly uneasy. I didn't feel safe at the school anymore; I always felt like someone was watching me, or that something bad was about to happen. The worst part was that I knew I was powerless to do anything about it, for all the powers I had, if I intended to stay on target for my goal.

Then the day finally came.

My Ethics class was finished for the day, and we had turned in an examination. As all of us were gathering our books to leave, Father Peter said casually, "Miss Black, please go into my office. I need to speak to you for a moment."

The girls turned to look at me, glaring with jealousy, giving me the once over. I suddenly felt sick and cold. I looked at the door—should I make a run for it? *No,* I thought. *This is it—I have to face whatever it is he's up to...*

Slowly, I gathered my things, and stepped into Father Peter's office, in a room adjoining their classroom. I sat down in the chair across from his desk. Father Peter spoke to a couple of students, and then began to gather his own papers. Once all the students left, he closed the classroom door. Then he came into his office, and closed the office door.

"Miss Black," he said. "I've been wanting to speak to you."

"Yes?" I said, staring blankly at him.

He paced back and forth in the room behind where I sat. "You are a very lovely girl, Miss Black. Very lovely." He walked over to me, and touched my hair. I instantly recoiled.

"What do you want?" I asked frostily.

He stiffened. "I want to have you, Miss Black. And I intend to have you, just the way I want you. I already know about your situation here in school, and your situation at home. You have no one at home to protect you here, and I have the school Headmistress wrapped around my finger. If you try to complain to the administration, they'll just say you are trying to get attention from the most popular teacher in school. And believe me; you won't be popular if you try to oppose me. Never mind that I can ruin your chances of getting into university."

"Some Ethics teacher you are," I retorted.

"You'd do well to keep your cheeky remarks to yourself" said Father Peter, now annoyed with me, wanting to punish me for spurning him. I did not look at him, and did not respond. This was way too overwhelming.

As Father Peter walked behind me, I felt him pull my hands behind my back, and before I could respond, he had cuffed me. He then tied a scarf over my mouth, and then bound my ankles. He pushed me from the chair onto my knees, drawing me up in front of him, looking down at me with triumph and disdain. "Remember that you are my slave now," he said, "and you will come to me when I tell you to. You'd best be responsive too—being unresponsive will make things worse for you." He unzipped his trousers and pulled out his cock. Pulling the gag from my mouth, he forced me to take his cock and suck on it. I was revolted, but acquiesced. When he finally came, he forced me to swallow it. Withdrawing from me, I coughed, and he pushed the gag back into my mouth. I felt dizzy, like little explosions were going off inside my head. Father Peter grabbed my hair and pulled my head back, forcing me to look at him. He stared at me for a moment.

"I am going to send you away now," he said. "You will not tell anyone what happened here today—no one will believe you if you did, and I will go out of my way to hurt you if you try. You will come to the rectory on Saturday night, at 7:00 sharp. Do you understand?" I could only nod.

He untied me, and pulled me to my feet. I said nothing; I simply picked up my books and moved toward the door. He grabbed me before I turned the handle; "Remember what I said." I just looked at him. He held me tighter. "Don't just look at me—tell me." "Yes I will," I said, my voice a rasp at this point. He relaxed his grip and I fled.

Up until now, I had gone through so many feelings and thoughts. I was devastated by what my father did, mystified, depressed, gloomy, followed by being ultra-rational and non-emotional.

But now I had lost it.

That part of me that I knew my father feared, though he never saw it…it was coming to the surface. I was not going to be held back any longer.

I had to put up with Father Peter for a short time, and he made that day in his office look like nothing. I noticed that he kept a diary of his sadism; I don't think my name was mentioned, but he delighted in all the ways he tried to torture me. However, my body doesn't bend, break, or bleed, and this clearly bewildered and angered him. He just tried to hurt me more, wanting to see the effects of his power on me, to no avail.

Somehow I got through that time, finished my A-levels, and passed my exams with flying colours. I finally held the acceptance letter to Oxford's Physics programme in my hand.

Now I could be done with the Cedrig School, and burn it all down.

And everyone there who contributed to my pain was going to suffer far worse than they made me suffer. Starting with Father Peter.

9

We were in the last two weeks of the term before graduation. I had no interest in graduation; I wanted my papers saying I was done, but I had no interest in the ceremony. Ceremonies were for families and friends, to celebrate a milestone. For me, there was nothing to celebrate, except my freedom, and I would do that elsewhere.

At this time they were still holding classes, though we only had half days at this point, and there was no real work to hand in. I remember that it was about 11:00 in the morning, and I was sitting in one of my last literature classes. The day before I had broken into the rectory, and ransacked Father Peter's closet— I knew he had been stealing money from the church where he also pastored, so no one knew about this box. I had discovered it when he'd forced me to come to the rectory. I stole the box, knowing that it would never be traced, and if he tried to find it or get it back, he'd have to admit he stole it from others. It seemed ridiculous that the only way I could get money for new clothes, train fare, and renting a place before starting school required a theft. But it really didn't matter to me.

On this day, sitting in the classroom, there was a sudden cry as a lightning storm came up suddenly, and we could see that the rectory was on fire. All the students were ushered out of the building, to a designated spot, and counted while the frantic Headmistress called the fire department. By the time they were able to get the blaze under control, most of the rectory had burned. The storm stopped as suddenly as it had picked up; the Headmistress cautiously went to the wreckage where the police and fire companies were gathered. The word "rapist" was seen on the walls, and the police had taken a hold of his red leather diaries, and had already read some of their contents. All all that remained of Father Peter was the charred screaming head, and the contorted skeleton, elevated on spikes.

There was an immediate investigation of the school after this event, and everything was thrown into chaos. It was discovered that the Headmistress had been embezzling from the school funds, and it was rumoured that she had an affair with Father Peter. Graduation was canceled, and all the students were told to pack up and leave as soon as possible. I was already packed up and ready to go; I had purchased some new clothes in the ensuing days, and also pre-purchased my train ticket for that Friday. I no longer had any fucks to give about Cedrig, so I broke into the office and used their office phone during off hours to negotiate a rental in Oxford, found copies of my diploma, and made copies of my transcripts, put on official letterhead. I knew that none of this would survive, so I wanted what was mine. No one suspected I had anything to do with it; the girls were all too upset and fearful to pay attention to anything but their own dramatic sobbing and "trauma" at the loss of this stain on humanity.

Some of them might have had a guess, though, at the end. It was a large group of us leaving at once; pretty much all of them were being picked up by their parents, except for me—I was walking to the train station. As I was leaving, I turned to them, and felt the sky darken behind me. I spoke out loud, very clearly:

"Except for the teachers—every last one of you will be gone within six months."

The girls stared at me, not knowing what to say or think. When lightning crashed behind me, they jumped, and I could see the colour starting to drain from their faces. I smiled for the first time in a long time, and walked off to the train. I learned that the entire premises of the school burned down not two weeks later.

10

From Wikipedia:

The Cedrig School Curse

The Cedrig School was an all-girls boarding school located in the Southwest of Wales a few miles outside of Llanelli. The school was founded by Gwyneth Lewis in 1954 as Christian school for young ladies. The school was funded from an endowment provided by a local baronet [*citation needed*], and mysteriously burned to the ground on June 20, 1990.

The school was considered prestigious, and attracted students from upper class families, who cited the exceptional education, the beautiful surroundings, and the private student rooms as reasons for sending their children. The school thrived for many years; however, at the end of the 1980s, with the tenure of Headmistress Eve Collins, the school began to decline in reputation. The tragedy of the school's burning was surrounded by scandal, as it was revealed that Collins had been embezzling from school funds, and allegedly having an affair with the chaplain-in-residence, Father Peter Walsh.

The mysterious burning of the school had been preceded a month earlier by the horrific death of Peter Walsh, who was found with his head and body impaled on separate stakes, and apparently burned alive. The burning of the rectory on May 20, 1990 led to the discovery of Walsh inside the burned building, spurring an arson investigation. A series of diaries in Walsh's hand suggested that he had been sadistically raping and torturing at least one of the students at the school, though the student was not named. All students at the school were accounted for when the obvious murder was supposed to have taken place, so the death remains a mystery. Graduation ceremonies were canceled, and students were sent home.

The Cedrig School Curse is the local legend that one particularly bullied student cursed the rest of her classmates as they were leaving, saying that they would not live more than six months, nor would the Headmistress. There is no first-hand verification for this story, but it's often used to explain the death of 20 out of the 21 classmates, and Headmistress Collins, within six months.

The Deaths:

Headmistress Eve Collins: decapitated in a car crash, October 10, 1990.

Lindsay McCarthy: bitten by an adder while hiking through Europe, September 5, 1990.

Hope Robbins: crushed by falling rocks while visiting ruins in Scotland, July 13, 1990.

Elisa Wade: Drowned in an undertow while swimming in the Atlantic Ocean on holiday, August 15, 1990.

Audrey Reynolds: Slipped on a staircase while touring a historic property in the Lake District and broke her neck, October 1, 1990.

Gwen Summers: Attacked and fatally wounded by a mountain lion while hiking in Northern California, USA, July 30, 1990.

Joanne Morton: Plunged to her death from Overtoun Bridge while attempting to keep her dog from jumping, September 23, 1990.

Sophie Dunn: Stabbed to death by a burglar who entered her home, November 6, 1990.

Jamie Burns: Died from smoke inhalation at a fire in her parents' home, December 4, 1990.

Alexis Barker: Mysteriously disappeared when investigating a "rath" site in Kerry, Ireland. The body was found on October 20, 1990. Cause of death still undetermined.

Stacey Nelson: Crushed to death by a steel beam in a construction accident in London, July 30, 1990.

Holly Sharp: Body was found dismembered and dumped into the Tyne River on the outskirts of Newcastle, December 5, 1990.

Darlene Frank: Accidentally ingested a fatal dose of arsenic, December 2, 1990. How the arsenic came into her possession was never determined.

Mary Nelson: Caught in the crossfire of a shooting incident while visiting family in Charleston, South Carolina, USA, on August 4, 1990.

Kelly Hoffman: Admitted to the hospital on October 24, 1990 for complications from anorexia; died on October 27, 1990.

Terri Pearson: Died of hypothermia after falling through cracks in the ice while skating on the pond on her family's property, December 19, 1990

Sonya Carpenter: Crushed to death in a head-on collision with a lorry on November 8, 1990

Theresa Bridges: Fell from the balcony of her family's New York penthouse after becoming too inebriated at a party, July 28, 1990.

Molly Mills: Trampled to death by a bull while visiting Western Ireland, September 30, 1990.

Regina Young: Fell over the side of a cruise ship which was headed to Norway and drowned in spite of rescue attempts., August 19, 1990. Young was pregnant at the time, and lost her child as well.

Eileen Howell: Developed an aggressive brain tumor that killed her within 3 months of diagnosis, on November 17, 1990.

There is no apparent connection between the deaths, as some were accidents, and only a few were regarded as homicides. In all cases the perpetrators were found and brought to justice. Out of 21 students, the only survivor was Layla Black, now a physicist at the University of Manchester, and allegedly the originator of the curse. Dr. Black has never commented on the deaths of her classmates, or directly answered any questions on the curse itself. In spite of the curse legend, she has never been considered a suspect in any of the deaths, as she has never been anywhere near the sites of the tragedies at the time they occurred. The connection to Cedrig is viewed as an uncanny coincidence by most, though some are convinced of the legitimacy of the curse.

11

Layla's Reflections told to Laura Wood

Oxford, move-in day, 1990

So, I had escaped, and I had mixed feelings. On the one hand, I felt like I could breathe again after years of choking. I got a stipend from the university, so I finally had money that wasn't stolen to pay for things. I had a room in Exeter College, and it just felt so much better than the gloomy lodgings at Cedrig. The latter felt more like a prison cell. Exeter was laid out in quadrangles, with windows facing an inward courtyard. My room had a large window that looked out at the Exeter Chapel. An attractive building, I suppose, though I didn't really want to think about churches. However, I was not likely to get away from those in any university town.

I'd met some of the other girls who lived in my residence hall, and they were very friendly; they'd invited me out for drinks after we had supper in the dining hall. It was a very pleasant change after years of having absolutely no one, but it was also a bit jarring, like coming out into bright sunshine after living in a hole in the ground.

The most outgoing of the girls I'd met was called Wendy; she was blonde-haired, blue-eyed, and didn't seem to wear a lot of makeup—mascara, I think, but not much more. She was rather conservatively dressed, and she always looked happy. I liked being around her, though I felt like her polar opposite; it was hard to shake the gloom out of my soul. I'd hoped I wouldn't end up scaring her off. From what I could tell she was very smart in the sciences, and would likely be a good student, but she was also hung up on checking out the boys. I honestly didn't know how I would handle that; I doubted anyone would look twice at me, but if they did—well, the whole thing at Cedrig, plus the thing with my father, I was absolutely revolted at the thought of anyone touching me in—those places. But I didn't want to explain that to Wendy right off; I didn't really want to explain it to anyone. If I'd learned one thing about the human race, it was that no one was interested in your problems, unless they wanted some kind of control over you. Or, I guess if they were a therapist, but then they would be getting paid, and would just label you as a nutter.

In any event, I was now free of the school, and free as an adult to make my own way in the world. This lightened my load considerably. But I was still saddled with everything I'd lost, and I felt like I'd lost the ability to relate to people. I no longer wanted to listen to music, or watch television, or read fiction books; everything reminded me of what I'd lost. So where would that leave me with making friends? People ask you about yourself, about your interests. I didn't have any but my schoolwork; everything else seemed alien to me. I couldn't tell people about where I was from, about my background, and I didn't want to depress everyone with the tale of my lost family. I mostly got by with asking questions about others.

I was quite amazed at how uninteresting I had become.

12

Wendy Thornton's Diaries—Oxford University, Exeter College, 1990

I love everything about Oxford; the college is beautiful, there are so many places to go, lots of good-looking men about —and I really love my mates in the residence hall. They've grouped those in the Physics course in one corner of the quadrangle, which is handy when you want to study together, or talk about assignments.

Layla lives in the room next to me, and she is the sweetest thing—a bit shy, very placid all of the time, but would help you with anything if you asked. God knows I would not have made it through some of my maths classes without her help. Her brain— it's unbelievable, it's like she knows everything. I feel like I'm struggling along a lot of the time, and for her everything is second nature. And she's such a dedicated student; I'm fretting most of the time about papers or laboratory reports that are due, and she's got everything done well in advance. She should definitely get a university job; she could probably even teach the course here better than most of the tutors. It's clear to me that they're also amazed by her.

What saddens me about Layla is that she is so introverted. She will come out with us when we go to the pub, or to the movies, or just down to the Common Room to play games. She's absolutely gorgeous; I have never seen eyes that color before. I asked her about her parents; she said her father was English, and her mother was Scottish. I've never seen anyone of either descent with such deeply violet eyes. And her beautiful black hair…there's something very exotic about her. The boys are mad about her, but don't know how to approach her, and she doesn't seem to want to be approached. I've tried to act as a matchmaker in the past—and there were some REALLY good looking blokes who wanted to approach her, I was a little jealous, truth be told, though I completely understood the attraction. But I really wanted her to be happy with someone.

She seemed confused by the idea of romance. It really made me wonder about how she grew up. She never talked about her family; she said she didn't have one anymore, which I found shocking. I asked if they had died, and she said no. She'd also let slip at one point that she's been on her own more or less since she was thirteen. How was that possible?

I finally decided that one night I had to get a couple of drinks in her, and get the story out of her. In one sense, I felt a little guilty, because it really is none of my business, and she should be able to have her secrets. On the other hand, she seemed like a very lonely person in spite of everything, and it just made no sense at all. She should have had everything.

We sat in my room with a bottle of wine. The conversation started as usual, with a discussion of projects for our courses, and upcoming exams. I edged my way into talking about the blokes who liked her, and finally just had the nerve to say what I thought.

"Layla, I have to be honest. You're a lovely, lovely girl and it makes me sad that you don't have anyone. I'd like to be able to set you up with someone."

She gave a half-smile, and sighed. "You're always very good to me, Wendy, and I know you mean things for the best. But I just can't bring myself to get involved."

"Why not?"

She fingered the wine glass thoughtfully, as if she was trying to make up her mind about something. Finally, "Well, I could tell you about it, but I don't like to discuss it with people. It's hardly the thing to bring up when you're making new friends."

So, that was when the story came out. Her father had sent her away abruptly, and she was essentially abandoned at the boarding school. She had no friends there, as everyone seemed to hate her for some reason, though she could never figure out why exactly. And then she told me about Father Peter...I was horrified, because I'd just read about this in the Mail. It sickened me to think that she was the victim. But I also marveled at her, because she was able to retain such poise. She did not complain, or make herself a victim; it was simply that bad things had happened, they had traumatised her, and she'd rather not be touched right now, thanks anyway. I don't know how I would react if I was in her situation; the whole thing was over-the-top in its horribleness, it was almost unbelievable. This was when I found out that Malcolm Black was her father. This was also a huge shock; I'd always been a fan of his music, but knowing that he could do something like this, I've felt very differently since.

"Well," she said, "I'm sorry to unload all of that—I have to admit that I'm still a bit dazed by the whole thing, and I have a lot of trouble with trust, and a lot of trouble thinking that there's anything about me that would interest anyone. After years of being hated by everyone, you start to wonder if there isn't something really terrible about you." This was the first time she'd ever shown signs of wanting to cry. But she pulled herself up, and wiped away any potential tears. "I'm glad I know you, and I'm glad I have friends here, things are so much better. But I wouldn't know what to do with a bloke. I don't want to be touched, and I could be wrong, but I don't know of many blokes who don't want to get physical. I'm not even good at conversation—outside of schoolwork, I'm just so hopelessly lost when it comes to the culture. I don't even understand most jokes. It's embarrassing, really."

I reassured her that there was nothing wrong with her, and that things could change and get better. She assented that it was possible, but didn't seem entirely convinced. When we said goodnight, I remember laying in bed feeling heartbroken for her. Because that's what she was—heartbroken, possibly beyond repair. How do you live through something like that and believe that things will be all right?

Then Andy Spencer came along.

13

Andy Spencer's Journals, 1997

I started my course at Oxford University during the Autumn term, 1990. I was studying Political Science at Oxford, and I think there was some expectation that I would follow in my father's footsteps in Parliament one day. It was far from unusual for a member of the upper class to attend either Oxford or Cambridge, so it still amazes me how much flack I took for it among my classmates. I certainly had my friends, but being "posh" was a liability among some. Maybe they are right, I don't know.

All I do know is that I had a reasonably comfortable flat near Balliol College, not too far from where the Political Science department was located. Many of my friends liked to go out to parties and on pub crawls; I didn't mind sometimes, but on the whole I was something of an introvert, and something of a romantic. You were more likely to find me in a bookstore than watching a football match. Still, I can't say that I was a misfit; I had friends who suited me, and who could relate to my tastes and sentiments.

I didn't lack for female attention while I was at school; in retrospect, I suppose I was quite a good looking young man, with brown hair on the long side, blue eyes, and a very youthful, almost effeminate face. Women really seem to like that in men, for some reason. Still, I often found myself in doubt; I didn't know whether women were attracted to me for my looks, or because I had a lot of money. In any case, very few women held my attention for very long; I was very attracted to beautiful women, but I also wanted someone I could talk to about deeper matters. I intensely disliked superficial small talk, and thus the whole dating cycle was frequently just a bore to me.

Then there was that day; I don't know if it was the best or worst day of my life, looking back. My friends and I met at the Eagle and Child, which was an extremely popular place for Oxford students. We always tried to get there early enough to get a table in one of the smaller rooms in front, and would spend hours discussing politics, philosophy, and literature. And, truth be told, we were also keeping an eye on the birds who came in.

On that afternoon, the most beautiful bird I had ever seen walked into the pub with some friends. She did not look our way, but she and her friends had grabbed one of the booths that faced us diagonally, so we could see all of them clearly. She wasn't very tall, but she was willowy; she wasn't voluptuous, but her body was gently curved at the waist and breasts, and she was rather petite overall. She had long rippling waves of black hair, and then I caught a look at her face. Her skin was like porcelain, and her eyes were a deep violet colour. I stared at her, completely enchanted; she looked like something out of a Rossetti painting.

She got up to get a pint with one of her friends, a rather wholesome looking blonde girl. My friends noticed that I had stopped talking, and they all peered out to see what I was looking at. When they saw her head back our way, they gasped; one of them whistled to himself. "Where did that bird come from??"

The girl who was the object of my fancy didn't look over our way at all, but her friend noticed us staring. She grinned, and then nudged the black-haired beauty, and whispered something to her. She turned slowly and looked at us, with a strange look on her face; she appeared to be puzzled. I couldn't take my eyes off of her, but I was too shy to go over. My friends were needling me to get up and go talk to her, but there was no way I could do it. I'm not sure I could have talked to her alone, never mind with a group of girls sitting there together. It was clear that her friend was keen to try to spur her to action, but she seemed reluctant. I felt somehow that she was also introverted and shy, and this just made me even more interested in her.

Well, the impasse was finally broken when her friend got up about a half an hour later to walk toward the bar. My friend Geoff stood up and said, "Okay, there needs to be an intervention here. I'm going to go talk to her about her friend." And before I could say anything, he made his way down the narrow corridor toward the bar. He was probably gone for about ten or fifteen minutes, and when he returned, he was grinning.

"Okay," he said, "I spoke to her friend, who is called Wendy—they are Physics students at Exeter College. The very lovely lady with the black hair is called Layla, and she is very much single. She is however, extremely shy, and Wendy says that she's a bit blind when blokes are looking at her. But I think she's keen to help set something up, if you're willing."

I could feel the redness rising in my face. I didn't know if I fancied being "set up." On the other hand, I was desperate to talk to this girl, and knew I'd likely make a fool of myself if I tried to confront her on my own. I looked over at Layla; Wendy was talking to her earnestly, and I could see that she was also blushing. Finally, Wendy looked at me and winked, and dragged her friend away from the table, heading toward the back. I knew that was my cue to follow them. As they waited on line to get drinks, I came over, trying to appear casual in spite of how self-conscious I was, and frankly, very nervous. Wendy immediately introduced herself and was very pleasant; she introduced Layla to me. "Hello," I said to her. "I'm Andy. Can I buy you ladies a drink?"

She smiled and blushed. "That's very kind of you." Her voice was soft and melodious, and her accent was definitely from the South of England, but I couldn't place exactly where. I was extremely grateful for Wendy, who moderated our small talk while we made our way to the bar. Finally I ordered for everyone, and when I got drinks, Wendy suddenly had to "do something" and left the two of us alone. I looked at her, and indicated an empty table at the back of the place. "Can we have a chat?"

"Um, okay," she said. She was pulling a bit nervously at her hair. I didn't want to frighten her off, so I started by asking her questions about herself, how long she was at Oxford, and her school course. She readily answered these questions, and asked me about myself. When I told her that I was doing a course in Political Science, we ended up starting a conversation about politics, and she was obviously not empty-headed. In fact, she spoke so intelligently, I wondered if I was out of my league. Any of my friends who had worked in the sciences weren't quite so comfortable with non-technical topics.

"You're so well versed in cultural subjects, it surprises me a bit that you're in the sciences. Do you like Physics?"

"Oh yes," she said. "It's…well, it's challenging, and I like to occupy my mind. I find the maths easy, which helps a lot."

I laughed. "I'm absolutely dreadful with maths. You will have to teach me." She smiled and blushed. "It depends on how dreadful you are—some people say that I'm dreadful at trying to explain it. But if I want to work in research and teaching, I guess I ought to get better at that."

"Is that what you want to do?"

"Yes, I think so. I like Theoretical Physics quite a bit."

I then shifted the subject to her family. "Where are you from?"

Her face tensed slightly. "I was born near Inverness in Scotland. I was raised in various places in the South of England, Esher being the last one. Before I came here I was at school in Wales."

"What school did you attend?"

"The Cedrig School. It was a boarding school."

"Wait...wasn't that place in the news recently? Did something happen there?"

"Yes," she said. She didn't elaborate right away.

"It burned down, or something?"

"Yes, that's exactly what happened."

"Were you there when it happened?"

"I was there when the rectory burned down. I was already here in Oxford when the rest of the school burned down."

"Do they know what caused it?"

She paused, and took a long sip of her drink, and stared into space, away from me. "Not a clue."

"Was your family upset?"

"I don't know. I haven't seen them in years."

This surprised me. "Oh…I'm sorry. I hope I'm not getting too personal."

Her face softened, and she smiled at me. "It's OK. It's a normal question to ask. But I'd rather not talk about them right now, if you don't mind."

"Fair enough." I wanted a hasty change of subject. "Do you like living over at Exeter?"

She was thoughtful. "Yes," she said. "I do. Everyone there is very nice, and it's not too rowdy. I hate being woken up at night by loud noises when I have class the next morning."

We talked about various things for awhile, and finally it was getting toward closing time. I saw that her friends were still there, looking in our direction. She glanced over at them. "I guess I should get going. Thank you for buying me drinks, I had a nice time talking."

I was not going to miss this opportunity. "We should do it again. Soon. Can we meet again tomorrow night? I could even pick you up at your residence hall, and we can go somewhere a bit quieter, so we can talk."

"Tomorrow? What day is it, Friday? Yes, I think that would be alright." She seemed to be comfortable around me, which I saw as a huge victory. She had looked very uncertain earlier that evening.

"Great—let me come by around sevenish? I'll meet you in the lobby of your hall. I have a chauffeur, so we can go anywhere that we like."

She looked at me for a moment, and I couldn't decipher what the look meant. But then she said, "Alright then. I'll see you at seven tomorrow. Ta."

I wanted to give her a kiss goodnight, but it seemed too presumptuous. So I just said goodnight, and we left with our respective friends.

As we walked home, I felt absolutely high as a kite. I could not believe I was able to talk to her, never mind get a date. I knew there was no way I would sleep that night.

Little did I know that Layla would cause me many sleepless nights.

14

Wendy Thornton's Diaries, 1990

The lot of us walking home from the pub that night must have looked like a bunch of besotted giggling idiots. I was absolutely thrilled that I was able to get Layla to talk to Andy, AND that she had agreed to go out with him again. I had gotten up to watch them a few times, and I liked that he was just talking with her, not trying to push her in any way in terms of touching her or kissing her. I hear all kinds of things about posh blokes, but he seemed to have proper manners.

It was hard to gauge Layla's reaction. She smiled and blushed a bit, which I'd not seen her do before. But she didn't seem to be ecstatically in love; in fact, the whole encounter seemed to leave her dazed. When we got back to our rooms, I implored her to stay up with me a while longer; there were no Friday classes for us, so we could sleep in late the next morning, and I would treat her to breakfast in town if we woke up too late. It didn't take much coaxing to get her to agree. So, she came over to my room, and I made us some chamomile tea; we'd certainly had enough to drink, and I didn't want anything that would make us too wired to sleep all night.

"Layla, I can't tell you how happy I am that you spent time with Andy, and that you're going to go out with him."

She looked at me, with that same puzzled look. "Really? Why?"

"Because you've had such a shite time of things. Andy seems very classy and respectful—and he is definitely a catch. He's gorgeous, and has a lot of money. Yes, I realise that the last part doesn't have to matter. But he's obviously crazy about you. So many blokes are such bungling idiots, I want you to be able to go out with someone who will treat you well."

"But…do you think he actually likes me?"

I nearly spit across the room. "Layla! My dear, you can be quite blind to these things! I think he'd do just about anything you'd say—he's totally smitten by you."

'Mmm…" she said, as though she were pondering this. "I don't know. I mean, he is attractive, and I don't mind going out with him. He's not been pushy with me, which I also like. But I don't know if he will always be respectful."

"What do you mean? Are you afraid he's going to push you toward sex?"

"Well, not exactly. I mean yes, if we do end up getting together, I'm sure he's going to want that, and I think I could overcome my aversion to it. I know I WANT to—I don't want Father Peter defining my sex life for me. But in the longer term, I think he's going to see me as his possession. To be fair, I think most blokes tend to do that. But I'm not okay with that."

I sat down next to her. "Layla," I said as gently as possible, "try to stay in the present. It's true, not all relationships end up being totally right or working out. Right now, you have someone in love with you who you think you could also feel for—give it a try! Even if ultimately things didn't work out—you know the old

277

saying, 'It's better to have loved and lost than not to have loved at all.'"

She looked at me. "Do you think that's true?"

"Absolutely! That's how love is anyway; it's up and down. And right now, this is an 'up'; try to enjoy it, take it as it comes."

She sat back drinking her tea. "Well, maybe you're right. I'll try to do that. But he comes from a posh family. He may like me, but they may not."

"Why wouldn't they like you?"

"Because I'm not the sort of woman they'd choose for their son. My father may have money, but I'm not from the right kind of family—and the fact that I'm estranged from my family won't go over well. They want another aristocrat, and they want someone who will properly marry him, have babies, and take up gardening. That is definitely not me."

"Well, you could marry him…"

"No, that is definitely out of the question."

"But why?"

"For starters, I'm not able to have children; that will be a strike against me. For another, I don't want to be a 'kept' woman. I've had enough trouble with men controlling my life, I definitely cannot have that situation going forward. And as nice as his family may turn out to be, you can bet that my life would be controlled in that situation. Aristocrats are like animals in cages; they're on display, and expected to do certain things."

I sighed. "Layla, please don't suck all the romance out of your life. You're incredibly sensible, and I admire you for that. Try not to think about that for now."

"Well, I did say I would try."

15

Andy Spencer's Journals, 1997

I picked Layla up at her residence hall at Exeter College. I still couldn't believe we were going out, and I was afraid she might not show up. But when I came to reception, she was coming down the stairs to meet me. I was flooded with relief, but I was still nervous. She seemed different from other girls, and I didn't want to screw things up.

I got the sense that she wanted to move slowly, and even though I was anxious to touch her, I didn't want to push her away. We went out on that first date alone to a quiet set of rooms and a private bar near my own quarters. I was astounded at the range of knowledge she had of various subjects—history, languages, philosophy, religion—and on top of that, I found out that she was First Class in Physics. She was both gorgeous and intelligent, and I was madly in love with her.

At the end of that first date, when we went back to her hall driven by the chauffeur, I looked into her eyes when I said goodnight; I wanted a parting kiss, and fortunately she did not disappoint me. But her kiss just made me want more of her. For the time being, I had to wait.

Soon we became an item on campus; it was known that we were in a relationship. I loved being around her, and being with her. But what I wasn't used to was her unwavering dedication to her course. Physics always came first, and school always came first. Yes, I realise that this is how it ought to be, but

I hated being separated from her. The more time she spent in the labs and studying for exams, the more I wished I could just whisk her away, and make her forget about her plans to go into research. But she would not budge. Still, I'd hoped that things would change over time.

Eventually the story about her family life and what happened to her at the boarding school trickled out, and it left me feeling profoundly disturbed and angry. It was no wonder she was so cautious, so reticent and sometimes distrusting. It didn't take me long to realise that this probably contributed a lot to her sense of independence; she'd been screwed over by two men she ought to have been able to trust—her own father and a chaplain. If I were in her shoes, I'd also be suspicious of anyone trying to plan any aspect of my life. Of course, even without these things, she was clearly brilliant. Why should she play second fiddle to anyone?

She had nowhere to go for the summers that we were at school, and had planned to rent a flat for the few months we were off. I told her that was ridiculous, she should save her money and stay with me at our family estate. It took some coaxing, but she finally agreed. My family got to meet her, and I could tell they were very impressed by her, in spite of the fact that she wasn't born into the aristocracy. She had impeccable manners, and was clearly well educated. I felt like I could overcome the hurdles to making her my wife.

But I didn't bet on the biggest hurdle—Layla herself. We'd been dating for three years, and I was keen on popping the question, but I wanted to feel her out first. It became very clear to me that she had no intention of marrying me, and this left me feeling very hurt and frustrated.

I was frustrated by her in general, to be honest. I felt she was mine, and I didn't like other blokes flirting with her or trying to spend time with her. I found that I was even bothered when she was studying with classmates for an exam, if any of them were male. I didn't want her spending time with anyone else, and certainly not any blokes claiming to be "friends. "

As for Layla, whenever I brought this up to her in any situation, she told me I was being ridiculous; she had no interest in pursuing multiple relationships, and she had a right to be friends with someone regardless of what they had or didn't have between their legs. "You always claim I'm distrustful," she said, "but I think you're the one who is not trusting me. And, like my father, you have no reason to not trust me."

This really stung; I did not like being compared to her father. But she reiterated her feeling—he sent her away apparently for some perceived slight that she never committed, and here I was, trying to control her interactions because of some perceived feelings for blokes that she didn't have. We would argue from time to time, but I was still optimistic we could build a future together.

Then the day came when it became very clear to me that this would never happen.

16

Wendy and her other friends had graduated, and Layla stayed on to do her doctoral work in Physics. She had chosen the most difficult professor to work with, as she wanted someone who would thoroughly criticise and vet her work. As it turns out, she passed her defense with flying colours, and graduated First Class. I was extremely proud of her.

What I didn't know was that she was looking for opportunities to do research at institutions all over Europe. So, the day came when we met up for a drink, and she gave me the bad news.

"Andy, I've got something to tell you."

"What?"

"I've got an offer to work on a project in Copenhagen. I'm leaving next Tuesday."

I felt my heart sink, and it was as though all my organs would fall down to my feet. "I can arrange to be there with you," I said.

She shook her head. "No. I think it's time we moved on from each other. I've enjoyed my time with you, and I'm grateful that I got to have a love relationship that was not tainted by my past experiences. But your family expects you to marry and produce heirs; I will never be able to do that for you."

I felt my face getting red. "The hell with them! I'd leave it all behind for you—I don't care!"

She looked at me, dismayed. "Yes, you do care. You're just upset right now. And you would resent me if I kept you from your family and your fortune."

"Layla, I cannot let you go!"

"I'm sorry Andy. But you have to—it's best for both of us."

My mind reeled. I didn't know what to do; I was angry, hurt, determined to keep her—everything at the same time. But all I said was, "When are you leaving? I at least want to say goodbye."

"Tuesday morning. I take the 8:00 train to London, and then I transfer from there."

I took a deep breath. "Fine. I'll come to say goodbye to you the night before."

She squeezed my hand and left.

After she left, I knew I had no intention of letting her leave. I was willing to do whatever it took to keep her, to bring her back to my family home, until she changed her mind. But she threw me another curveball.

On Tuesday morning, I came by her flat early. I knocked on the door, but there was no answer; the place was dark. Her landlady heard my knocking, and stuck her head out the window, looking cross.

"What is it you want?"

"I'm sorry—I didn't mean to bother you. Layla said she is leaving today; I'm thinking I missed her."

"You certainly did. She left yesterday."

I was stunned. "Yesterday??"

"Yes. Now, if you don't mind, I'm going back to bed." With that she shut the window.

I never saw Layla again. I didn't think I would ever recover from the heartbreak I felt when I lost her, and I was angry at her— angry that I'd ever met her, that I'd wasted so many years. Eventually I did do what my father wanted—I married an aristocratic woman and settled down. I never did go into politics. In retrospect, I think Layla was trying to spare me from having a scandal; she seemed to know everything, and I'm sure she knew my intentions. But I've never really gotten past it. All I've been able to accept is that I was somehow out of my depth with her.

17

Layla's Reflections as told by Laura Wood

Wendy had wanted me to take a chance on Andy, and I did. We did have a lot of good times together, and I was grateful to him for helping eradicate some of the pain of my adolescent years. But he had the problem that I know I will always have with men—they become obsessed, and they want you as their possession. I told that to Wendy then, and it came true.

I knew that he was not going to just let me go; he would do something highly illegal, try to kidnap me. He might even get away with it, given his class and his family connections. But he never realised what I was capable of; he didn't know how much I had to do with Father Peter's death. He would not have been worthy of the same fate, but it could have been a disaster.

So, I told him I was going to Copenhagen on a Tuesday. In fact, I was going to Berlin, and I'd left the night before. It was better that I just slipped away, rather than having a confrontation.

I've seen Andy's father in the House of Lords since, when I've had to go to Parliament to look for funding. He's always been very nice to me, and I can tell from the look in his eyes and in his general demeanour toward me that he is grateful I did what I did. While I think the family liked me, I would have been an uncomfortable fit, and they knew it. I could have pulled him away from the family, but I knew that wasn't right for him—and I was not looking for a spouse.

The Berlin project was the first of several that I got involved with before seeing the job opening in Manchester. In that time I managed to publish some papers of my own, and collaborate on others; I had built up enough of a CV to push for the tenured job I wanted. And this was how I ended up here.

18

Laura Wood's Reflections on Layla

When I finished listening to Layla's whole story, I was gobsmacked. It really worried me that she would not go to therapy; what had happened to her was so traumatic, and no one had been there to support her. Her hermit-like ways and personality now made sense to me. I was glad to hear that her Oxford years were something of an improvement; I imagine it gave her some balance and stability after what she'd been through. But I was sad that this seemed to be the last time she had close friends or a lover.

I also marveled at how she'd managed to survive her teen years emotionally and physically. It didn't sound like she managed to eat much during that time, she ought to have been terribly ill. I also wondered, if I had been in her shoes, if I would not have contemplated suicide. I would never have dared mention such a thing to her—I wouldn't want her to think it—but it seemed like that would be a crushing load. And the business with Father Peter—I'm surprised she didn't go mad. But the business about his death...I felt like she'd said a bit more than she intended, and I really did not know what to think. It was possible that she was exaggerating some of the story, but that didn't really make sense, either. Why should she tell me any of this at all? It certainly wasn't a story that she shared with others; she only told it to me because I'd pressed her on it. I also realise that she was basically suggesting she'd murdered someone, but it seemed so preposterous, I just couldn't believe it had any truth.

She was not a hysterical or overly emotional person; she kept all of it bottled up. It was obvious, because if her voice started to rise slightly, she would take a stiff drink to keep herself in check. It was as though she was determined not to let her past ruin her life, though I'm not sure she succeeded, at least not in an emotional sense.

But I also realised that there was a lot more to the story than she was telling me. I knew her father neglected her, but I still didn't know who he was, nor did she talk at all about her mother. Who was her mother? It was as though she was raised by her father alone; surely if her mother had been there, she would have something to say in the matter, or she would have been there to take her in. The events themselves were baffling; why would her father just suddenly send her away, after being close with her? If she wasn't making it up, then there were a lot of gaps. It was clear that she herself did not know how to explain or fill some of them, but others...

I went home that afternoon much later than intended. Chris met me at the door.

"Where have you been all afternoon? I've been worried about you."

"Sorry, love—I went to drop off some things at Layla's flat around lunchtime, and I ended up staying and talking to her for a bit."

"Quite a bit, I'd say—it's already 4:00. What did you find to chat about for so long?"

So, I told Chris about my conversation with her. We ended up having a long discussion about her before we sat down to our own tea.

"I don't know, Chris," I said. Everything in me believes her story, but I really don't know what to make of some of the loose ends, and the business about Father Peter is really disturbing to me."

"Well, yes, rape IS extremely disturbing, and may go quite a long way in explaining some of her behaviours."

"Yes, of course—but more than that. How his life ended... she basically implied that she caused it. Not that he didn't deserve it. Either she's making that up or..."

"Or what?"

I sighed. "I really don't know. If I believe every word—and I don't really want to—then Layla is capable of some really dark things."

Chris let out a long breath. "I'm sure she's making that up, or perhaps has deluded herself into thinking that's what happened—like you say, it was so traumatic, her mind probably concocted some story like that as a kind of compensation. On the other hand..."

"What?"

Chris shook his head. "I don't know. There's something uncanny about her. I've written a lot of it off as related to her being a genius, but...well, what am I saying? I'm starting to sound very unscientific."

I smiled, but didn't laugh. "There seems to be a lot going on here that is hard to explain with science."

I expected Chris to rebuff this thought, but he didn't.

19

Malcolm's Reflections, shared from an Anonymous Friend

1985 had to be the worst year ever. I was constantly ill, and very much addicted to cocaine at that point. I was starting work on an album with my friend Steve Abbott, who was an incredible blues singer. I was glad to be playing and writing songs again; it was one of the few things that helped put me back in balance.

But this was also the year that things were falling apart with Layla. I loved Layla more than anything; I still do. But that year I was caught in a real emotional trap; I was really desiring her sexually, now that she was blossoming into womanhood. But at the same time, I loathed her; she filled me with absolute terror for no reason. I felt like a voice was in my head, telling me to get rid of her. Of course it didn't mean to kill her; that's not even possible. But as the year went on, I had a more and more urgent sense that she was a problem.

When I think about it, it really DIDN'T make any sense. The sexual desire WAS a problem—I was seeing a therapist about that. It was as though I thought she was deliberately tempting me to do the unthinkable. Again, in retrospect, that is an extremely stupid idea. Layla was very gentle, sweet—and really, behaved no differently than she had in previous years. She was affectionate, but could also be very detached. I already knew… well, there are things about her…things that might give me reason to think she could be dangerous. But I never saw any hint of any dangerous tendencies. Still, the thought plagued me night after night when I tried to sleep. For awhile I could shake off the feeling during the day, but then I just found it difficult to be around her all the time. Something kept telling me it was her fault, though my rational mind told me that this was absolute rubbish. I couldn't let go of Layla; she was unique, and I felt like an appointed guardian of her. Of course, in my drug-addled state I felt I was doing a shite job of that, and this realisation only added to the idea that I should send her away. After all, I was too much of a failure as a parent to take care of her.

Well, I struggled with these feelings for a long time, but finally things came to a head. I got the not-so-brilliant idea of trying to give in to my desires, to actually have sex with her. My rationale was that if I allowed myself–just once–and I could put something in her food to make sure she slept, so she didn't have to know–I would get over this crazy feeling. You know, "the thrill of the chase", the idea is more interesting than the actual event. At the time I felt a great relief; I felt like shouting to the roof tops. Clever me, I had found a way out of this emotional conundrum. It had not even occurred to me that I could just talk to her about my feelings; we pretty much talked about everything else in the past, even when she was really only a child.

So, I planned it. I put a sedative in her food, and watched carefully to see if she would notice. She did seem to notice how I looked at her, so I had to really stop being so conspicuous. But the plan went off without a hitch, well–except one. The most important one.

You see, I woke up the next morning, and realised that not only had I not cured myself, I'd made the situation one hundred times worse. My emotions were all magnified, it felt like hundreds of times. The voice in my head said that she did this, she would have her revenge on me. And I suddenly became angry.

I didn't waste any time. I recalled a previous discussion about boarding schools in which someone mentioned the Cedrig School in Wales to me; I had my assistant get the information on the place. I set things up in a hurry, and sent her there that same day, if you can believe it. I really hadn't researched the place, it was just far away from our home, and that was good enough for me. Naturally she was very upset and clearly baffled at what was happening. But I found that if I tried to talk about anything, I just became angrier and angrier. This wasn't just with her—it was with family, with friends. She just became an explosive topic for me; I resented that I had to do anything for her care at all.

After everything that later happened at the Cedrig School, I realised I'd made a horrible mistake. But then I was in mortal terror of what she would do. I heard how the priest there died…I knew this had to be her…and there was no reason in my mind why I shouldn't be next.

20

Malcolm Black's Reflections, Shared from an Anonymous Friend

Sending Layla away turned out to be the first in a long line of extremely bad decisions. I had a hard time kicking my drug habit, and I almost died a couple of times. I took a holiday, and met a woman called Lisa who later became my wife; we had a son together. She turned out to be possessive to a maniacal degree; I could not go anywhere without her tracking me, without her calling up any female I'd spoken to, for any reason—and she would start threatening them. Eventually I had to break free from this situation, and we got divorced. Because of my problems, she had full custody of my son. The judge was not particularly in favour of me, and I lost a lot of money. I had to sell off a lot of assets, and decided that I needed to record a new album. I did manage to produce a solo record, and had some collaborations with a few lesser known singers. The album was not a success; in fact, I think I lost more money on it.

I managed to hobble through financially for a time, with an occasional increase here and there—and then I met another woman, Celestine, while traveling abroad, and decided to get married to her. There was a huge age gap between the two of us, and we proved to be extremely different people. We had several children together, and then everything busted up. Financially I was in the hole once again. But that wasn't the worst of my problems.

You see, ever since Layla left, there was a kind of heavy feeling in the house. I attributed it to her, that she might have cursed me as well. I ended up moving back to London, buying a house there; I thought it would be a fresh start, that things would be better. I had taken down all of my photos and memories of Layla, and put them in the attic. Again—something inside me wanted to burn it all, get rid of everything. But I fought back against this urge; I just couldn't bring myself to do it. I figured that hiding it was good enough, and someone might eventually find it when I was dead. It did not occur to me that Layla would ever be back in my life, or that I should ever invite her back in.

The new house proved to be as oppressive in its vibe as the old house. I found myself going through frequent bouts of depression; I was losing money, I was not as attractive anymore to women, and even though my children visited me, there was still a sense of distance from everyone and everything. I would start music projects, and find that I had no will to write songs, or even just play music. This was devastating, as music was my whole life. I bounced from one distraction to another, but there was always a feeling—was it fear? Insecurity? I didn't know, but I was sick of feeling anxious all the time. My doctor prescribed antidepressants, and I started to become addicted to them. The weird part was that they didn't really help. I started taking them with alcohol, and then my health started to go into a downward spiral. I'd never had the best constitution to begin with, so it was yet another really stupid decision.

In my moments of lucidity, I found myself missing Layla a lot, but every time I wanted to make a move to find her, it was like I was hit with blinding chest pain; sometimes I couldn't breathe. When this happened for the fifth time, I suddenly had a creeping fear come over me. I now started to wonder if my decision to eject Layla from my life was my own—and if it wasn't...

What the hell was it that had a hold over me?

296

21

Malcolm Black's Reflections, Shared from an Anonymous Friend

I remember the afternoon that I decided to take a walk away from my house, to get out and clear my head. My health was not good, and recently I'd had thoughts of suicide. I was starting to feel overwhelmed by the choices I'd made, and feeling profoundly disturbed about my inability to think of Layla.

I was now trying to be objective. What made me send her away? As I thought through the events, I realised that I had absolutely no rational reason for it, in spite of any feelings I may have had about her. I could blame being on drugs to some degree, and the erratic way I felt at the time. But I knew now that there was something else.

I had dabbled enough in the occult to know a few things about the other world—hell, that was how Layla came into this world—so I had to figure out a means of contacting whatever this was without harming myself further. I decided to go visit my friend Darryl, a long time practitioner of voodoo, and a much more serious occultist than myself. Someone who was able to communicate with and negotiate all types of spirits would be needed to find this out. I was too afraid of my own frailty to try this on my own.

Darryl lived in the East End, near Shoreditch. We shook hands, and he offered me a joint, which I accepted. We talked a bit about things—world events, personal events—and then I got to the reason for my visit.

"Something's not right. I feel like something has been around me. For a long time." I explained to him my recent symptoms, and my reflection on the long list of bad decisions I had made—and my fears about what I'd done to Layla.

Darryl looked at me, and his face was somewhat grim. "Yeah, I never understood why you did that. That girl—she's a powerful one, you really had some serious shite protection there from someone who could slice you up like an Easter ham." I shuddered at the analogy, though I was also tempted to laugh.

He took out a box of shells, and threw them out, blowing on them as he did so. He closed his eyes, and tried to tune in to what was going on. When he opened his eyes, he had a wild look on his face.

"You definitely have something around you—it's not a demon, but it may as well be. It's some kind of being I'm not familiar with. My own spirits are calling it a "dark elf"; sounds like something out of Tolkien to me. But whatever it is, it hates the Morrigan."

I felt my blood start to freeze, and I was conscious of my anxiety. "So, you mean it hates Layla."

He nodded. "Wherever she comes from—she is some kind of queen, you understand? She's managed to bring three warring groups under her, and I think most of them are fine with that. This thing…it's not. It wants to be in charge. But she's stronger than it." He took a breath, then continued. "So, he's tried to get her another way—he perceives your weakness, and he's attacked you instead. And he has so far managed to keep himself hidden from her, so she doesn't know that he's the one doing it."

"What is his name?" I asked, trembling.

He shook his head. Something like "Dunclunan, or something like that. Sounds like some Gaelic-type name, and I don't know those languages."

"What can I do about it?"

"If you've destroyed your relationship with her, I don't know what you can do, other than try to appeal to her. Did she ever give you anything for protection?"

I thought about it. "I don't think so..." My head started to feel fuzzy. Somehow I felt that she HAD given me something... but now I couldn't remember what it was.

"Well, I don't know then. I can give you a protective charm, but ultimately, she's the only one who can help you."

Darryl then stood up, and went through the process of making me a gris-gris. After what seemed like a long time, passing it through a foul-smelling incense and reciting incantations I did not know, he handed it to me.

"This is the best I can do. Take care of yourself; if this thing realises you're trying to get rid of it, it will go after you. Keep this with you, and try to think of other things while you are figuring out what you're going to do."

"Well, that seems impossible."

"Yeah, it's hard. But you've got to try." He paused. "And get yourself off those damn drugs—they are not helping you. Call me if things get worse."

I thanked him, and headed back toward my house with some trepidation, and not terribly reassured. However, the gris-gris must have had some effect, because I had a sudden moment of lucidity.

Layla HAD given me something for protection. And she had told me how to use it too. I just needed to be able to go into the attic and get it…

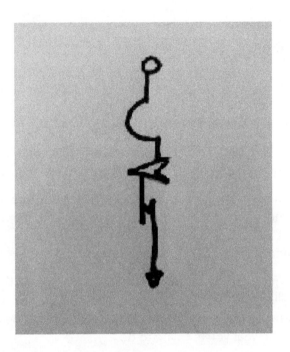

22

Mila's Vision

It was a crisp October evening, and the days were getting shorter. By the time Layla pulled up to the Cheshire House, the sun was setting. She looked at the front of the house, with its dark crisscrossed beams and peeling white paint. The property was a bit overgrown, and she could see the purple-orange glow of the setting sun at the back edge of the yard if she looked over the mildewed gate. She could hear the sound of the brook pattering, though she could not see it from the front. The trees on the property swayed gently in the wind, scattering colorful leaves across the grass.

She turned away from the gate, and headed to the front door. The lock was a bit rusty; she was going to have to replace it. Really, she was going to have to replace everything. But she didn't mind. It gave her something to do besides sit up all night drinking scotch and distracting herself by reading Physics journals, which was only so much of a distraction.

The floors creaked beneath her as she turned on an electric lamp that she had rigged up in the house. She headed to the kitchen, where she had been replacing rotten beams in the floor, and laying a new stone surface. She wanted to do any hammering or drilling at an hour that would not annoy the neighbours.

Layla could not say exactly why she purchased the old Tudor that was outside the village of Chester. It was falling apart, and had a reputation for being haunted. It had served as a tavern, and a lot of unsavory characters were said to have stayed there, and some murders had taken place there as well. Layla was not daunted by any ghostly activity; it was the sheer amount of work involved in putting the place back together that seemed questionable. But she knew she spent too much time in the office on projects. She needed something to work on that allowed her to connect to others, something entirely normal, that would create a safe topic for discussion. The renovations would be extensive and would take some time; at the end of it, she would finally have a home of her own.

This was a departure from her previous mode of thinking. She'd never considered really settling down anywhere, which is why she had so few possessions. And why did she want a big house? It wasn't like anyone else was going to live there.

But that was the thing. She suddenly had the feeling that someone else WOULD live there with her. And the surprising part, at least to her, was that she sensed it would be her father. But she still did not know how this was going to come about. Nonetheless, she trusted her feelings, and went ahead with the project.

The project turned out to be a relatively short one; she had done most of the renovations, including the electric, the gas, and fixing structural issues, within nine months. She did all the work herself, and had to have contractors in to verify that the work was up to code. All of them looked at her, and were sceptical that she was capable of doing the work, but they all left surprised. Everything had been perfectly completed.

Once she was able to secure a certificate of occupancy, she spent time on final details, and decorating the place. She'd never owned real furniture in her life, but she managed to put together a cosy house, a very earthy retreat from the outside world. Initially she felt strange in the house, as she was the only occupant. If her solitude had been evident before, the effects were magnified now. But something was changing; she could feel it. She just didn't know what to do with it yet.

23

Mila's Vision

Layla had been living in the Cheshire House (as it was now called) for about a month. She had altered her routine to make the longer drive home, and tended to work fewer hours to make up for commuting time, and doing errands on the way home.

She came home one night around 10:00PM, and her senses were immediately on edge. She went into the house, dropping off her groceries in the kitchen. After locking the front door, she peered out into the back yard. She had about ten acres of property that stretched into woods, and a creek ran nearby, on the eastern side of the property. A small English garden was near the back doors, where she had put French doors in one of the rooms facing the backyard. Her sharp vision picked up an unfamiliar movement coming from the woods, and close to the house.

She watched the figures as they tried to slip by in the shadows. They were tall and extremely thin, with spindly limbs and long fingers. They were hairless, completely white, and had dark hollows where eyes should have been. She could hear them make a kind of muffled grunting sound. Immediately she slipped into her room, and reached under her bed; she pulled out her massive battle axe, a quiver of arrows, and a bow. Then she made her way downstairs, changing shape so that she only appeared as a whiff of black smoke. And she watched her quarry.

The figures began to come close to the house, and peer in the window. She drew an arrow, and shot the first one clean through the chest. It cried out, and fell to the ground. This alerted the others, who were obviously confused. Layla realised that they were not particularly intelligent creatures; they just sort of ambled around, devouring things in their path like zombies— but they were not zombies. These things, in fact, had never been truly alive, from what she could sense. But this also meant that no one else could kill them. Her weapons could destroy any type of being, so they were not immune to her attack, and this clearly jarred them and sent them running.

Layla did not let a single one get away. She let out a horrific roar, and ran after them. Some of them were taken down by arrows, others had their heads hacked off by her axe. In a short time, she had destroyed every one of them—about nine of them in total. She made her way along the property, scanning for others—but there were none. She then walked back and looked at her prey.

The bodies were already starting to shrink and decompose, and they suddenly collapsed as a pile of dead leaves, which then seemed to burn themselves up and disappear. She did another thorough walk around on her property, and returned to the house after retrieving her arrows.

She poured herself a drink and sat in the living room. What the hell WERE these things? She had seen every kind of being in almost all dimensions—these were new to her. They weren't much of a threat to her, but she felt they would be a threat to humans.

But then the inner voice came to her—these things were created BY humans—from human consciousness, which was becoming increasingly devouring and destructive, and not in a natural way. And someone was rounding them up and setting them on their path. But who?

She realised that whoever was doing it could not be another human. It had to be someone with a mission contrary to her own. In the Otherworld, they could see impending disaster, and knew they had to mobilise to meet the threat. That was why she was here, after all. But who would be in favor of destroying this universe—and at least a thousand others?

A name jumped into her head. But she was ready to dismiss it—surely he was not stupid enough to oppose her? It then occurred to her that he would not directly oppose her; he would work behind the scenes. She was starting to connect the dots between different events in her life that had been a mystery even to her. And it made her extremely angry—angry enough that she had to willfully calm herself down. She had to reserve that anger for the right time.

24

I'd reached a point where things were going from bad to worse. Previously I'd felt a heaviness in the house, and a depression. But after my visit with Darryl, other things started to happen.

For one thing, I started hearing voices and seeing shadows in the hallway. I'd hear doors open and then slam shut. Sometimes I would get up to investigate, and there was never anything there. Once I would go back to bed, the voices would resume, and footsteps. I was too exhausted, and frankly terrified, to try to find out more.

I had resolved to go into the attic and find the amulet that Layla had given me, but I had put it off. Something kept holding me back. First, I would think that the gris-gris was sufficient for now, I didn't have to take that step yet. But as things got worse, I knew I had to act, and I was afraid. I didn't know if I'd survive the visit upstairs. And what if it wasn't there?

Every time I would decide to go to the attic, the activity would stop, and it would stop for days. Looking back, it seems like the thing plaguing me was buying itself time, trying to make me weaker. My health was not improving, and I was finding my support dwindling away. My children stopped coming over, my phone conversations were interrupted by a weird static out of nowhere.

All at once, activity escalated. Now I was seeing items being thrown across the room of their own volition; I had to be careful that I didn't get slammed in the head by something. Books flew off of shelves, and the temperature in the house became intolerably cold. I went to bed scared to death, and if I managed to sleep, I woke up scared to death as well. I was barely eating, and trying to stay holed up in my room with my protection. I didn't really know if it was working at this point.

Then letters started coming in from creditors; my money wasn't covering my payments, and I was in serious danger of administration. It made no sense to me, until I logged into my accounts. Inexplicably, my money had been disappearing. I called my bank, and they saw the large withdrawals, but it was impossible to see who was taking them out.

This was too much; I was really ill at this point, had no help, and was now in danger of losing everything. I pulled together the last of my nerve, and made my way up to the attic.

25

Layla's Account, told to a Gathering of Family Members

The university was about to embark on a huge international project in quantum mechanics, which was going to require new facilities with newer technology. In particular, we needed new high-level computers for research into artificial intelligence. I was also working on some other projects related to holographic universes. My colleagues of course didn't know that I already had a full idea of how all of it worked; it was just a matter of making it demonstrable in these dimensions, under laboratory conditions. This was a rather expensive proposition.

So, I was sent with Chris and a couple of others to Parliament, to see if we could lobby the Science and Technology Committee for funding. It was not the first time I'd been sent on such a missive, and I was usually successful at securing funds for different projects. Much of it was demonstrating how the potential results would be useful to the nation at large, and the government in particular. I found this kind of salesmanship to be tedious, honestly, but it was necessary.

Chris wanted us to go down together, but for some reason I decided to drive myself. We were put up in a hotel in the West End, a bit outside of Central London. We had been given security clearance to enter, and spent a couple of days making presentations. It appeared that we were going to be successful in securing about two million pounds for the work at hand. I wish I could say I was excited by the result, but I was rather restless these days.

Maybe it was restlessness and boredom, but I had a hard time focusing once the task at hand was done. I felt like something was not right, something needed my attention.

I would find out what the trouble was soon enough.

26

Malcolm's Account told to an Anonymous Friend

My heart was beating, and I was sweating, but I was determined to not to be beaten. Taking a deep breath, I charged up the stairs and opened the attic door, propping it open with a box. I looked with some dismay at all the boxes with Layla's things—photographs and other mementos. It did not appear I was going to find it quickly. Oh well, I needed to make a start…

I started ripping open boxes and going through them as fast as I could. I was sneezing like crazy from the dust, and my eyes were watering. I went through almost every box…and then I opened the last one.

And there it was. Sitting at the bottom.

"It" was a strange kind of object on a chain. It was long and slender like a rod, but with various curves in it, ending in a shape like a sloping "M" with an arrow. As soon as I held it in my hand, all hell broke loose. Boxes started moving in front of me, trying to block my way out of the room. Panicked, I frantically pulled things out of the way and headed for the door. A large box suddenly moved in the way, and I had great difficulty in moving it.

I am NOT going to come this far and lose…I will NOT let this thing win…

I stopped and took some deep breaths. My chest was starting to hurt. Nonetheless, I shoved as hard as I could and managed to slip through the opening into the hallway. As I reached the stairs, I felt like someone behind me was trying to push me down; I held on to the railing for dear life and made my way down. Doors slammed as I ran, and I made my way to the room where I had done my crude magical practices, frantically grabbing for a piece of chalk to draw a circle around myself for some kind of meagre protection.

And then I saw it for the first time.

Outside the circle, the thing materialised. I expected it to be something tall, but it really wasn't–it seemed to be just under six feet. The eyes were a yellow color, and the skin was leathery and a strange dark colour, almost a greenish, brownish, blackish look. It had long yellowed fingernails, and bared teeth at me that were long and sharp, like fine needles. I pissed myself at the sight of it. It growled at me, and I could hear it speaking, but I couldn't understand the language. It gave off a foul odor, like decaying flesh. I would have assumed it was a demon, but something told me it wasn't. It was something else.

I could now hear it speaking to me in my head. It told me that my efforts were futile, that I was done, and it was going to have its victory over me–and over the Morrigan. As soon as I heard this, it confirmed for me what I'd suspected since visiting Darryl; this thing, whatever it was, had insinuated itself between Layla and I, trapping me in a weak position and keeping her away. But this also made me realise in an instant that she was more than a match for it.

My terror turned to anger, and I clutched the amulet tight, my hand bleeding from the sharp edges. I had to remember the words–I gasped them out in syllables–"Cusnin Macha may chay go will igla urm."

It was only a few moments, but it felt like an eternity. The thing gave an angry hiss and started to move toward me. I felt

like I was suffocating, and it swiped at me. I felt a burning
sensation on my arm where it hit me. I was losing consciousness.

27

Layla's Account, told to a Gathering of Family Members

    The group of us went to a pub not far from the hotel for drinks, not only to celebrate getting funding, but to sort out any last minute details among ourselves. I felt a strange static in my head, and I could not focus on anything anyone was saying. I knew something was very wrong.

    Then suddenly I heard the words--*Cosnaíonn Macha mé cé go bhfuil eagla orm.*

    I immediately grabbed my things and ran for the door. Chris followed after me, but I told him I'd call him later. I left the bewildered group and headed out like a shot.

    That was what I taught my father to say if he was in trouble.

    Fortunately, we were staying very close to his neighbourhood, and I was able to get to the house in no time at all. I burst the door open and ran in; the stench of decay was everywhere, and I already knew what was happening. Once again, for the second time in my semi-human life, the Babd took over.

28

Mila's Vision, in Layla's Voice

I saw my father, nearly dead on the floor, and a familiar form standing over him.

Duncluan.

Now I was purple with rage. He was too cowardly to fight me face to face, he and his ilk had lost the battle with me, so he was going to try to have his revenge by destroying my mission, my father, and in some fashion—me. I grabbed him by the neck and dragged him out of the room, kicking the door shut. I then gave out a roar that nearly shook the house to its foundations. I could see the look of anger, hatred, and terror on Duncluan's face. He fought back, but he was no match. I shifted into my battle form, and drove my axe through the middle of his forehead, and then cut off his head and smashed open his ribs and his innards. I then called out the song that opened a portal to the Otherworld; when I saw through the gates, I was looking at his piece of the island, on the North side. I took his body and tossed it over. Then I stepped in, took his head, and placed it on a broken down, wizened tree. I then returned to the other side, and closed the portal, drawing my sigil on the wall.

I pushed open the door to the room where I'd left my father. He was barely conscious, but I knew he was alive. I could see the bloody marks on his arm; he was pale, almost a sickly green in his skin. His breathing was laboured. I lifted him up, and he opened his eyes and looked at me. There was a sadness and a fear in his face. I could hear his thoughts; he was grateful that I had come, and ashamed of his own weakness. I could see that he'd also wet himself. I picked him up like a baby and carried him to the bathroom. "Come on," I said gently. "I need to get you cleaned up and treated."

29

Mila's Vision, in Layla's Voice

I undressed him and threw his clothes to the side, turning on the shower and helping him in, holding him up with one hand and washing him with the other. When we finished, I dried him off and treated the claw marks on his arm. I got him fresh clothes and dressed him, putting him in his bed sitting up. The entire time he was trying to talk to me between gasps and sobs; he was trembling. He continually repeated to me, "I am so sorry. I am so sorry."

Finally I said, "Enough! We will not speak of that now. There will be plenty of time to talk about what's happened. I need to get you sorted out. Does anyone else live here besides you?"

"I've had various girlfriends in and out, but no one has been here in awhile—not even any of my other children."

I glanced around the house. The place was a mess. "When did you last eat?"

"I can't quite remember. I've been too sick to eat."

"Are you on medicines?"

"Yes, for my heart and blood pressure, and for depression. They're in the cabinet in the bath."

I went to the cabinet and found all the bottles, bringing them in. "This is what you've been taking?"

He nodded.

I examined the pills. I am not a medical doctor, but I realised that something wasn't right. I looked at the labels on the bottles. "These are the bottles they came in?"

He looked at me with some puzzlement. "Yes…yes they are. Why?"

I shook my head. "Because I do not think that what it says on the bottle is what is actually in the bottle. In any case, you're not taking any more of this rubbish." I took all of them and flushed them down the toilet." I went back to the room and stared at him. "You're in my care now."

He looked at me, and I could see some ambivalence in his face. On the one hand, I think he was deeply relieved that I was there. On the other, I think he wasn't sure if I wasn't going to rake him over the coals for his treatment of me. For the moment I did not solve his conundrum.

I handed him his phone. "Call Anika, tell her to come over." He obeyed, and she turned up about an hour later. She came running up the stairs toward me, and grabbed me in a hug, tears streaming down her face. "I never thought I'd see you again." I was tempted to note that I'd been around for years; early on it may have been difficult, if not impossible, to find me. In later years, I had a career and a reputation—even a Wikipedia page. I was not that hard to locate. But, like my father's apologies, I let that go by for the moment. In all truth, I had missed my family, and it soothed my broken heart to be there with them again, and to be wanted.

We chatted briefly, and then I started asking both of them questions about Daddy's state of affairs. When he told me about everything—the financial issues, health issues, the things in the house—I knew I had a huge mess to clean up. I sat down and sighed, trying to decide where to begin. I looked at Anika. "Could you do me a favour?"

"Yes, anything!"

"Could you run to the store and pick up something for us to eat, something takeaway? Daddy hasn't eaten—I'd get something lighter for him. And if you would for me too—and yourself, if you haven't eaten."

"Yes, of course! I'll head out now." I was going to give her money, but she waved it away. "No worries, I have it covered. I'll be back very soon."

After she exited, I pulled out my own tablet, and set it up on my own hotspot network. I brought my father into his office, and we sat down together, logging into his accounts. I took a lot of notes, and examined the losses on his accounts. I then logged into Tor on my own computer, and began my own rather nefarious journey through the world of stolen funds. My father watched me, wide-eyed.

"Are you…are you on that deep Web thing?"

I did not turn my head. "Yes."

We were both silent, and to make the long story short, I managed to recover his funds and put them back into his account. I then added myself to all his accounts, and changed his passwords to really complicated ones, setting up duo authentication where I could. There would be no more hacking into his accounts.

"Now," I said. "Let me get these outstanding bills settled. But you are going to sell the house; I don't think you should be here by yourself at this point."

"Where will I go?"

I looked at him pointedly. "You're moving in with me."

He blinked at this imperative, but he did not argue with me. All he said was, "It will be strange not to be in London..."

I shrugged. "You will like the area. Chester is the closest town, and it's decent; there's enough around. No, it isn't London, but frankly you need to be out in the country, in better air. And it's obvious that you make shite decisions by yourself, so I need to watch over you. And..."

"And what?"

I looked at him. "You owe me."

I saw a flash of fear in his face. "Oh, stop with that," I said. "If I'd wanted to destroy you, I would have done it a long time ago. Now that we both know what caused the split—well, that does ease up a lot of things. But we will still have to talk. And there are still things you need to help me with."

"Like what?"

"Don't ask me now. Let's finish getting this sorted." I called his creditors, and got the bills taken care of right away. I then called a local realtor, and a moving company. When I was finished, I turned to him. "Okay. You're sorted out financially. I'm having the realtor put the house on the market this week; it will probably sell quickly. And the movers are coming over the next two days; I'm getting boxes tomorrow morning, and they will take everything away the next day. Your furniture will go in storage, we'll bring valuable things in my car, and the rest will be brought up by them."

"In two days? That's really fast, isn't it?" I could tell he really hadn't had time to absorb what just happened. Anika appeared with dinner, and we went downstairs to eat together. I reiterated the plan, and she had a similar reaction. But I shook my head.

"If I hadn't come today, you wouldn't be alive. While there were external factors that weren't your fault, a lot of what has happened occurred because you're weak, both mentally and physically, and make poor decisions. I never should have left you, and your life would have been very different. However, here we are, and honestly, things could be a lot worse."

Anika turned to me. "What exactly has been going on? I've really hated coming here lately, and I'm seeing what a mess the place is now. I feel like…I don't know, like something has been here that doesn't want us here."

Malcolm explained the chain of events that lead to my coming here, and I could see Anika turn pale. Anika understood very little about who I was or where I came from, so I doubted she really understood what it all meant. I leaned over. "When we all get together to talk about everything, I should be able to fill in some gaps for you. For right now, let's just focus on getting Daddy sorted out. You can come visit me in Cheshire; there's a train that goes there from London, I can pick you up and you can stay a couple of days, once everything is settled."

The conversation then turned to more mundane matters, and we talked for a surprisingly long time. I realised that I had not been back to my hotel, nor had I touched base with my colleagues. Anika had to leave soon, so I hustled over to the hotel to check out and get my car; I would now be staying with my father until we left. Anika stayed a little longer when I returned, and then left for home, promising to return the next day to help out. I then got my father upstairs and into his bed.

"Layla?"

"Yes?"

"Will you stay up and watch telly with me?" This was something we did all the time when I was a child, and one of the things I had missed.

"Yes, I will," I said. "Just let me straighten things up a bit first." The house was still a wreck with thrown books, furniture, and broken objects. It took me about an hour, but I got things in some semblance of order. In the last room—where I'd found him —the amulet was on the floor, with some blood around the edges. I picked it up, wiped it off, and brought it into the bedroom. I then went out and called Chris, to give him a very brief rundown of events; I only told him that my father had needed help, and that I needed to be here for a couple of days. If I had any other business for work, I could take care of it tomorrow. He assured me that we could talk again back in the office; it was clear that he wanted more information about what was going on, but there was no time. I wasn't really sure how much I should tell him anyway.

30

I remember the day my sister Anika called me, to tell me that our father was moving out of London. He had not been well for some time, and I knew he was having some problems. I tried to go to see him as often as I could, but work obligations had kept me away. I'd wondered how long he would stay in that house; I guess the idea that he would move was not a surprise.

What was a surprise was that I had another sister. Anika told me about Layla. I thought I'd heard her name spoken in the past. In fact—I think my father was in an argument with Steffan Brown, and her name came up. I was very young at the time, and had no idea who or what they were talking about; all I knew was that Steffan was very angry with my father, and that we didn't see him again after that.

I could not imagine why my father would not have told me about my sister; it was bizarre. Anika tried to fill me in on some of the details. She didn't know much herself, all she knew was that Layla had been very suddenly put out of the house at the age of thirteen, and sent to boarding school. The one time she did come home for Christmas she was met with hostility, and she had not returned again, until now.

"Wait, I'm confused—why was he hostile to her? What did she do?"

"As far as I can tell, nothing," said Anika. "I was not allowed to talk to her, and I was scared to death of what was going on. I managed to talk to her for a few seconds, and asked her what happened. She told me she didn't know, and it was clear she was devastated. My heart just broke; I couldn't understand what was happening, and she and I had been fairly close. She was definitely Daddy's favourite, so this made no sense at all. And I worried that if I stepped out of line, he might get rid of me, too."

"That is really fucked up, if you don't mind me saying so."

"I don't disagree. But we all gave the subject a wide berth. In retrospect, I think we were all cowards. But things seem to have really gotten bad for Daddy after she left, and when I got to the house yesterday, everything was in a disarray—it was like he was attacked by something. And somehow he knew how to call Layla for help, even though he hasn't been in contact with her in years. He was lucky, because she happened to be only a couple of blocks away—she had business at Parliament, apparently, and was staying nearby."

"Does she work for the government?"

"No, I don't think so—she's a theoretical physicist. I think she was with a group from her university looking for government funding."

I whistled. "She must be very smart if she's doing that for a living."

Anika's voice became very serious. "Yes, she's smart. In fact, she knows everything."

"I beg your pardon?"

"You'll see when you meet her. I'm going over to Daddy's tomorrow to see if I can help at all with packing."

"Wait—he's moving now?"

"Yes. He's moving in with her. She lives up in Cheshire in a big house, apparently."

"Is she married?"

"No, I don't think so."

The whole thing seemed really weird to me. "Okay, I'll make a point of coming over tomorrow. I'm very much interested in meeting my sister."

So, it was settled. I headed over the next day, just after lunchtime. The whole house was almost fully packed already, and the furniture had been corralled in one room for the movers. Anika was there, so I greeted her. My father came into the front room, and greeted me. "Hello Mal! Glad you could drop in before I go."

"Yeah, Anika told me yesterday. This seems sudden. And who is this other sister I have?"

"Ah, yes—Layla. You need to come and meet her."

"Why did I never know about her?"

My father's face changed; he had a rather sad and almost guilty look on his face. "I made some terrible mistakes. Layla has asked me not to discuss them now, but we will get a chance to all talk about everything. Here she comes."

I was not prepared for the woman who came down the stairs towards us. She looked a lot like my father, but there were some key differences. Her eyes were a deep purplish-violet colour; I'd wondered if she wore fake lenses. As it turns out, she didn't. She had long rippling black hair, and she was about average height, and very slender. But she gave off—I don't know what you call it—some kind of aura, or energy or...something... that hit you like a tidal wave. She was unbelievably beautiful, but there was also something unnatural about her—I couldn't put my finger on it. When she came over and we were introduced, we shook hands, and I noticed her long fingers—and she only had three on the right hand, kind of like a claw. She was soft spoken like my father, and very even tempered.

We exchanged pleasantries, and she told me that she was moving my father to her house. She wanted all of us to come up once he was settled in. I had a lot of questions for her, but it was clear that for today she wanted to finish up business before the movers came. She went back to moving boxes, and that's when I noticed that she was unnaturally strong. She could pick up very heavy items like they were nothing at all and move them around. She found some things for Anika and I to help with, and we all got busy.

We had a long day at the house, and I decided to crash there rather than go all the way home. I slept in one of the bedrooms that still had a bed in it. The movers were coming around noon the next day, so I would have to be up early and have it ready to be packed. I slept very easily, as I was exhausted.

When I got up the next day, Layla was already up, and my father had recently awakened. She was sitting in front of a mirror in her room, brushing her long hair. I saw my father come up behind her, and he spoke her name, as a question. "Layla?"

"Mm-hmm?"

"Can I…I mean I've missed doing it…can I brush your hair?"

She shrugged. "Okay, if you want to." She handed him the brush, and he began.

I watched them from across the hall, and a weird, unsettled feeling came over me. Why was he doing that? Maybe he was just feeling sad and nostalgic for when she was a little girl, when in all likelihood he did brush her hair every day. But something about it bothered me.

Later, we went downstairs, and Layla prepared a rather meagre breakfast for us, as most of the kitchen stuff was already packed away. But as she was working at the counter, I saw my father go up behind her, and touch her back. I got that unsettled feeling again; there was something in the way he looked at her, and stroked her…it just felt wrong. I looked at Layla, and she didn't seem to react one way or the other.

Soon we had cleaned up from the morning, and the movers came. Anika had also dropped by again; once everything was done she was going to bring me back home. The whole process was amazingly fast; Layla had done an excellent job of organising everything, so that things could easily be loaded in order, and taken out again in the way she wanted it at her place. She stood there in a long-sleeved black boatneck shirt and jeans; very ordinary attire, but it somehow made her seem magical. Or—maybe that's just how she was…I really did not know her yet. But I was starting to form some ideas about her relationship to my father, and perhaps why they hadn't spoken in years.

Anika and I watched as they got into her Mercedes, and with a final wave, they took off.

***

Now that they were gone, we left the empty house. The keys had been put in a lock box for the realtor, and a chapter was now closed on our lives. Now that we were away from the house, Anika and I talked more about the events of the last few days. I hesitated as to whether I should tell her what I thought; I finally decided to just say it.

"Anika?"

"Yes?"

"You grew up with Layla; what was her relationship with Daddy like?"

She was thoughtful. "She was with him all the time. He took her on tour with him, and it kind of felt like he was afraid to leave her in anyone else's care. She was even tutored for years, rather than going to regular school, because he wanted her around all the time."

"Did he…well, I mean…was he very physical with her?"

Anika gave me a surprised look. "What do you mean?"

I sighed. "Look–I don't know her as well as you do, and I didn't grow up around her. She seems okay to me, though I just have a really strange vibe about her–like there's something…" I was searching for the word–"Supernatural."

Anika nodded. "Now you know what I mean when I said she knows everything."

"Does she?"

"Oh yes. Most things. She can tell you what will happen before it does. She's gotten Daddy out of a bind I don't know how many times, and it appears she's done it again. I guess the only thing she didn't know was why he abandoned her–unless she knows now."

"Hmm. Well, okay, there's that–and something else." Anika looked at me expectantly.

"I don't like the way he touches her."

"Really?? I hadn't paid any attention, to be honest."

I related what I had seen that morning, and Anika gasped. "My God—do you think—I mean she is REALLY beautiful…but he is her father…our father…"

"Yeah, well I hate to say it—he's our father and we love him, but he's not always had the best sense of ethics in that area. It's like he's transfixed by her, but she's not doing anything to encourage him. She seems to act like it's normal."

Anika tapped her finger on the steering wheel thoughtfully. "You know…" she said slowly, "I'm starting to think…and you may be right, that may not be something new. He did some odd things to her at times, things he didn't do to me. But he mostly did them when he didn't think anyone was looking."

"Like what?"

"Well, it's hard to describe. He would pick her up and put her on his lap, and it was the way he held her, like he was pushing himself against her…I thought it was weird, but I was too young to think of it as anything else. But I guess it made something of an impression on me. I also remember Layla mentioning offhandedly to me once that she always slept in Daddy's bed if my mother and I were away. That doesn't mean anything went on…but…Jesus, I hope not!"

"Okay, this whole thing is just really—disturbing. And now he's going to live in her house? If she knows everything, she must know that. But I wonder if it's just normal to her, if he's always done it? And did he send her away because, well because he possibly got out of control with the whole thing?"

"Out of control?"

"Yeah—as in—maybe he took a step he shouldn't have taken. Hugging and kissing is one thing, there's still a line, but that's up for interpretation. Beyond that…"

Anika looked a bit shaken. "You know, I just don't want to think about it. It's possible you are right, but I really hope there's another explanation. We may be just reading into this. Daddy may just be really glad to have her back and really regretful about sending her away—that may be why he's so touchy with her now. And I was only a child—I could have misread the whole situation."

"Maybe. I don't know. I'm sorry I brought it up, I'm not looking to accuse Dad of anything, I have no idea that he's actually guilty of anything. But it was just unnerving. Maybe it's just me."

***

Malcolm's Reflections as told to an Anonymous Friend

As we pulled out of the driveway, I knew I probably wouldn't see London again—or, at least not very often. I felt a twinge of nostalgia, and I was a little nervous about what was ahead. Layla had not shown any anger toward me in these last few days, but she was also somewhat chilly. She was all business and had showed very little emotion in either direction. In any event, she was hard to read, and it made me a bit uncomfortable. Would the floodgates open once I moved in?

I knew Layla could read thoughts, but if she read mine at that moment, she didn't comment on it. Instead we talked about her job, and about the house she'd just renovated. She gave me a very abbreviated version of her movement from the Cedrig

School to Oxford, and had mentioned she'd had a boyfriend there—the last time she'd bothered dating anyone. I was glad to hear that she had some kind of love relationship, but I couldn't understand why she chose to be so solitary.

She gave me a look. "Maybe because I'd spent my teen years learning not to trust men." Then she relented. "No, I shouldn't bring that up. We will have that conversation later. Honestly, I've learned more in the past few days than I had in thirty-five years."

"But who—or what—was influencing me?"

"His name is Duncluan. You know that I come from the De Dananns. Well, the De Dananns aren't the only ones in the Otherworld. Fairy lore didn't arise out of nowhere. There are fairy folk of all types, and Duncluan belongs to a group known as *dulbodach,* which roughly translates to dark elves or bogeys, or something like that. De Dananns were always at war with Firbolgs and Fomorians, but now they've been united—and I am the queen of all groups. For the most part this is fine, but you can't please everyone, as they say. Duncluan was a very powerful member of this race, and he was furiously angry when Fomor made a treaty with us. He and I have gone at it in the past, and he has always lost. He doesn't have any friends among most of his Fomorian kin, though he does have a few allies from his own tribe, as you might imagine. So, he doesn't dare try to challenge me directly. Apparently what he has done—and he did an excellent job of hiding himself, because I truly did not see it—is influence you, because he knows I am attached to you, and that you are not, well, not exactly…" she searched for a diplomatic word. "…the strongest person or best decision maker." She glanced at me, and I could only nod my assent. I liked to believe I had it all together, but if I was honest, I'd bungled my way into everything in life.

She continued: "When you were really addicted to the hard drugs, he made his move, and did he ever manipulate you—you were like a marionette on strings. All of the vile things you said—I even felt at the time that they couldn't be coming from you, but I couldn't see where else they were coming from. If he was looking to blindside me, he succeeded." Her face was grim for a moment. "In any case—once he had a hold of you, he thought it would be fun to destroy you slowly. That's the way he thinks. And he kept up the lies about me that you told yourself, because it kept me away. Once you started to have an awareness of what was going on, he got more forceful, and tried to finish you off. I guess it's to your credit that you got your shit together and found that amulet." I shuddered, thinking about those last moments before Layla arrived…

"What happened to him?"

"Oh, I finally finished him off, and tossed his various limbs into the Otherworld—I opened a portal, which has been shut again—the new owners of your house will not be affected by it. Once I realised what was going on I was enraged—furiously enraged. There has only been one other occasion where I have felt that much rage, enough to obliterate my enemy."

"When was that?"

She shook her head. "I will tell you about that, but not now. As I said a few days ago, you are still regaining your strength. I want your heart, your breathing, and your general health to be better before we get into the details of anything."

31

Anika's Reflections, told in an Interview with Mila Fell

My father had moved in with Layla at the start of Autumn, so it was mid-October before we headed up to Cheshire. My brother Malcolm and I took the train together, and Layla met us at the station, to drive us back to the house. It wasn't a long drive; we were there in about fifteen minutes. The house was on a side road in a neighborhood that was not entirely rural, but Layla's house was the last one on that block, and it bordered some woodland and a stream, so she had a few acres of property. The house itself was gorgeous, and much larger than I would have thought. Layla said it had been a tavern in the 1500s, and had been in and out of use for years before falling into decay. The building and property were cheap; her main expense had been fixing it up, but she saved a lot by doing it herself. When she showed us photos of the original property, I could not believe how much work she had done; it seemed clear she could do anything.

When we came in, my father was in the parlour, and came to greet us. I was pleased to see him looking well; he looked rested, his colouring was good, and he even seemed a bit younger to me. It reminded me how ill he'd been for so long. His strength and energy seemed to be back as well. The inside of the house was beautiful, and the shared space was very cosy, with a sunken-in floor and a fireplace. She showed my brother and I to our rooms, as we were going to stay for a couple of days. The view outside was breathtaking; you could see her

English garden below, and the fields and trees beyond it. It was a very restful scene, and it made me glad I was away from the bustle of London streets.

We were not the only visitors; several of my father's close friends, including Joe, Tom, and Steve Abbott, were coming over. Steffan Brown was also coming over, the first time he was really going to speak to my father again after all those years. This was shaping up to be a potentially emotional and explosive gathering. While everyone exchanged happy greetings, there was still a sense of underlying awkwardness and tension. Everyone had so many questions, and I could understand why Layla wanted him to be in better shape before having a conversation. But we all had questions for Layla as well.

After some drinks and a late lunch, we all sat down in the front room to talk. Layla first told her horrific account of things at the boarding school, and how she managed to get by after that. It shouldn't be surprising that there was a lot of alarm and anger at my father for his neglect of her. As for my father—he looked absolutely distressed about the situation. She had already had a conversation with him before the group met, apparently, and it nearly broke him in spite of his improved physical condition. Everyone in the room was looking to him for an explanation. He sat with his head in his hands, but finally he raised himself up and spoke.

"I don't...I don't even know how to address this. I guess I have to start by saying that everything I did in this case was wrong. Layla had not done anything that should have caused me to treat her that way. And many of you," he said, looking over at Steffan, Tom and Joe, "confronted me about her welfare, and I also did not respond in a way that should make you ever want to speak to me again. I know that no one has any pity for me, and they really shouldn't. The only thing I can say in my defence is that I was not myself when I made all these decisions. It was like something was driving me away from Layla—something external."

Steffan, who was somewhat unconvinced by this speech, asked "What do you mean 'something external'?"

My father gave a deep sigh. "I don't...I don't know how to explain it to you. It was like a constant voice in my head telling me she had to go, that some of the issues I was having...with her...was her trying to hurt me."

Steffan leaned forward. "What issues?"

"I was afraid you would ask that. Well, I may as well admit it—I was going to a therapist, because I started to really desire her in a way that was inappropriate. She's a beautiful girl, and as she was now becoming a woman and growing up...I don't know. I started to think and feel things that alarmed me. I wanted to keep her away from me, to not do anything that I shouldn't. Ultimately, that put a rift between us."

"But," Steffan went on, "why then, didn't you both go to counseling? Or, why didn't you tell her the truth, and send her away for her safety, but try to work on it?"

"Well, that's just it—that would have been the right thing to do, I agree. But I felt like I was influenced by something else—some other voice..."

"Are you saying you're schizophrenic? Or possessed?"

"I don't know. At the moment I don't think I'm either. But I definitely had a rage in me, that she had somehow wronged me and I had to keep her away. I hated being questioned about it, because the reality was that I had no cause. When I look at it now, I'm horrified—I drove away the girl who was one of the best things that ever happened to me." He put his head down and began to weep. Some people felt sorry for him, but it was clear that many were not convinced.

"Look, Malcolm," said Tom. "You were pretty set on not talking to her, and on keeping others away from her. I agree that it didn't seem like you at all. I know you were doing a lot of drugs then, maybe that affected you, but it really doesn't add up. Like Steffan said, I could see you keeping a distance, and working with her on it, but not just totally abandoning her with no support."

My father didn't make much of a reply to this; it was clear that there was some piece of this that he was not sharing. "You're right Tom—as I said, it was the totally wrong thing to do, but I couldn't stop myself from doing it."

"Why not?"

Layla suddenly jumped in. "You know, I'd wondered for years what happened. I think the reason I did not totally write my father off was because I felt there was a missing piece, there was something not right. I'm good at seeing all angles of everything, but I just couldn't see what was happening here. As it turns out, there is a reason he did what he did—and he's not giving you a line of bullshit. He was influenced, as I saw firsthand."

Now we were all interested, but Layla was somewhat cagey about the details. "Let's just say when I got the call for help, I came into the house and found that—something else was there. Something really trying to do him in. And I recognised that something, and realised that this was what I was missing all along."

"Wait—first, how did your father contact you?" asked Steffan.

Layla gave him a rather mysterious look. "I just heard him. It was ringing in my ears. He didn't use a phone, or anything like that. I just heard him."

"You mean like you had a psychic intuition?"

"Something like that." Steffan was sceptical, but he also remembered that Layla did seem to have some strange abilities. He pressed on—"But it seems to me that you're not angry with him. If you'll forgive me—it would be hard for me not to be angry with him if I was in your shoes."

She nodded. "I wouldn't assume that I've just brushed everything aside. Daddy and I have talked about all of that already. He still owes me. And that's why he's here."

***

Collected Reflections, and Notes from an Interview with Steve Abbott

A lot of questions were asked that day, and there were some answers, some closure—but many felt that there were still gaps in the narrative. Malcolm had always been secret about Layla's origins, and it seemed like this filtered over into the situation in some way. Overall, it was good that Layla and her father had made amends to some degree, but they wondered about why she wasn't angrier about the outcome. They couldn't buy Malcolm's "possession" story, and it was hard to believe that she would either, given her obvious intelligence. But ultimately it was between the two of them, and if "all's well that ends well," it wasn't really their place to argue.

337

But Malcolm Jr. still had a lot of questions. His father's account of his feelings when she was younger just proved to him that he was right, and he doubted that his father was set on "doing the right thing" ethically. Something was still unbelievably off, in his mind. But they both seemed to behave normally during their visit on the whole; he didn't see evidence of his father's uncomfortable touching, so maybe he'd imagined the whole thing, or was just very intuitive about the initial problem.

Over the next couple of days the visitors filtered out. The last one remaining was Steve Abbott. Steve had not been particularly close to Layla; he'd seen her a few times on tours, and spent a little more time getting to know her before her father sent her away. But he didn't have the kind of relationship with her that Malcolm's other bandmates had.

Steve had plans to leave that afternoon; he was taking a later train, to get to his mother's house by dinnertime. It didn't make sense for him to go home first. After having breakfast with Malcolm and Layla, she motioned for him to come into the front room, and turned to him with a very focused look.

"Steve, we don't know each other very well—at least not here—but I should tell you that you're very important to me, and to my work."

Steve stared at her; he was not sure how to respond to this. "Okay…"

Layla sat down and leaned forward. "Do you understand the idea of multiple universes? Parallel ones?"

"Um…er…I've heard of it. I can't say I know anything about it."

"Well, it's a bit like this. We are running on a timeline, with certain events, in this universe that we're experiencing. But this is not the only one. There are many others—in fact, the number of possibilities is so huge, there's not even a nameable number for it—it can only be expressed exponentially. Still, the possibilities are finite. Which means that at least in some of these universes, the people and things in them repeat, though not necessarily the timeline."

"Okay…" I sort of understood, but I wasn't sure where she was going with this.

She sat back. "Right. So—the things that have happened in this life have happened on a particular timeline. But—in another timeline—a pretty critical one—all of us are there, but the whole situation is playing out differently." She paused. I still did not know how to respond, so I waited for her to continue. "In this other critical universe, you have a huge role to play in the timeline."

"I do?"

"Yes."

"In what way?"

"Well, first of all, you need to understand what's different about me. I was very hesitant to tell the group at large, and frankly, I doubt you're going to believe much of it either. But there's a reason my father and I don't talk about my mother." She then rose up. "Wait here—I am going to show you."

I was still confused, but now very interested. I didn't know why I should be the person to learn the secret, but I had a feeling more was coming. She returned with an old photo album.

"Okay," she said. "My father and mother are the same person. My father is the one who gave birth to me." I stared at her in disbelief. "Here, I will show you."

I paged through the photo album she showed me. They were somewhat gruesome photos, as it clearly required a surgery to remove her from…a womb? He obviously wouldn't have had one of those, but it was also obvious that a child was taken from the lower part of his body. I was speechless.

"So…what does this mean?"

"Well, I didn't just come from nowhere. You know my father dabbles in magic; or at least you may have heard rumours. In any case, he's not terribly good at it. He was doing an evocation, and opened up a door—I took the opportunity to slip in and be born into this world."

"But then…what were you before?"

She smiled "I am the Morrigan."

The name was familiar to me, but I had to ultimately profess ignorance. "If the name is known to you at all, it would be as the Irish goddess of war. All the writings about me that are still around are transcriptions made by Christian monks, so as you might imagine they are barely accurate. A tremendous amount is left out, and everything left in is designed to create a narrative that glorifies Christianity and debases the rest of us. But my reason for coming here now is that you're all in trouble."

Malcolm had been hovering in the background, but now he sat down and joined us. He seemed a bit nervous, and I'm not sure he was entirely comfortable that she was giving me all the background. He was a bit puzzled, and honestly, so was I.

"What kind of trouble?" Malcolm asked.

"It's a lot to talk about—I'm not sure I want to get into it at the moment," said Layla. "But I do want Steve to know why you sent me away."

Malcolm and I looked at each other; he looked at me curiously, his eyes saying, "Why you, of all people?" Not her siblings not the people who had known her forever…

Layla leaned forward, looking at me. "Just as there are different universes and worlds, there are different kinds of beings. In another world I am Queen, and I am queen over two different tribes who had always been at war. One subset of that tribe has never accepted me, and has been determined to bring me down, to interfere with my mission. Their leader is the one who influenced my father."

"What—you mean like a demon of some sort?"

"No, not exactly. The term 'demon' tends to be a catchall for every type of being that humans don't understand and perceive as negative. He is definitely negative, and has definitely been a nuisance, if not an outright threat. But I have finally destroyed him. In another timeline, a human warrior who I bring over to the other side destroys him. You are the one who helped me do that."

"Really?" This was getting to be very strange. I was uncomfortable; I wasn't sure if she had gone crazy, and if she hadn't…what did this mean to me now?

Malcolm spoke up. "I know that sounds insane. But it's true—I saw this…this…whatever it was. It was terrifying. And it tried to kill me—my other children were a witness. It wanted to separate me from her, and it did a good job of it. I had no idea I was being influenced. I would never have thought it was that kind of a creature; I'd given up on things like evocations several years before. It wasn't exactly the product of an evocation anyway."

"Then where did it come from?"

"It came from the same world as Layla, apparently. It's easier for them to come here than to go there, apparently. I can't tell you how weak and foolish I feel, opening myself up to that kind of deception for that long. My treatment of Layla was inexcusable, but I somehow just accepted it; it was like I couldn't think about it like a caring human being."

"Steve—the reason I want you to know about this, even if you think I'm crazy, is because we're all coming up on a rather significant event," said Layla.

Malcolm and I both looked at her with surprise. "What is that?"

"The timeline where you, Steve, are one of three individuals instrumental to the continued existence of this planet and universe is going to cross with ours very soon."

"I don't understand."

"Timelines do cross from time to time, but we often don't notice. This is going to be a much more significant crossing— there will be two of all of us, merging into one timeline. You both have to be informed about what is coming up."

I was "informed", but still understood no more than I had when I came for the visit. I frankly wondered if Layla was mentally disturbed. And I wasn't sure if I should humour her in her fancies or not.

32

Chris Wood's Reflections

When Layla just up and left our gathering in London, I was very concerned. What kind of emergency could it possibly be? When she mentioned her father, I was more curious than ever; she alleged that she didn't have a family, or that there was a decidedly permanent estrangement. And I hadn't heard her phone ring, nor did I see her check it; her facial expression had just changed, and she bolted. When she finally returned my messages later, she said she was checking out of the hotel and staying with her father. I was absolutely mystified.

Well, it didn't take long for me to learn that her father was Malcolm Black. I was gobsmacked; when I saw them together, it was obvious that they were related. The news media felt the same way, apparently–a photo of them walking to dinner in London went viral, and people were saying to themselves, "How did we not connect these two as related?" You would imagine that someone would have done it at some point.

From what I'd learned from Laura about her past and what her father had done, I really could not understand why she accepted him back into her life so readily, even enough to let him move in with her, after being reunited for less than a week. When we spoke about it, Layla would only say that things had happened out of her father's control, for which she now had first hand evidence, and thus she was inclined to help him. However, she'd also implied that he was not entirely off the hook with her. I did not know what that meant. Was she punishing him in some fashion? And how would she do that?

They certainly didn't seem to be at odds. In fact, Malcolm's behaviour towards her made me uncomfortable. I couldn't say why; just something in his body language, his way of interacting with her. When I did a little soul searching, it occurred to me that I was jealous. Was I just jealous of their closeness—maybe something, in some way, I'd wanted for myself? Or was there more to it?

One thing seemed to be certain to me: Malcolm Black had really been showing his age, but now it seemed like he was getting progressively younger. I was not aware of him going for any kind of plastic surgery, or any other kind of treatment that should produce that kind of result. In any case, if he had been getting plastic surgery, it would have been very noticeable on someone his age; there would be skin-tucks, or something like that. It never looked quite natural. However, Malcolm looked like he might have been thirty years old again, and he was at least seventy.

I casually mentioned this to Layla; her only comment was that getting out of London and being cared for by her was obviously doing him some good. I could understand an improvement in health with proper diet, exercise, and medical treatment; I could not understand how one would suddenly look so much younger. He had never been overweight, in fact he was quite skinny—and while this tended to look good on someone more youthful, it tended to make older folks look more wrinkly and aged.

So, what exactly did I think was going on? It was impossible to say; I had no scientific explanation for it, that was for sure. Maybe I was just imagining things. But Layla was

344

changing too; she'd always been a bit uncanny before, and now she seemed really strange. She informed me that she was planning to retire from the university, which was upsetting to me. She was going to stay home with her father full-time; for what, I wondered? If he doesn't need round the clock health care, there's no reason for her to be there all the time. But it seemed that Malcolm was the lynchpin in her life; now that he was there, everything else was going to come together in a different way. I just had no idea how different it would be.

33

Malcolm's Reflections as told to an Anonymous Friend

After Steve left, I had dozens of questions for Layla. What exactly was happening? There was the situation between us, and the dark elven figure that had managed to cleverly come between us. But it appeared that there was a lot more going on. Really, what did I expect? Layla clearly didn't intend to come into this world just for my entertainment. Gods don't make appearances like this without good reason.

We sat outside in the garden; everything was very neat and manicured, and even the wild fields and woods beyond seemed to fit into a perfect romantic landscape. It was hard to imagine that anything could be wrong.

But Layla assured me that not all was as well as it appeared. "Duncluan and his forces may be a minor threat, but there's also a major one coming from elsewhere."

"Where is it coming from?"

She looked at me gravely. "From humans."

I frowned. "Do you mean bad human behaviour on the planet?"

"Sort of. That's part of it. It's more about what's embedded in collective human consciousness. It's like a zombie race; everyone is looking to devour everything, they want more, they take more, and don't replace, don't honour what's already there. And it's manifesting as an entirely new race."

"Wait—how does that work? I mean, actions are one things, but thoughts are another."

"That, my love, is where you are wrong. Thoughts are extremely powerful. Didn't you do magical workings? You should know that. And what Duncluan did to you—there was no action, no physical attacks until the end. He just had to manipulate your thoughts and feelings. Thoughts are extremely powerful."

I sat back, absorbing this. "What's this about another race?"

"Ah—I call them White Watchers; I think popular culture refers to them—at least some of them—as rakes, or wendigos. They are these creepy, tall white beings with spindly legs and arms, and they are nothing but devourers; they destroy property, plants, animals, everything, and also attack humans. The problem is that humans are unable to kill them; it requires the weaponry of the Otherworld to get rid of them. I know this, because I've destroyed several myself."

"So—what does that mean? Are they planning to attack?"

"I think they are manipulated by other forces, some perhaps related to Duncluan's people, but I don't think they're the main culprits. Just as there are creative forces in the universe, there are ones looking to destroy. They're not always wrong, you know; sometimes you need to wipe clean and start over. But these are not the forces seeking to rectify any imbalances; they just want to destroy. If they destroy this world, they'll destroy the chain of connected worlds—and the Otherworld."

I felt a distinct chill in the air, and I wasn't sure if it was getting cold, or if I was just reacting to what she said. She went on. "As Queen and Protector of the Otherworld, it's my responsibility to try to stop it. In the parallel universe I mentioned, the other Layla has already gone a long way towards this goal. In this one—my role has really been to prepare the world intellectually, through what the sciences are learning and can work with. But there's a lot more that I would have liked to have done. Duncluan managed to throw a wrench into that."

"So, what does that mean? Are we doomed?"

"Fortunately, I don't think so. I think the other Layla was more outgoing, and action oriented; I think my role has been to focus more on the inner issues, the pain and emotional suffering that is also part of things. The fact that we were able to get rid of Duncluan and come back together is a big victory in itself. I would have liked to have brought Steve along a little more, and not dropped this on him at what may really be the last moment. There's not much he has to do—he only has to not resist the merging when it happens. The same goes for you."

"When is that going to happen?"

"Sooner than I would like."

PART III: MERGING SPIRALS

1

It was a beautiful day in the Northeast of Wales, along the border with England. One might say it was average; between the towns of Chester and Wrexham, the areas in between and heading north and west were no busier than usual, and there was nothing to indicate that anything was out of the ordinary.

Well, there was one thing.

Weather on the Irish Sea is often unpredictable, so when a sudden storm came up, it really didn't draw any attention. It was night time, and all it represented was a miserable evening, and staying indoors at home was the best plan. Most people did just that, and the glow of computer screens, phones, tablets, and television sets cast a bluish violet light in most homes in the area. Anyone who had been driving through at the time would have nothing to really see except the driving rain reflecting off any street lights or light from nearby houses, and their own headlamps.

What was strange that evening was not what was seen, but what was heard. The sea battered the coast as usual, but there was a strange sound, a kind of watery slurp, like something was being dragged—or dragging itself—out of the water. The dragging sound began at the shore, but it continued throughout the countryside, and the sound moved from North to Southwest. Most people didn't notice, as the noise from their own homes and the sound of the rain was sufficient to drown out everything else.

But a few people did notice, and looked out their windows. The lights were not much help in the rain, but it seemed as though something large was moving through fields and forests, but they couldn't quite see what it was. It was definitely something long, and almost serpentine. A few folks called the police, but the report wasn't taken that seriously. Others assumed that the light was playing tricks on their vision, and that it was really nothing at all.

The next morning, along the route of the sound, people who were out jogging or walking their dogs noticed a strange flattening along the fields, and downed trees in forested areas. If they had gotten closer, they would have seen a blackish substance covering these flattened areas. The only thing that really got anyone's attention was the negative reaction of their animals if they got close to the area. Dogs would start snapping and snarling, or would whimper and pull their owners in the opposite direction. It was very strange, but no one felt inclined to investigate. There was probably a rational explanation for it.

Not too far away was the hill where the two Laylas and two Steves met, unbeknownst to the locals below. As morning crept toward afternoon, more sounds could be heard, this time coming from underground. Figures began to appear from densely wooded areas, from caves, or from manholes underneath the streets. They were a milky white color, but had a glossy, slimy appearance. They looked something like humans, but their limbs were elongated, and if it wasn't for the slimy skins, they might have looked like a collection of skeletons. Their faces were horrible, and they had long jaws that hung down. All of them seemed to be moving toward the same place—toward that same hill.

As more and more of these creatures appeared, and closer to the cities, people now began to raise an alarm. Some had been curious, trying to take videos or pictures with their phones, but soon the creatures were too close, too frightening, and social media was lighting up with these images. What the hell were these things? They pushed away any obstacles in their path, and wherever they walked, any vegetation beneath their feet died. They made a horrible sound in their throats, which made them even more terrifying. People now began to flee, taking shelter wherever they could to stay out of the path of these things. No one knew what they were, or what they were doing.

What started as a few of these creatures eventually multiplied into hundreds, and soon the area was taken over. The military was dispatched, and started to fire on these creatures, to no avail. They seemed impervious to bullets and just about everything else. And all at once, all communications went dead. Electricity went out, and all Internet connectivity just died in an instant. There was widespread panic, and many injuries were sustained by people trying to get away, pushing others out of their way in desperation and falling over themselves. Some got into fights. This was not supposed to happen in these predictable Northern towns; whatever dangers might lay there were well-known ones. The scene that suddenly erupted in the middle of an ordinary Saturday, when everyone was out doing morning errands, did not seem possible. In fact, it was totally impossible. Responses were poor because no one could process what was going on.

Then all at once there was another sound.

At first there was a loud blare like some kind of trumpet. This was followed by a loud singing voice. It was a male voice, and the man was singing in an unfamiliar language. As the sound drifted closer to the crowds, and the mobs of creatures, there was a kind of hush that came over everything. No one knew where this music was coming from, but it was unearthly. Some people crossed themselves and began to pray; they felt that the end times must be here.

Then a bigger shock came, as there was a tremendous burst of light in the nearby hills, like an explosion. The fiery ball turned into what looked like a gate, and the gate swung open. And to everyone's astonishment, a very strange looking army marched through the gate. They were too far away from the city for people to see details, but many of the riders were clearly on horseback, and wore what appeared to be outfits of leather and fur. They looked a bit like Vikings, and they carried very old-fashioned but scary looking weapons; huge broadswords, maces, battle axes, all gleaming like silver in the light.

The sky overhead began to turn black and red, and a swarm of crows came rushing down at an impossible speed. The crows seemed to move together in a kind of dance, and they suddenly changed into a form—a dark form that hung in the sky, and split into three. These shapeless forms took the image of women—women with long dark hair, glowing red eyes, and terrifying faces. The middle woman gave out a scream that was so horrible, it caused bystanders in the towns several miles away to go into convulsions, have heart attacks, or bleeding from the ears. This seemed to charge up the army, and they raced down toward the white figures that had now taken over the countryside. Their weapons had an effect, as they sliced through the creatures, who gave out horrible cries as they fell to the assault of the army. Behind the army, a song was barely heard that seemed to close the supernatural gates behind them.

As this battle began to rage, some people took this as a cue to flee, others were riveted to the spot by this insane spectacle. The British military had backed off, and was left to try to observe what was happening, to try to figure out what this mysterious army was, and where it came from. They were clearly making progress against the apparently supernatural invaders, and they were a terrifying lot themselves, so no one was going to get in their way.

As the army drew closer in its assault, many of them did look like Vikings—men with long hair and beards, many seemed much older, but there were a few younger ones, most notably the blonde man who appeared to be a general or captain. They shouted orders to each other in an unintelligible language, and very quickly surrounded the white creatures, cutting off their escape and slashing brutally through their lines. There was another part of the army that was terrifying for a different reason. They all looked monstrous; some were giants, some were smaller creatures that darted in and out of the lines, but all of them looked like goblins of some sort, and when they flashed their teeth, they were long and sharp, and looked like they were made of iron. These creatures tore the white ones from limb to limb, or smashed them with great maces and axes that were made for these giants, who must have been at least fifteen feet tall.

The cacophony of the falling creatures and the roar of the army began to quiet down as the battle raged on all afternoon. It seemed like the menace of these humanoid creatures was contained.

But the army was suddenly faced with another problem.

A large, black, slithering creature was now coming toward them, breathing fire as it went out of three heads. Its skin was reptilian, and it must have been about fifty feet in length. It pulled itself along on front legs, and had a massive spiked tail. The eyes were a putrid yellow colour, and it dripped venom that hissed as it hit the ground, turning the green terrain into a sickly brown. It ambled toward the army, which paused for a moment, clearly in awe of the challenge before them.

However, it didn't take long for them to swing into action again, as they split before the beast moving toward them, flanking it from a distance on either side. The three women gave out another great roar, which stopped the beast for a moment. It seemed to glare at the women, and the women stared back at it with an equally baleful look. There was no fear in their faces; in fact, they seemed almost triumphant.

As these opponents locked eyes, there was suddenly the sound of singing again, and some shouted words in that same unintelligible language. The monster turned its head to find the source of the singing, but it was not clear who was singing. It gave a belch of fire in that direction, but the flames hit an invisible wall that turned back toward the creature, causing it to give a huge roar and back off as it burned itself. The apparent captain of the Viking-like army had drawn his bow, and charged in suddenly, shooting the monster directly in the center of its chest, and then he dashed away again with lightning speed. The arrow made a significant hit, because the creature suddenly lurched forward, spewing a blackish blood. It belched out fire again, sending the forests and the countryside up into flames. The armies were dangerously close to the flames and had to retreat, but suddenly a song came out again, and rain suddenly came pouring down, extinguishing the flames, but leaving large clouds of billowing smoke everywhere, causing anyone within viewing range of the battle to hurriedly cover their noses and mouth, lest they breath in the toxic fumes.

Finally several of the giants came along and smashed the body of the monster with their great axes, chopping it into bits. The creature was now dead, but its body was still toxic to anyone near it. The captain could be heard to call out, and everyone immediately retreated from the creature, heading back up the hill toward the three women.

The three women suddenly collapsed into one, a woman with long dark hair and violet eyes. She gave out a command, and the armies stood at attention. All at once a man wearing black appeared at her side; he was older, with short graying hair and a beard. He began to sing, and the ethereal gates opened again, the armies marching through them as he sang, and the gates swinging shut as the last warrior walked through.

The dark haired woman and the man now stood on the hill together, looking at the area, which was completely destroyed by the toxic nature of the beasts. The toxic flow had spread into the towns, and there was general panic, as emergency medical attention was needed in the area, but there were no working communications. British military soldiers had to drive to nearby towns to get any kind of help. As it turned out, telecommunications didn't just go down in the surrounding towns of Chester and Wrexham; they were out all over Britain, and much of Europe.

The man and woman conferred with each other briefly, and then went their separate ways. The woman seemed to vanish entirely, and the man went off to the West, into the woods North of the battle area. While the two had been observed, there was no time at the moment for anyone to look for them.

Army officials ordered people to stay in their houses while they investigated. The only things that remained of the great battle was the swirling ashes in the wind, a toxic odour in the air, and rows of empty wooden stakes where the severed heads of the white creatures had been.

2

Everything was quiet.

The rolling green hills were littered with broken trees and ash, and nearby towns and villages looked like natural disaster zones. Buildings were destroyed, power lines were down, piles of rubble filled the streets. A few places here and there escaped the ravage, but everyone was still without power and without any telecommunications. People wandered around in the streets, huddling in groups, trying to find out anything they could about what happened, and what was going to happen now. No one knew the extent of the damage or the death toll, and no one knew when anything like normal life was going to be restored. It was a void of smoke and ash.

Not surprisingly, there were government agents and military convoys in the area, trying to keep people out of the "ground zero" site of the battle. The whole episode was too incredible for words; two armies that didn't appear to be human battling each other, and not a vestige of either side was left on the site. Soldiers were sent to look for bodies, and they could not find a single one. There were still stakes in the ground, but the bloody heads atop those stakes had disappeared. This was not only a national emergency on the ground; it was a test of everyone's sanity.

For starters, forces had been deployed when the battle started, but had to fall back when none of their weapons worked. Not a single machine gun, assault weapon, grenade, or chemical weapon made any impact at all on the battle. It was like they were throwing rocks at a mirage. The armies on both sides were impervious to the assault; and it was like they weren't really THERE. The figures witnessed by absolutely everyone were almost entirely non-human or humanoid; no lame Defence Ministry story would be able to cover that up. But this very fact made the whole thing dubious; surely there were no such creatures, no rational person could believe it. They would have been willing to write it off as a mass hallucination if it weren't for the very obvious destruction that went on for miles. None of it made any sense.

Some postulated that some enemy force might have tainted the water supply with a hallucinogenic substance, but that was just as crazy as what was witnessed. What enemy would do that, and why? Still, the theory was pursued, but no scientist could come up with a hallucinogen that would do something like that. The water was tested, but no evidence of any nefarious substance was found.

The agents in charge of the investigation knew they could not go back to their superiors and say that "there's a lot of damage but apparently nothing happened." Answers were wanted, and it would require more digging that looking around at the site. In the meantime, those who returned to London said that there was an "assault by unknown agents" that had turned the area into a disaster zone, and immediate relief was requested.

Both the agents deployed to the site and many of the townsfolk had a common experience; they could hear singing. The voice sounded like it carried on the wind, and it was in an unfamiliar language; certainly not English, but also not any other language that anyone could identify. As soon as anyone could hear the sound, they stopped to listen. The voice was haunting, almost magical, like it was casting a spell over the landscape. It sent chills down the spine of the listeners; the terrifying visions of the day before seemed like less of a hallucination, and there seemed to be more to the world and everything they'd ever experienced encompassed in that voice. Both civilian and military alike went to look for the source of the song, but it always seemed to be just out of reach.

The singing went on for the next three days. Underneath the ruined landscape the vigilant observer would have seen shades of green starting to reappear, as though nature was reinventing itself inside the apparent scene of death. As uncanny as the voice was, it gave the listeners hope. They could not say why; it was more felt than understood, and it felt like a song of renewal.

At the end of the three days, the singing stopped. Investigators had found their way to the top of a hill, the same hill that the two Laylas and two Steves looked down from before the battle started. And it was here that they found a little cottage that was so well hidden it may as well have been invisible. Here would be the beginning of the real investigation.

3

Steve Abbott's Reflections to the Rescued Friends and Family

The time had finally come. Or perhaps I should say, the "times" in plural.

Layla had spoken about the crossing of the timelines. I had spent years preparing for this day. After my initiation into her priesthood, I took the learning I'd gained from the priests of the Otherworld, and combined it with other songs and incantations taught to me by Layla.

You see, the world is a vibration; the universe is a vibration; all universes are a vibration. Things exist on frequencies, like radio waves. There are some mythologies that describe the world as being created by song, life emerging from silence. It turns out that this is not metaphorical; things really DO come from sound, and can be manipulated through its use. It's why yogis and meditators recite mantras in their practice— reciting the sounds changes the vibration of things. It can change your DNA, it can change your brain. It can also change the world around you.

The songs I learned were very old, and in a language that was equally old. How old? Thousands of years, maybe almost a million years old, songs that existed among races that were on the earth and in nearby universes long before humans. These songs were retained, but they were secret, only entrusted to those who were initiated.

I have spent my life as a professional singer, and whatever else I may or may not be known for, my voice was always considered legendary. The Morrigan knew this in her Otherworld, watching over the descendants of Duagh. She could have tapped other descendants to get rid of the curse, but she tapped me because of my voice. There were no more kings, but she still needed a singer, and not to entertain–she needed me to change things. This is why she said that lifting the curse was about much more than me or my family. She knew someone would come in a future generation who could help with her mission, and I've only been too glad to do it.

Many years had passed since my original initiation, and when I stood on the hill, facing two Laylas, facing another version of myself on another timeline–a version totally ignorant of what was happening–I knew the projected moment had arrived. The power of human consciousness had now reached an ugly and destructive peak; it could only be tamed and taken out by armies of the Otherworld.

The Morrigan did not want me to participate in the battle; I am very old now, and she knew I would be a prime target for the enemy. But I couldn't not be involved. If I could warn our warriors about potentially being surrounded, or threats going on behind the battlefield, I wanted to do that. There are songs of invisibility, and I used those to my advantage, so I could move through the scene without being noticed. Not only was I able to warn about counterattacks, I could use my song to set up barriers to the other army if they tried to retreat or surround our army. I was honestly surprised at my own energy; it was as though I had left myself and moved as a force throughout the battle. When it was all over, I sang the song that opened the gates to the Otherworld, and our army retreated. I remember looking sadly at the destroyed landscape; how much had been lost in this fray? But I couldn't spend a lot of time mourning; I knew it would take several days of singing the songs of renewal to put things back on track.

So, I hid myself in a valley, and began singing. I knew others would hear the song, and come looking for me, but I remained invisible to avoid being interrupted. I was exhausted, and I hoped my voice would not give out. But I was filled with the fire of determination; I was going to finish this mission, the last one I would have on this earth, on this side. I knew that rest awaited me in the not-too-distant future, in the Otherworld, a land that I'd come to love more than this one. Life in this universe felt oppressive, like breathing in wet mud all the time. Still, there was a chance it could be as beautiful and clear as it was many, many eons ago...

When my song was finished, I picked myself up and came back to the cottage where Layla and I had taken care to hide you, our loved ones, to keep you from the ravages of battle. You would have been targets for the other side, and you were entirely innocent of everything that was going on. I remember the astonished looks that I got when I returned; Malcolm and Anika moved to get me something to eat and drink, and to get me cleaned up and into bed to rest. I was too exhausted to speak about what had happened, but I felt like I was glowing; my whole being felt alive with the work of renewal. I was tired, but I was filled with joy.

4

The Farewells of Layla, Steve, Aaron, and Malcolm, in Mila's Vision

They sat around the fire in the living room as usual. But they had two other guests—Judas and Aaron. The two who had been living in Tir na nOg were not thrilled about being back on the human side of things, even for a short time. But Layla had decided that this was the best place to review what had happened. She felt that Malcolm and the others needed the complete picture of what was going on. After all, with the house on the market and family members and friends prepared to take on final details, it was also going to be Malcolm's last days on the human side of life. Malcolm was old, and it was very close to his time.

Malcolm could actually hear the violent rumblings from the battle, but was not close enough to see it. He did, however, get a view of the monster from a distance, and was anxious to know what went on. There was surprisingly little coverage of the event in the papers, though social media was abuzz with questions—what happened? What were the monstrous things that attacked them? Where did the defending army come from? What about the monster? And even more distressing—did it happen at all? There were few remnants of the combat, and the military was anxious to hush it up, though one could be sure they were investigating behind the scenes. What was obviously real was the widespread outage of all technology, and for those in the village that was the centre of the attack, there was no way that anyone could tell them that it didn't really happen. Many of the villagers were severely traumatised, and some even died from the shock.

But these were not the questions of the group. The discussion was of the battle itself. Back at Tir na nOg, the three were hailed as heroes. The Dagdachoris was untouched. Steve, though not a warrior, used his Druid skills to protect the group from unpredicted attacks. And Judas, the half-Fomorian who felt he had no battle skills at all, showed an incredible knowledge of strategy, and was extremely brave on the battle front. His communication with Aaron was flawless. The three additions from the human world to the Tir na nOg ranks had fought with tremendous strength, skill, and fortitude.

"I'm very pleased with all of you," said Layla. "I expected that you would all be brilliant fighters, and you came through better than expected. And Steve went well beyond his intended role."

"So, what exactly happened?" This was Malcolm talking.

Aaron spoke up. "We had been preparing for this battle in the Otherworld for some time; even before I got there, it was under discussion. I really did not know what kind of enemy we were facing, even though it had been explained to me. And I had never fought in a battle before, so I didn't know how this was going to work. A lot of it is an exercise in letting go, really; you only have so much control in these situations. Fortunately everything went well, and we all worked together to keep our own side protected. Steve was a tremendous help."

"What did Steve do, specifically?"

Steve joined the discussion. "I am only the magician, I am no warrior. But I was able to use some of the spells I'd learned to keep the White Watchers from running off. They're not very intelligent, they're just destructive, so I wanted to give the army the chance to pick them off. The black creature was another matter—that one was dangerous even in death. But I had an intuition that they'd have to make a direct hit in the chest to kill it, and this is what I called out to both Judas and Aaron. Aaron immediately made the dash, and hit it right in the bullseye. It was an incredibly brave thing to do."

Aaron demurred from the praise. "Well, it did have to be done, and I was glad you spoke up. Things could have been a lot worse, but as you say, there was no escaping the damage from that one. I'm amazed that none of our warriors were taken out."

Malcolm listened to the discussion with interest. "It almost makes me wish I was close enough to see it," said Malcolm.

"Oh, I don't know—it was quite a scene, it might have driven you mad," said Layla.

This raised a question for Malcolm. "Where were you during all this?"

Layla smiled. "Right behind the troops. My role is to open the gate of war, and to get them into a frenzy with the war cry. I tend to maneuver things indirectly. But the warriors make or break themselves; I don't usually step in directly unless there's a critical reason to do so."

Aaron leaned forward. "I have a question, if you don't mind, your Excellency." Malcolm looked at him with wide eyes, and had to suppress a giggle in spite of himself; he was not used to Layla being addressed in this fashion.

"Certainly. Ask."

"What was that monster? Where did it come from? What is it called?"

"It has no name, and it's best not to give it one, as that gives it more power. It came from the depths. It popped up in the Irish Sea, but it really could have popped up anywhere. You see, it's a psychological being—kind of like a living poltergeist, only very much manifest."

Aaron was puzzled. "But if it was psychological ... I mean, it was certainly real enough when we were fighting it."

Layla smiled. "Yes! And you were indeed fighting a real monster. But here's the thing—there are more beings in the universe besides humans and the flora and fauna that you know. And of course, you know that; Allette is your wife, and she is certainly a different kind of being from yourself. But a lot of what drives the universes are the thoughts of its occupants. Humans have always been a strange lot, and the more technologically advanced they get, the more hubris they develop. As their light gets brighter and brighter, the darker thoughts become even darker."

"Are you saying that the monster is a manifestation of the dark thoughts of humans?"

"One of them, yes."

"One of them? There are more?"

"Well, you saw what happened at the end of the battle. Everything disintegrated, because once it has been destroyed, it really has no existence anymore. But that doesn't make the thoughts go away, and that doesn't mean they won't regroup. This is not likely to be a one-time thing, and as humans advance in one way, the problems will become more severe in another."

"But why does Tir na nOg even bother supporting humans? I mean—all of us have links to this world, but for most of the residents, the world is a dim memory."

"Because we are reliant upon them. Our dimension is supported by their universe. To a certain extent, we are a creation of the thoughts of this universe, and that creation was so strong, it didn't go away when belief went away. Some of us pre-date human existence, so we are part of their original thoughts. But they need us more than they realise—and we need them, if we want to continue to exist."

Aaron grew silent. The whole thing was very strange, and yet made sense in an odd way. "I'm sorry to be full of questions—but then is our world at Tir na nOg no more real than this one?"

"Hmm, that's a good question. It depends on what you define as real. Would you say that what's happening to you is not real? It's not a dream; no one will pinch you and you'll wake up."

"I certainly hope not," said Aaron.

"Agreed," said Judas.

Layla laughed. "Well, obviously you prefer the Otherworld to the human one, and who can blame you? I'm glad I have not made any of you suffer too terribly."

Steve grinned, but then he looked at Malcolm, and a thought came to him. "So, if we all go back—I mean, we can't stay here anymore. You've said that the military officials who were there did recognise us, or at least had some kind of intelligence regarding who we were. What will happen to Malcolm? If we're not here, surely they'll come for him."

Layla looked at Malcolm. "Your years are almost over—your cord is to be cut. You're actually ill right now and don't know it. But, I will bodily take you to Tir na nOg, so it won't matter. He will be healed and regain his youth there."

"So—we are all just going to disappear, including Malcolm?" Steve asked.

"Just so. We've already talked to family about getting affairs in order and passing on the house and property to Anika. But for all intents and purposes, it's goodbye. Does that trouble you?"

"Not in the least," said Steve, grateful to be returning to what he felt was his real home.

5

The team examined the battlefield near the Northern Welsh border, with surprisingly little evidence to report. The area was clearly decimated by a disaster, but there was no evidence of weaponry, any bodies, or anything left behind that would give us a clue about the destruction or its cause. There was a lot of ash in the area; samples were sent to the lab for evaluation, but no conclusions could be drawn from the wreckage.

Several soldiers and civilians reported a strange singing coming from the hills where the alleged battle began. An initial examination of the area did not reveal the source of the sound. However, a secluded cottage was discovered in the woods, and in this cottage were a group of inhabitants. None of them were permanent residents in the house; all said they were told to go there or were brought there by a Ms. Layla Black or a Mr. Steve Abbott. Both of them had warned the inhabitants about an impending battle, but the group had very few details; they had only heard what sounded like explosions or felt rumblings in the earth, so they were inclined to go along with the hasty exit without questioning either Mr. Abbott or Ms. Black too much. When asked about the whereabouts of either Ms. Black or Mr. Abbott, they indicated that both had turned up at the house about twenty-four hours prior, but had left again, taking Ms. Black's father, Malcolm Black, with them. They confirmed that Mr. Abbott was the "singer" heard on the hillside, and that he had come in at the end of his singing rather dirty and looking

369

exhausted. Ms. Black returned to the house with two others; one was Aaron Langley, the musician reported missing a year earlier after briefly reappearing under mysterious circumstances to purchase a large quantity of gold. He had also disappeared before he could be questioned by authorities. The other man they did not know; he was referred to as Judas, and they said his appearance was "less than human", as he seemed to have strangely sharp teeth and long pointed fingers. However, he was not threatening to the group, and it seemed that both Langley and this Judas figure were part of the defensive army that appeared out of nowhere.

In order to further the investigation, the group that was present agreed to individual interviews, to discuss everything they knew about Layla Black and Steve Abbott, who seem to be the central figures in this unprecedented situation. No one at the house could say where they had gone, and subsequent searches turned up nothing. Ms. Black's house outside of Chester had been vacated, and she had left instructions for her sister, Anika Black, to dispose of any furnishings and sell the house.

While we had hoped for a very fruitful investigation that would explain the "Phantom Cheshire Battle" and provide some kind of new strategy for this type of event, we in fact have to admit that this is an extremely complicated situation, and more time will be needed to separate fact from fiction.

6

Mila Fell

And thus, my work is finished.

The Defence Ministry conducted their interviews. I conducted many of my own, and Steve Abbott's diaries were invaluable. What has been presented here is the best untangling I can do of tangled events. I have stayed out of them as much as possible, letting the stories tell themselves. As for the gaps in the story, the places where interviews and diaries don't go...I like to think that the Morrigan was inspiring me from whatever divine abode she now lives in.

We appear to be looking at the same people appearing in two timelines that managed to cross at the so-called "Phantom Battle of Cheshire," even though Cheshire was to the East of the actual event. The Ministry was reluctant to release the account, as it sounded too fantastic, and often too unscientific. But we have no other account of events, no evidence to the contrary—in fact, the change in the world since the battle is very much evident.

No one has seen Layla Black, a.k.a. the Morrigan in all her guises, or Malcolm Black, or Steve Abbott, or Aaron Langley since the battle. If there is an "Otherworld" as indicated, then it might be assumed they now reside there.

I cannot help but to think about Layla Macha Black. She appears in one timeline as a kind of femme fatale, though one clearly on a mission. In the other she is more of a hermit, more isolated, and living a much sadder life. But even in this timeline she works as a scientist, attempting to bring the world along via another method. Some of the discoveries she made have sadly been lost; many have yet to be understood, even with the mathematics spelled out by her, right in front of our eyes.

If Layla was in fact the Morrigan—and I have no reason to believe she was not—then she is a goddess that the Christian priesthood described as monstrous and terrifying, a force to be defeated, but in fact proving that she cannot be defeated, nor should she have been defeated. All would be lost if the Phantom Queen ultimately lost. She makes us think about the nature of the universe—this one, and other possible ones—and what we think we know about life and existence. She is the antidote to a world overrun with sociopaths and patriarchs, reminding us that it is really the Divine Feminine that has power—all efforts to conquer and subjugate her will fail.

Moladh do Macha. Longaiter tromfoíd.

CPSIA information can be obtained
at www.ICGtesting.com
Printed in the USA
LVHW081658180422
716540LV00014B/349